"S-sorr
Didn't mean

Maxwell White rose from
itting, clutching a batter
high. Once again, Hattie realized y
was.

"What do you want?"

"I just wanted to see— Is he all right?"

He stumbled over his words, and she almost felt
sorry for him. Until she remembered that his very
presence in Bear Creek might upset her carefully
aid plans.

"He's alive."

Hattie noticed a dark stain on the midsection of
Maxwell's white shirt. Had he sat here all afternoon
waiting for word on the man's recovery?

"You've got blood on your shirt," she said.

He looked down, nodded. "It's not the first time…."
He glanced up and their eyes connected.

Hattie, heart suddenly pounding, quickly severed
the moment by opening the front door for him.

"Thank you for…telling me the man made it,"
Maxwell said, and rushed out the door.

Hattie shoved it closed and leaned against it. Yes,
she could see Mr. White being a distraction. One
she desperately didn't need.

Books by Lacy Williams

Love Inspired Historical

Marrying Miss Marshal
The Homesteader's Sweetheart
Counterfeit Cowboy
*Roping the Wrangler
*Return of the Cowboy Doctor

*Wyoming Legacy

Other titles by this author available in ebook format.

LACY WILLIAMS

is a wife and mom from Oklahoma. Her first novel won an ACFW Genesis Award while it was still unpublished. She has loved romance books and movies from a young age and promises readers happy endings in all her stories. Lacy combines her love of dogs with her passion for literacy by volunteering with her therapy dog, Mr. Bingley, in a local Kids Reading to Dogs program.

Lacy loves to hear from readers. You can email her at lacyjwilliams@gmail.com. She also posts short stories and does giveaways at her website, www.lacywilliams.net, and you can follow her on Facebook (lacywilliamsbooks) or Twitter @lacy_williams.

Return of the Cowboy Doctor

LACY WILLIAMS

HARLEQUIN® LOVE INSPIRED® HISTORICAL

Recycling programs for this product may not exist in your area.

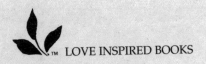 LOVE INSPIRED BOOKS

ISBN-13: 978-0-373-82994-1

RETURN OF THE COWBOY DOCTOR

www.Harlequin.com

Printed in U.S.A.

Be sympathetic, love one another,
be compassionate and humble.
—*1 Peter* 3:8

As always, to Luke, who inspires me.

And for my sister, who has seen way too many doctors but still manages to be positive and brave. Love you!

Acknowledgments

With grateful thanks to my critique partners Regina and Mischelle. Still can't do it without you gals.

This book also never would have come about without all the helpers and babysitters in my life. I hope you know how much I appreciate all of you.

And thanks also to my editor, Emily Rodmell, who makes each and every book better than I ever could.

Chapter One

1897—Wyoming

Home. After five years away, Maxwell White was finally coming home.

Two years too early.

The *clack-clack-clack* of the train rumbling down the tracks had an entirely different feeling than when he'd left home for college. At eighteen, he'd been excited and anxious, ready to conquer the world—or at least achieve his goal of becoming a doctor. Now the rocking, dusty passenger car bore him home, but he had not completed his education. How long would he have to work to get the funds he needed to attend his last two years of medical school? Could he return in the fall—or spring at the latest?

The scenery rushing past outside the train window offered him no solutions, only pushed him toward Bear Creek, and his family. While he'd been gone, he'd missed his adopted brothers and sister, all seven of them, more than he'd ever thought possible. Exchanging letters just wasn't enough.

Next thing he knew, the train had stopped and he disembarked, hauling his small travel case onto the platform. With late springtime in full bloom, he hadn't expected his pa or brothers to greet him. Ranchers needed every hour of the day to get their jobs done. And, according to the last letter from his younger brother and jokester Edgar, his ma couldn't lumber up into the wagon without assistance, being far along with her third baby.

He'd see if he could get the livery owner to let him borrow a horse to get him the rest of the way home.

Before he could leave the platform steps, a voice rang out.

"Maxwell!"

Sam Castlerock, his best friend of eight years, hurried down the boardwalk toward him. Sam's wife, Emily, was on his arm and he was wearing a wide smile.

His friend looked very different from when Maxwell had first known him. Back then, Sam had worn fancy duds more suited to city boys. Now he wore denims and a worn chambray shirt, dusty boots and a Stetson. He looked like the cowboy he was. And he looked confident, happier than Maxwell remembered.

Maxwell accepted a back-slapping hug from Sam and a buss on the cheek from Emily. He'd been sweet on her during his teenage years, but before he'd left for college they'd grown to be simply close friends. Maxwell was glad Sam had found love with the shopkeeper's daughter.

"You look tired," his friend said, stepping back and claiming Emily's hand as if he couldn't bear not to touch her. Maxwell noticed and tried not to feel the twinge of envy in his stomach.

"That's what sixteen-hour days of classes, labs and studying will do to a cowboy like me. Plus, I've been on a train for two days straight."

"Do you have time for lunch before you head out to your pa's place?" Emily asked.

"After forty-eight hours of train fare, I'm more than happy to stop for a quick meal." He nodded his thanks to her and looked away quickly from the small bulge at her waistline. Sam and Emily were starting a family, it seemed. He felt another of those twinges beneath his breastbone.

"Do you have luggage?" Sam asked.

"A trunk full of medical texts."

Sam grinned and motioned toward a wagon along-side the plank boardwalk a ways down. "I guess I'll trust you with my wife. Meet you in a few minutes."

Maxwell knew he should probably have helped his friend wrestle the heavy trunk into the wagon but was just as happy to escort Emily, who had remained a dear friend. She chattered about their homestead— Sam had already told him via letter that it was close to his pa's place—and how Sam fussed over her because of the baby. Her expression shone with joy and he had to avert his face.

You'll never have that came a painful whisper from the past, one he did his best to ignore.

Looking up Main Street, he saw many of the store-fronts had changed in five years. Different business names. Some wore a new coat of paint. The street extended farther than he remembered. New stores must've been built, as well.

Everything was the same, and yet everything was different. Or maybe he was the one changed by his time away.

Suddenly, three whooping cowboys thundered down the dirt-packed lane on their horses, and Maxwell shifted Emily toward the nearest storefront, away from the commotion.

"There's a new saloon in town," Emily said, her tone apologetic. "The sheriff claims all the trouble-makers are getting their courage there…."

He didn't have time to answer her before a wave of people swept toward them, crowding the boardwalk and stalling their steps.

"Gunfight!" a man in a suit shouted.

"It can't be." Emily frowned. "Not in Bear Creek—"

Above the heads in the crowd, Max could just make out two men squaring off in the street.

"Get low." He folded Emily close to the ground and pushed her back. They were still too far from the nearest store to duck inside.

Sam didn't have to be present for Maxwell to know his friend would want his wife as far away from the event as possible. Nearby, a knot of schoolgirls craned their necks, trying to see the action. Maxwell checked twice to ensure his younger sister Breanna wasn't among them and shouted at them to get down.

He hadn't had occasion to see many gunshot wounds in the laboratories he'd observed, but his education had taught him the kind of havoc such an injury could have on the human body.

With the crush of people surrounding them, it was almost impossible to move, but Maxwell persisted, using his shoulders to push forward, keeping one hand on Emily's bent back. They'd almost reached the corner of a nearby alleyway when shots rang out above the crowd's murmurs, silencing everything. Beneath his hand, Emily flinched.

A woman screamed.

More hoofbeats sounded, and Maxwell saw a man wearing a silver star on his chest gallop past.

"Bystander's been shot!" The blacksmith, a tall man wearing a thick leather apron, shook his head in disgust.

With Emily tucked safely in the alley, Maxwell looked back. "I've got to help, if I can."

She turned frightened eyes on him but nodded. "I'll wait for Sam."

She'd be safe where she was. With the sheriff present, likely nothing else would happen. Hopefully, Sam would forgive Maxwell for leaving her.

He pushed his way back toward the commotion. The crowd had thinned now that the fight was over.

When Maxwell rushed forward, he saw one body lying prone on the dirt-packed street. The sheriff scuffled with another man farther down the lane, but neither had a gun drawn.

It was the knot of people surrounding a man laid out on the boardwalk and the woman kneeling over him that caught Maxwell's attention. He ran toward them, feet pounding against the ground, adrenaline pumping.

He was over a yard away when he caught sight of the man clutching his stomach, blood seeping through his fingers.

"Ma'am?" The woman who crouched next to the

victim was shaking and pale. Probably his wife. Not doing anyone any good just sitting there. Maxwell didn't wait for her answer but knelt beside the man.

"Shot went wild," one of the onlookers grumbled. "It could've been any of us."

A woman in a fancy dress gasped and pressed a hand to her forehead as if she would faint. Maxwell wished the people standing nearby would go away— they weren't helping.

"Can you get me a towel or some clean rags?" He directed his question to a teenage boy standing wide-eyed not two feet away, frozen with horror. He was thankful to see the lanky kid rush into a nearby store.

"I'll get the doc!" someone else exclaimed and rushed off. That left only three or four gawkers standing over Maxwell's shoulder.

"Should we move him to the doctor's office?" a male voice asked.

"No—"

"No." A crisp female voice overlapped Maxwell's as a shadow fell across him. A pair of small, neatly kept hands appeared in his vision, followed by a dark blue skirt and the bottom of a wide white apron. The dainty hands didn't hesitate to push a towel against the injured man's abdomen, with enough pressure that the man gasped.

"Not yet," she continued in a clipped voice that brooked no argument. "We'll wait for Papa to make a quick examination. We don't want to make things worse. Take this—"

Maxwell followed orders and replaced her hands with his. The man groaned as Maxwell applied the same hard pressure—enough to hopefully stem the flow of blood.

"Good." The woman glanced at Maxwell briefly, and the tilt of her head drew his gaze up for the first time. Her blue eyes were straightforward and sharp, and instantly he felt as if he'd stuffed his mouth with cotton pads. She leaned over the man, and wisps of her chestnut hair fell from the bun behind her head, curling gently across her cheek.

She was much younger than he'd supposed from the authority in her voice. Even younger than his twenty-three years.

Maxwell forced his gaze back to the life beneath his hands. To focus on the human body, not the pretty girl. "He's hemorrhaging from the upper left flank. The bullet could've hit his spleen."

She looked up sharply at him. "Are you a doctor?"

It was a struggle to keep his eyes on the patient and not respond to her melodious tones.

He wished he could answer differently. "No. A medical student."

What a waste of a beautiful day. A gunshot wound. Senseless. And it would likely take all afternoon to tend.

Hattie Powell had heard the commotion from inside her papa's medical clinic and rushed out to help. Papa was on a house call and she could only hope someone had been sent to fetch him.

Now Hattie knelt over the injured man—she recognized him as a local farmer, John Spencer—and accepted the towels someone had procured from the general store and traded them out from the blood-soaked towel beneath her helper's hands. She couldn't help but note the strength of his wide, blunt fingers. They were more calloused than she would've expected from a medical student. And his dress was that of a cowboy—trousers and a woolen shirt. Even a Stetson. Unusual. And surprisingly, he hadn't acted prideful about being a medical student. Other than one comment, he'd been silent.

He towered over her as they both knelt next to the victim. Her hands twitched with the desire to take action.

"But we can't move him until Papa does a quick examination," she muttered to herself. "If the bullet is still inside, moving him could make matters worse."

The medical student—or was it cowboy?—nodded once. "Might be better to get him inside, though. Risk of infection..."

"Of course there is a risk of infection with any type of internal injury," she said. "But we don't dare move him yet."

The cowboy across from her glanced up with a quick flash of intelligent green eyes. She flushed. Likely he thought she was too bossy, but a man's life was at stake here.

No doubt she'd seen more of this type of wound than he had, in her years of assisting her father in his medical practice. What was taking Papa so long, anyway? Mr. Spencer continued to bleed.

"His pulse is slowing," her companion said. "Pupils are dilating. He's going into shock."

"An excellent observation," said a familiar voice. Relief flooded Hattie as Papa knelt beside her, nudging her aside. With his bristly white mustache and shock of graying hair, he cut a recognizable figure in town.

"You must be Maxwell White. I'm Doctor Powell," Papa said as he probed the victim's neck, then pushed his eyelids back to get a good look at his eyes. "Got to talking to your father a coupla Sundays ago 'bout you, and he said you were coming back into town."

"You did?" The genuine surprise in the man's voice was echoed by the shock in his face.

"Yep. We discussed how you won't want to lose your focus while you're rounding up funding for the rest of your schooling. Thought you might like to chat about helping out in my practice."

Hattie heard the sharp intake of breath but wasn't aware it had come from her until the keen green gaze flickered her way. Abruptly, she lowered her face. Earlier this spring, her papa had promised to consider allowing her to attend medical school. Did the fact that Papa was possibly getting help in the clinic mean he was seriously of a mind to let her go? She could only hope....

Unless there was a chance this Maxwell White's presence could interfere with her plans.

"Bullet's still in there. Let's get him over to the clinic." Papa looked up at the people surrounding them from a few steps back. "Oh, Samuel. Good. Can you help Mr. White lift him? Hattie, take his head."

Sam Castlerock, the husband of one of Hattie's friends, stepped forward as Hattie moved around Mr. Spencer to join Maxwell White on his other side. Her father's command put her immediately next to the medical student's shoulder. He towered over her even more than when they had knelt side by side. He must be well over six feet in his socks.

"Keep him steady, now," Papa murmured. "Don't want to make things worse on the inside. Hattie, keep pressure on that wound."

Hattie cradled the man's head in the crook of her right arm and used her left hand to replace Maxwell White's pressure against the towels. With the location of the wound, the action pressed her arm against her neighbor's surprisingly muscled chest. His height gave the illusion that he was slender, but it was—apparently—not so. He didn't just *appear* to be a cowboy. He must actually be one, in addition to being a medical student. How unusual.

The two men lifted Mr. Spencer without even a grunt to show their effort. Hattie rose with them, concentrating on keeping the victim's head stable, trying hard to ignore the way her shoulder pressed into Mr. White's biceps. It was a wasted effort. With each step they took, the contact between her shoulder and his arm seemed to burn fire through her nervous system.

For someone whose nerves occasionally experienced numbness due to a medical condition, the entire process was unsettling.

Intense relief spilled through Hattie as Sam and Mr. White deposited the injured man on her father's operating table in the rear of his clinic. She retained her position at the side of the table, continuing to put pressure on Mr. Spencer's wound as the other two men moved away. Sam went out the door, and Hattie heard the murmur of her father's voice.

Mr. White hesitated. "Do you need—"

She ignored him. Kept pressure on the wound

with one hand while attempting to unbutton the victim's shirt with the other. Her father would want it removed before he could start the surgery to save this man's life.

"I can help—"

She hadn't realized Mr. White had come closer, but then he was beside her and their fingers tangled as he attempted the same button that troubled her. Sparks zinged up her forearm as the warm, callused digits enclosed her fingers momentarily.

"I've got it," she insisted. And then promptly wished her voice hadn't sounded so breathless. What was it about this man that discombobulated her so?

Papa shuffled into the room, moving to pump water from the sink in the back corner and scrub his hands. Many of his colleagues sneered at his penchant for using running water, but her papa believed it helped prevent infection.

"Thank you for your help today, young man," Papa said. With his back turned, he didn't see how Mr. White had ignored her and was quickly removing the man's shirt, gently edging it out from beneath him now while Hattie maintained pressure on the wound. "We'll get together soon to discuss things."

It was an obvious dismissal. With the victim's shirt gone, Maxwell flicked one last glance at Hattie and stepped back. "Thank you, sir."

Papa didn't even seem to hear him as he approached the operating table, he was so intent on the injured man. The same as always. Focused on a patient to the exclusion of everything else. Hattie heard distinctive boot steps retreating out of the sickroom and toward the waiting room out front.

"Now, let's see if we can't remove the bullet and save this man," her father said as he joined her at the table. "Administer the ether."

They fell into the easy routine they'd achieved after years of working together, when Hattie's condition allowed. At age twelve she'd helped him stitch up a little girl's nasty cut, using the sewing skills her mother had worked hard to instill. Hattie's aid in dispensing medicines and calming young children had evolved into helping Papa set broken bones, and by age fourteen she'd assisted in her first surgery.

Medicine had become her passion. She'd avidly followed Elizabeth Blackwell's career and scoured newspapers for articles about women doctors. She wanted to be a doctor more than anything. And if her plans worked out this summer, *if* she could convince her parents, then she would be headed to medical school in the fall.

If Maxwell White didn't interfere.

Hours later, after they'd closed up the gunshot wound and her papa had snuck out the clinic's back door, Hattie finished tidying the room and setting the instruments back in their proper places.

Mrs. Spencer sat at her husband's side, holding his hand. Hattie would go home and rest for a while, then come back and spell the other woman during the night hours. It wouldn't be the first time she'd slept on a cot in the clinic, watching over a patient.

It was one of the arguments she planned to use when she spoke to Papa about her dreams of medical school later this summer—her papa's trust that she could take care of his patients.

She knew there was a chance he would refuse to consider Hattie's wishes; her mother had taken an adamant stance against Hattie receiving further education in medicine since Hattie had brought it up several years ago. She'd been fifteen when she'd overheard her parents' hushed conversation about Hattie helping her father in his practice. Her father had argued that if Hattie had been born a boy, her mother would have had no issue with furthering Hattie's education. To which Hattie's mother had responded that Hattie had *not* been born a boy, no matter how much Papa had wanted a son. And that wasn't even including Hattie's medical condition—something her mother used as a further argument to keep Hattie at home.

Before that day, Hattie hadn't realized that her father had wanted someone to carry on his medical practice. She didn't see why she couldn't be the partner he desired. The medical field wasn't particularly open to female doctors; however, there were now schools that admitted women. Hattie knew she could be one of them. Her father had promised to listen; now she needed to ease him into keeping his promise. She was getting older. There was a chance her condition could worsen as she aged. She couldn't waste what might be her only good years to practice. She needed her papa to agree now, this year.

Hattie's condition did not have an official diagnosis. It had symptoms similar to multiple sclerosis, where she would occasionally lose nerve function and have weakness in her extremities. But her condition was not as severe as the cases of multiple sclerosis her papa had studied. And he'd studied plenty over the years since her symptoms had first started manifesting as a young girl. She felt she could manage it, enough to attend medical school, enough to practice as a physician. But she also didn't want to waste time if there was a chance her condition could worsen. She wanted to make a difference in people's lives now.

Leaving the woman praying over her husband, Hattie slipped into the small waiting room to ensure that the outer door was secured. Movement from one of the chairs startled her and she whirled, one hand at her neck.

"S-sorry, miss. Didn't mean to scare ya."

The cowboy-turned-medical-student. Maxwell White.

Her shoulders came down, but adrenaline still rushed through her system, making her heart thud loudly in her ears. The combination of a long day of surgery and the burst of energy left her trembling, and based on her past experience, Hattie knew she needed some quiet time to regroup before her nerves rendered her useless to anyone.

He rose from the chair where he'd been sitting, clutching a battered Stetson against his thigh. Once again, she realized just how tall he was.

"What do you want?" The stress of the day and her fading energy made her words sharper than the situation warranted.

"I just wanted to see— Is he all right?"

He stumbled over his words, and she almost felt sorry for him. Until she remembered that his very presence in Bear Creek might upset her carefully laid plans.

"He's alive." She couldn't keep the pride from her voice. Her father, with her assisting, had saved the man's life, stopped the bleeding and stitched him up. "No doubt you know that infection is the next stage of the battle. If he can survive the next few days, he should recover."

The cowboy moved to the door and passed through a late-afternoon shaft of sunlight from one of the windows. As he did, Hattie clearly saw the dark stain on the midsection of his white shirt. From the little her papa had said, she knew the man had just arrived in town. Had he sat here all afternoon waiting for word on the man's recovery? Put off his homecoming with his family just to find out?

He must've sensed her appraisal, or perhaps he was just nervous, because he looked down at himself self-consciously.

"You've got blood on your shirt," she said.

He nodded, then glanced up and their eyes connected. "I'm sure I've got some chloride of lime stashed in my luggage. It won't be the first time I've had to launder something like this…."

She was surprised that he would admit to doing something that could be construed as a woman's task. When made into a solution with water, the chloride of lime would help bleach out the stain and could remove any infectious bacteria as needed. She had often laundered her soiled aprons, wanting to spare her mother's sensibilities. But to hear this cowboy admit that he did the same changed how she thought about him—unlocked a tenuous connection between them.

She severed it by briskly opening the door for him, heart pounding.

"Thank you for…telling me the man made it," he said.

He stuffed his hat on his head and rushed out the door. Hattie shoved it closed and leaned against it. She needed to get home but also needed a moment to compose herself.

Though the cowboy was awkward, part of him was endearing. He'd obviously cared enough to see if the injured man had survived the surgery. For a moment, and only a moment, she'd entertained the thought that he had stayed to impress her father. But his very manner struck the thought from her head. He was too sincere.

Yes, she could see him being a distraction. One she desperately didn't need.

Chapter Two

"Come back here, you rascal!"

Maxwell chased the small white dog around the corner of the doctor's two-story home on the outskirts of Bear Creek, but the animal evaded his grasp and slipped beneath a porch spanning the back of the structure. Maxwell kicked a booted foot through the dirt, frustrated.

Taking off the white dress Stetson he usually wore to church on Sundays, he slapped it against his leg. Running his other hand through the curls matted to his head, he blew out a long breath.

His frustration didn't entirely stem from his sister Breanna's ornery dog, who'd followed him into town this evening. It had been two days since he'd helped carry the gunshot man to the doctor's office, and he still couldn't forget the doctor's beautiful daughter. The nurse.

Since childhood, he'd never been particularly good at talking to ladies. Until Penny had got hold of him as a teen and coached him on what to do. Her help had resulted in his lasting friendship with Emily, but events during college had shaken his temporary ease with the opposite sex. And it seemed his innate shyness and discomfort increased exponentially when he found a woman attractive. Like Miss Hattie Powell, whose name he'd managed to finagle from Sam.

Apparently, the Powells had moved to Bear Creek less than two years ago, and Doc Powell had taken over the practice from old Doc Calloway. Maxwell hadn't known her before he'd left Bear Creek for university, and since his confidence with females was next to nil, it would be tough finding his feet in a conversation with her.

No woman will have you came the insidious whisper of his birth mother's voice. How many times had she said those words to him?

When the doctor had extended an invitation for supper with his family, sort of an unofficial interview before accepting Maxwell to help out in the man's medical practice, Maxwell hadn't been able to refuse. But if Miss Powell was at the table with them, Maxwell could be tongue-tied and awkward. And he desperately wanted the chance to further his education with hands-on practice, if he couldn't be back at medical school yet.

He would just have to find a way to bear Miss Powell's presence. And try not to humiliate himself in the meantime.

"Dog!" he called, bending to see beneath the porch steps, where the dog had squirmed into a small space. With evening coming on, Maxwell couldn't make out any movement in the shadows. Had the animal found another way out? "Come out, you little fur ball. I don't have time to hunt for you...."

He rounded the corner of the porch, eyes on the ground, looking for any place the animal might've escaped.

"Where are you, you flea-bitten—"

A softly cleared throat stopped him in midsentence and midstep. His eyes flicked to the porch, where Miss Powell sat in a chair. With a small white bit of fluff on her lap.

"Er, Miss Powell." Slight panic threw every thought from his mind. "How do you do this evening?"

The dog considered Maxwell from its perch and panted happily, its mouth stretched in what almost seemed a smile. It must've slipped out from beneath the other side of the porch and gone to her.

"Mr. White. I suppose this creature belongs to you?" She scratched its head, and the traitor arched up into her palm. Her chin dipped as she looked down on the dog, giving Maxwell a good view of her profile, the sweep of her golden lashes against her cheekbones. *Sweep, sweep away the tears that rest where my lips want to rest. Hide, hide from view the answer to your test. Would I be welcome there?* The unbidden line of poetry fell into his brain, unsettling him further.

He cleared his throat. Tried to remember what she'd asked about. The dog. "My sister, actually."

One of her brows arched above her deep blue eyes, as if she didn't believe him, and heat boiled into his neck, creeping up his jaw and into his cheeks.

"I'm usually in lectures all day—at university—or attending laboratory. Or catching up on reading assigned texts. I wouldn't have time to keep a pet, even if the boardinghouse where I stay—I mean, *stayed*—had allowed for them—" He cut himself off, knowing he was rambling.

Miss Powell looked down at the dog now curled in her lap, a slight smile turning up the corners of her mouth. Was she laughing at him? If it wouldn't have been considered rude, he'd have mashed his hat back on his head to hide his flaming face. The best he could hope for was that the pinkish light cast by the setting sun would cover his blush.

"Breanna loves animals and attracts all kinds of critters. That rascal—" Maxwell pointed to the dog, who appeared completely at ease in Miss Powell's lap "—followed me around the homestead all day and then into town this evening."

"Hmm." She didn't speak further.

He wished he knew whether he should join her on the porch on one of the several rocking chairs spread across the wide enclosure or if he should return around the front of the home and knock on the door. Maybe if he'd spent a bit less time studying and a bit more time courting, he would know, but after Elizabeth had broken up with him during his second year of college, he'd thrown himself into his studies as a way of forgetting.

Now he settled for propping his booted foot on the first porch step and looking up at Miss Powell. The fading light turned her fair skin golden and burnished highlights in her upswept chestnut hair.

He swallowed hard.

"How is the gunshot patient?" he asked when she didn't carry the conversation forward.

"Much recovered. He is in a lot of pain and had

some fever yesterday, but it appears Papa stopped the internal bleeding."

"Was his spleen hit?" The words were out before Maxwell thought perhaps it was inappropriate to discuss a man's insides with a lady like Miss Powell, even if she was a nurse.

But her face lit up. "It was nicked, but Papa thinks he was able to remove all the damaged tissue. So far, there has been no internal swelling that we can tell…."

Warming to the topic, Maxwell barely noticed when his feet carried him up two stairs so that his head and shoulders were level with hers where she sat. "One of my professors had a patient with damage to his internal organs—"

"Hattie, you'd better come inside. Mr. White should be here any moment." A woman's voice preceded an older version of Miss Powell as she peeked out the door that Maxwell guessed must lead to their kitchen.

"Mr. White has already arrived," Miss Powell said. "With a guest."

Mrs. Powell's drawn brows showed her confusion until she noticed the dog in her daughter's lap. Her noise wrinkled, and she smiled in the same way Maxwell had seen his professors do many times when faced with a student who tried their patience. "I suppose it can stay in a box in the kitchen."

"He can find his way home," Maxwell hurried to say. The ornery dog had better not ruin his chances of working with Doc Powell.

"It's fine," Miss Powell reassured him, sharing a smile that was decidedly warmer than when he had first arrived. "We've already got a basket inside for the house cat."

He thought she would urge the pet to scamper down off her lap, but she reached down to release a lever and then began to turn the two large wheels at her side, turning the chair itself.

And that was when he realized she wasn't sitting in an ordinary chair at all. It was an invalid's rolling chair, similar to those he'd seen at the hospital back in Denver.

Hattie knew the exact moment when Mr. White realized she was confined to the wheeled chair. It was barely discernible, but there was a definite shift in his expression.

She hated it.

Hated feeling like an invalid. Hated that the easy conversation they'd shared had instantly disappeared.

She wasn't a convalescent. Between being on her feet for the extended surgery two days ago and the long hours spent watching over the patient until her papa had sent him home today, her nerves had been taxed. The wheeled chair served mostly as a precaution. The sudden weakness overtook her most often in the evenings and had caused many a bump and bruise when she wasn't expecting it and resulted in a fall. The medical condition was Mama's biggest argument against Hattie working with her papa.

Only a few close friends, including Emily Castlerock, knew that Hattie was occasionally bound to the chair. She typically didn't go about in public when her nerves were weak.

And it galled her to be such when her papa had

invited Maxwell White to supper. If only he'd come around to the front like a polite visitor, she would've had time to transfer to the dining room chair before he'd seen her. Her pride had demanded she take her supper alone in her room—not join the gathering— but she didn't want her weakness to seem pronounced, not if it would give her papa any reason to deny her when she finally spoke to him about attending medical school. She should talk to Papa soon, but not when she was weak.

She needed to be at her best until Papa agreed. And while Mr. White might prove helpful to Papa while she was away at school, she didn't want Papa distracted by his new colleague, either. She had two months to prove her value before the interview with the scholarship committee. Two months to convince her father she could be a doctor herself, someone he would want to bring on as a partner. She'd taken a chance and applied to her chosen school, even put herself forward for a special scholarship offered by a committee of women doctors, with the assumption she could talk her papa into seeing things her way.

She didn't need Mr. White around to confuse things.

"Should I give you a push or just…"

A sharp glance over her shoulder silenced him midsentence. "I'm perfectly capable." And she was.

In the kitchen, she maneuvered around the work counter with the familiarity born of repetition. She was intensely aware of Mr. White's gaze on her as she reached down and settled the little dog in the cat's basket near the stove, with a ham bone to keep him occupied.

Her pride pinched at the thought that perhaps he pitied her now. Papa crossed the threshold to the dining room as Hattie moved her chair inside. He appeared preoccupied, twirling one side of his mustache with a far-off gaze.

"What's wrong, Papa?"

"Oh." He looked up, eyes focusing. "Hattie, dear. Just a phone call from a physician over in Pear Grove. A consultation. He may have a case of cholera on his hands."

Mama paused just behind Mr. White on the threshold between the kitchen and dining room with a steaming bowl in her hands. Hattie saw the immediate tremor go through her. Both women knew how quickly a case of that particular disease could result in an entire town being subject to it. And how very dangerous it was. They could only pray it stayed in Pear Grove.

Papa didn't register their pause or their concern, instead focusing on their guest. "Ah, Maxwell. You made it."

"Doctor Powell." The younger man reached out to meet her father's handshake, his dark suit coat stretching over his shoulders and reminding Hattie of the strength she'd inadvertently felt in them. Even dressed in Sunday clothes, he looked more like a cowboy than anything else.

"After your help the other day, I think we're past formalities. It's Matt or Doc," Papa said.

Hattie wheeled herself up to the only place at the table without a dining chair. The men waited for Mama to seat herself before they joined the ladies at the table. Her father bowed his head, signaling the mealtime prayer. Hattie followed suit, only to freeze as a warm, callused hand enclosed hers. For once, every nerve ending seemed to be in perfect working order—buzzing with energy in response to the man next to her.

She didn't hear a word her papa said until Maxwell released her hand at the final amen.

Why did she have to be so attracted to this particular man?

With shaking hands, she tucked her napkin into her lap and pretended that it was any other meal shared with her parents.

"So, Maxwell," Papa began as he passed a full plate to Hattie. "We relocated to Bear Creek about a year and a half ago, and I'm afraid I still confuse the names of your siblings. And I must confess, I had forgotten you were away at medical school until your father mentioned it."

"Keeping us straight isn't easy" came the quiet answer from the man kitty-corner to her. "We're a big bunch. Getting bigger soon."

"Ah, yes, your mother is expecting her...?"

"Third. Walt is six now and Ida four."

"Your stepmother must have unlimited patience to have married into a family with so many children," Hattie said softly. With so much time spent in her father's clinic, she socialized less than her mother would have liked. She'd never actually met them all but knew the White family took up an entire pew in church. "Not that I don't like children," she amended, realizing her words might've sounded unkind. "I imagine they can be a lot of work! How long after your father's first wife passed did they meet?"

She was acutely aware when Maxwell shifted in his seat. "Penny is my pa's only wife. Jonas adopted all seven of us boys after he'd left Philadelphia with his daughter Breanna."

"How interesting," Papa said. "You were all orphans?"

Maxwell nodded, shifting his legs beneath the table once again. His expression had closed off. Almost as if the topic was one he wasn't entirely comfortable discussing.

"And your father was willing to take on so many children?"

The cowboy spoke to his plate. "No one else wanted us."

The words were said simply, but Hattie felt there must be more behind them.

Knowing her papa, he would question the man until he'd unearthed Maxwell's entire life history. Whether Maxwell wanted to tell it or not. Perhaps she should intervene.

"How did you become interested in the medical field?" Hattie asked. It was a daring question, because she wanted the conversation to stay away from him helping her father at the clinic, but she well knew her father's tendencies to push, even when speaking of something made people uncomfortable.

He shrugged, only glancing quickly at her. "I guess it was something I wanted after I met Jonas—my pa. But I didn't think it was possible until Penny—my ma—pushed me to try."

How curious. She wanted to know more, but the way he kept his head ducked as he pushed his food around his plate made her think he was uncomfortable. Did the man not like talking about himself?

"And do you enjoy the medical courses?" Mama asked.

Finally, his expression brightened. "I love the lectures. Even the studying interests me. The human body is fascinating, and although there's much we don't know, it's incredible what healing we—and the Lord—can do."

"He sounds like you when you were in medical school and excited about learning," Mama teased, with a fond glance at her husband.

It sounded marvelous. Hattie tried not to be jealous, but she desperately wanted her chance to attend.

"How did you come to be a nurse, Miss Powell?" Maxwell asked.

"She isn't a nurse!" Mama exclaimed. "Her father allows her to help in the clinic—which I've discouraged, but no one wants to listen to me. It's high time Hattie finds herself settled and married. With someone to take care of her."

Hattie heard her mama's unspoken censure. It was her turn to suffer a flare of embarrassment. She and her mother didn't see eye to eye on suitors or a woman's right to be a nurse or physician. They never had. Hattie had never met a man who had interested her—and with her book learning and habit of speaking her mind, she'd never interested any man. And not to mention her condition. She'd never been close enough to anyone to share about it before.

Still, it was humiliating to have her mother say such a thing in front of a guest.

A glance at Maxwell revealed only a flash of curiosity in his eyes before his glance flicked away.

"I've been helping my papa with his work for almost eight years now. But I'm not a nurse." But she *would* become a doctor, if she could convince her father to let her attend.

His brows went up. "That's impressive. Your parents must be real proud of you, Miss Powell."

With a comment like that, what could they say in argument?

"Hattie," she said softly. She hadn't wanted to like him, but the man had complimented her on the thing she was most proud of, her work with her father.

From across the table, Mama smiled a secret smile. Hattie hoped she didn't get any ideas about matching up Hattie with the cowboy medical student.

She couldn't afford to befriend the man. If he edged her out of working with her father for the next month and a half, would her arguments for medical school mean anything?

Maxwell had intended to return to the bunkhouse directly, but as he rode past his brother Oscar's cabin, the other man waved to him from the porch.

Reining in, Maxwell dismounted and approached, hesitating when he saw Oscar's wife, Sarah, snuggled up on the porch swing with him. He didn't want to interrupt the couple's private time. Knew they probably didn't get much of it, not with three adopted girls to look after and an infant son of their own.

"How did it go?" asked Oscar.

Maxwell's thoughts went immediately to Miss Powell—Hattie—and how he'd botched things when he'd noticed she was in a wheeled chair. He hadn't known what to say, and her cool attitude toward him had flustered him even worse. Although she had seemed to warm to him a bit during their supper conversation, she'd retired soon after the meal. He had the feeling his reaction might have bothered her more than she'd let on.

He'd just been so shocked to see her in that chair. Two days before, she'd been active, with no hint that anything was wrong as she'd helped carry the man to her father's office. And assisted in the surgery, too.

He'd gotten the courage to ask her father about her health as they said their goodbyes on the front stoop. Dr. Powell had assured him it was a recurring condition and not serious as long as Hattie got adequate rest.

He couldn't help but be curious about it. If he had more knowledge of her symptoms, he might have an idea of what affected her.

The doctor had been protective of his daughter, telling Maxwell not to spread it around anywhere, not that he would've. Then he'd almost absentmindedly returned to their discussion, as if he'd put his daughter's condition out of his mind.

The funny thing was, Maxwell found her just as vibrant and attractive in the chair. He admired that she knew her limitations. When he'd had the chance to clasp her cool, small hand in his during the mealtime prayer, he'd been so distracted by his reaction to her he'd almost made a fool of himself by not noticing when the moment had ended.

"Did the doc offer you a job?" Oscar prodded.

Maxwell rubbed the back of his neck, hoping to

camouflage his inattention—once again, Hattie's fault. Of course, his brother had meant Maxwell's education. Not the woman he found irresistible.

"Yes. He wants me there whenever you can spare me, so I thought in the morning you and I could work out a schedule for training the animals."

Oscar had promised him that if Maxwell spent the summer helping break this year's crop of horses, he could have a cut of the profits. With cattle drives becoming rarer because of the railroad, Maxwell was thankful for the opportunity to supplement his income by assisting the doctor, no matter how small the payment might be. Even if his job was scrubbing instruments and floors, he could soak up knowledge from Doc Powell.

If he could keep his concentration off Hattie, he might be able to return to medical school next spring.

A soft cry from inside the cabin brought Oscar's and Sarah's heads up. Oscar removed his arm from around his wife's shoulders. "I'll check on him." He smacked a kiss on her cheek and disappeared inside the dark cabin.

Sarah smiled fondly, her eyes remaining on the doorway where his brother had disappeared. Maxwell averted his eyes from the display, feeling a little as if he was intruding.

He didn't know Sarah well. When he'd learned that Oscar had married the gal he'd teased mercilessly in their school days, Maxwell had been more than a little surprised. But in the couple of days Maxwell had been home, it was easy to see the love between his older brother and Sarah.

Maxwell wasn't jealous. He was happy for his brother. At least, that was what he told himself.

After all, he was the one who'd given up on finding love. It had seemed the natural conclusion after the events of his past. Didn't mean it didn't still hurt, though, especially when witnessing moments like these.

"Your brother might not say so, but he's very proud of you." Sarah's voice brought him out of his melancholy musings. "One of the first real conversations we had was about your family, and Oscar talked about how proud he was that you were in medical school."

Maxwell shifted his feet. "I never would've gone without him pushing me. I'm just sorry it's taking so long for me to finish." He'd lived as frugally as possible, but the private scholarship funds he'd received had still run out with two years remaining in his education.

She shrugged, and a softening in her expression told him she understood. "Oscar and I know you'll make it through. Even so, we are thrilled to have you home for a while."

"Who, this half cowboy, half doctor?" Oscar joked, stepping outside with a dark-haired bundle tucked against his shoulder. "He insists he needs his mama."

Sarah rose, took the softly fussing baby from Oscar and went inside.

"I'll see you in the morning," Maxwell said, trying to excuse himself.

Oscar stopped him. "You sure everything is all right? You seem a little…I don't know, off tonight."

Maxwell shrugged. "I'm all right."

Oscar and Sam Castlerock were his closest friends

and both knew that he'd had some courting troubles while away at college. But neither knew the full extent of it. And Maxwell didn't want to get into it now.

Hattie Powell was going to be in his life for the time being and he would have to find a way to interact with her. Be friends. Without making a fool of himself. Bringing his brother or best friend into it would only make things worse—they were likely to tease him mercilessly or push him at Hattie, and he didn't need that.

The house was dark when Maxwell arrived back at Jonas's place, but light spilled from the bunkhouse windows. After he'd settled his horse in the barn with a nice rubdown, Maxwell went inside to find his younger brothers cutting up. Seventeen-year-old Ricky had fifteen-year-old Seb in a wrestling hold, while twenty-one-year-old Edgar and twenty-year-old Davy discussed something intensely over the small table tucked between their two bunks. Seventeen-year-old Matty read by the light of a lamp but looked up when Maxwell entered.

"You have a good time with the doctor tonight?" Davy called out.

"The doc's daughter is sure easy on the eyes, ain't she?" Ricky teased. All of his brothers knew that Maxwell was shy around ladies. They'd all joshed him about it since he'd been sweet on Sam's wife, Emily, when he was fifteen. Since then, Penny had tried to help him overcome his innate bashfulness, something his birth ma had ingrained in him with her harsh words.

"You'd better watch out," Edgar cautioned. "Women ain't nuthin' but trouble."

"Aw, Ed!" chorused the others. "Leave him alone—"

Edgar shrugged. Since Maxwell had come into the family, his next-youngest brother hadn't made a secret of his distrust of women, including Penny when she'd come into Jonas's life.

Maxwell did his best to ignore them, but his brothers continued joking and guffawing anyway. It would be much worse if they knew the truth, that he wanted to get to know Hattie better.

Even with their teasing, he couldn't help but be glad to be home. He'd missed the camaraderie between all his brothers. With their similar backgrounds, theirs was a brotherhood of family ties, not blood. But Maxwell almost thought their bond was stronger for the fact that they shared similar difficult pasts and had chosen to be a family.

It had been awkward when the doctor and his family had questioned Maxwell about his childhood at supper. He didn't talk about the family he'd been born into with anyone. And until Hattie had intervened, it had seemed as though the doc was going to dig until he uncovered everything.

He'd rather forget those days.

Maxwell retreated to his bunk and pulled out one of his medical texts. After he'd flipped the tome open, he slid out the small leather-backed journal he'd taken to carrying on his person now that he was back home.

His poetry.

He didn't count himself a talent by any means, but once Penny had taught him how to read when he was sixteen, he'd fallen in love with books. Then, at university, he'd found poetry. Considering the ribbing his brothers would give him if they ever found out he wrote poetry, he hid his little notebook as if it was pure gold. Writing his poems helped him release some of the emotions that tended to get bottled up inside. When he thought about his past or worried too much about school, he found solace in creating the rhymes.

And now, apparently, it helped when he was befuddled by a beautiful woman.

He scribbled down the lines that had popped into his head when he'd first come upon Hattie on the back porch of her parents' home, knowing he would never show them to another soul. They were too private, too personal.

But he had to get his feelings down. He would never tell Hattie Powell that he found her attractive, but at least he could write his feelings here, in his private notebook. It was the best he could expect.

Chapter Three

With Thursday morning came Maxwell's first chance to work with the doctor. He arrived at Doc Powell's practice as the rest of the businesses on Bear Creek's main street were opening for the day, excited and anticipating how he might help the good doctor.

The inside of the clinic was quiet, except for a soft rustling from another room.

"Hello?" he called out. "Doc?"

But it was a woman's voice who answered. "Yes?"

Hattie appeared in the doorway between the waiting room and the short hallway that led to both a small examination room and the room where he'd taken the other man for surgery last week.

Her welcoming smile faded at the same time his heart registered her presence and sped up.

"Maxwell," she said curtly.

It wasn't much of a greeting, but he tipped his hat and smiled. "Morning, Miss Hattie. Is the doc in?"

"Not yet. He had an early-morning call and asked me to see to things here until he arrives. I suppose you can wait."

She turned on her heel and disappeared into the back of the clinic.

Could she still be upset about his reaction when he'd first seen her in the chair? If so, perhaps he should apologize, but how did he know? What if she'd had a spat with her mother or was just busy? He wished he knew more about women. Wished he wasn't so hesitant to follow her down that hall.

He went anyway. He was determined to learn everything he could under Doc Powell's tutelage, and it wouldn't hurt to familiarize himself with the clinic. If Hattie was cool toward him, it might help him keep his head around her. Even if it did sting a little. For the past several days, thoughts of her had sneaked up on him as he'd worked the horses with his brother. The deep blue of the sky just before twilight reminded him of her eyes. He'd see the chestnut mare out of the corner of his eye and imagine a glimpse of Hattie's hair in the sunlight.

Apparently, she'd entertained no fond thoughts of him in the interim.

He found her in a back room past the exam room and the surgery, in the middle of unpacking a crate of supplies. Several brown bottles of various sizes stood on a counter against one wall. A cabinet above hung open, where several more bottles were lined in orderly rows.

As he watched, she bent and took three more flasks from the straw-packed crate. They clanked together, and she stretched to reach the high shelf.

"Can I help?"

She startled and one of the bottles slipped.

He darted forward.

It toppled on the edge of the counter and Maxwell reached out and grabbed it before it could hit the floor and shatter.

Hattie turned to him, fire in her eyes. "You really shouldn't sneak up on people and frighten them!"

"I'm sorry." He set the bottle on the counter and backed up, palms in the air. His face flushed with heat. "Can I help?" If he learned where the doctor kept all his medicines, it might make it easier if he needed to retrieve them for a patient.

"I'm perfectly capable of unloading a crate of medicines."

She turned her back and reached for the bottle he'd left on the counter. Her hand was shaking.

Had he really scared her that badly, or was she still offended about the other night? How could he make things right?

She sighed—more of a huff—and said, "There's another crate on the back stoop. I suppose if you want to make yourself useful, you can fetch it inside."

Back into the hall Maxwell went. He turned past the exam and waiting rooms and found the back door. Outside, a second crate was on the stoop. So was a small boy, seated with feet dangling toward the dirt-packed ground, holding a rabbit.

At Maxwell's appearance, the child jumped up.

"Who are you?" Maxwell asked. Was this child supposed to be here?

"Who're you?" the child responded. "I'm waiting on Miss Hattie."

"She's inside." Maxwell waved his thumb over his shoulder. "You wanna come in and talk to her?"

"I guess." The grubby, barefoot boy kept his eyes

on Maxwell even as he passed him to slip inside. Maxwell hoped he wasn't making a mistake letting this boy into the doctor's office.

Maxwell shouldered the crate and followed the kid inside.

"Hullo, Miss Hattie."

"Good morning, Jeremiah. What are you doing here?"

Maxwell set the crate on the floor in the hall. The tiny storeroom was too small for all three of them, but he could hear everything the two were saying. He couldn't help noticing that Hattie's greeting for the boy was noticeably warmer than the one Maxwell had received minutes ago.

"Hopsie hurt his foot th'other day" came the boy's voice. "See here, this scratch? It's all red and puffy."

Maxwell peeked around the corner of the storeroom door. There. The pry bar Hattie must've used to open the other crate lay in the corner. He reached in to get it. Didn't mean to glance at her, but her head came up and their eyes met. She looked away quickly, almost as if she was embarrassed.

"Yes, it does look inflamed. Swollen," she amended.

"He ain't hoppin' right on it. You reckon it's something you can fix?"

With the lid off the crate, Maxwell found gauze, catgut for stitching wounds and more medicine bottles inside. He took out an armful of the supplies and slipped back into the room, going to the cabinet. Hattie had vacated it to kneel next to the boy. Maxwell opened drawers and the lower cabinet doors until he matched up the surgical thread with where it belonged.

"Who's he, Miss Hattie? You got a new beau?" Though the boy whispered, in the close proximity of the room, Maxwell heard every word.

"Certainly not!" she muttered.

Maxwell passed her on the way back to the crate, but she kept focused on the rabbit. In profile, her cheek and ear were an interesting shade of pink. She hadn't needed to sound so adamant about his not being her beau.

"Maxwell is a medical student. He's going to assist my papa in the clinic when he's not working with the horses out at his father's ranch."

"Didn't think cowboys was real smart," the kid mumbled. "He's really going to school to be a doctor?"

Hattie coughed. To cover a laugh? "Yes, um…yes, he is."

Face flaming and loaded down with another armful of medicines, Maxwell passed the two again. This time the boy scrutinized him. Maxwell nodded, wondering what he was looking for so hard.

"You know anything about rabbits?"

Maxwell knew how to make a nice rabbit stew, but he doubted the boy wanted to hear that.

"Not really."

The boy shrugged and returned his attention to Hattie as Maxwell continued unloading the supplies. "So, Miss Hattie…Hopsie's inf—inflamed leg. Can you do anything for him?"

Maxwell watched from the corner of his eye. Hattie considered the animal gravely, treating the boy's request as important as if he'd consulted her about a human patient. As if she did this kind of thing every day. "I think we can try some antiseptic on it, see if we can get the infection to go away. That should make him—Hopsie—feel much better."

Maxwell made several trips between his crate and the storeroom shelves while she applied antiseptic to the rabbit's wound and dressed it in a small bandage. He couldn't keep his eyes from the graceful movements of her hands. Stanzas of poetry about her hands and fingers filled his head, but he tried to shake them out. He needed his concentration today to help the good doctor.

Finally the boy left with a thank-you and a small hug around Hattie's waist.

Maxwell's intense curiosity wouldn't let him keep silent. "Do you treat a lot of pets, then?"

She kept her face averted and returned to unloading her own crate. "Some. Papa thinks it creates rapport with the children, and if they later come into the clinic to be treated for an injury or sickness, they aren't frightened."

Maxwell could understand that. But her care for the boy had seemed to go above and beyond what her words implied. She'd taken time with him, been patient and pretended that a rabbit was important. Made the boy feel important.

Her actions tugged at a part of Maxwell's heart.

A bell jangled, and his head came up.

"Must be a patient, coming in the front," Hattie murmured. Before she could turn to go, the back door opened and closed.

Doc Powell peeked in at them. "Oh, good. You're here, Maxwell. And good morning, Hattie dear."

"Just trying to familiarize myself with the clinic," Maxwell said, shooting a look at Hattie. Willing her to know he wasn't trying to get in her way or step on her toes.

She looked away, brushed by him on her way out of the room. "I'll go see who came in."

Obviously, she was still sore at him. Whether for his reaction to seeing her in the chair or scaring her this morning, he didn't know.

He would do well to get her on his side of things. She could be an invaluable ally as he tried to learn as much as possible from the doctor. But she would barely speak to him.

He needed to find some way to bring her around. Without making a fool of himself.

It was midmorning before Hattie truly felt as if she'd gotten her feet under her.

She hadn't meant to snap at Maxwell this morning, but his presence had immediately overwhelmed her. The moment she'd seen him in the waiting room, all the attraction she'd felt at supper the other night had rushed forward.

He seemed to fill the storeroom just by standing in the doorway.

And she hadn't wanted him to think less of her for seeing her in the wheeled chair. It was prideful but true.

She took solace in the familiar routines of setting up and wiping down the exam room between patients, greeting patients and bringing supplies when her father needed them.

Maxwell remained by her papa's side during the exams. Hattie's usual place.

Perhaps she shouldn't worry so much. The cowboy had another job for the summer, and if they shared the duties, Hattie could still prove her worth.

She just needed to make sure that, if there were any advanced cases, she was there to prove her knowledge to her papa. She had another four weeks before she had to be in Omaha for the scholarship interview.

The usual morning spurt of patients had thinned by lunchtime, and Hattie stuck her head into the surgery, where Papa and Maxwell had retired. She found them in the middle of what seemed to be a friendly argument.

"My professor insists that vaccines save lives," Maxwell said from where he sat on top of the surgery table, legs dangling. Except for how very tall he was, he looked like a child, his expression open and eager to learn. She probably often looked the same.

"And yet, I've seen many cases of tuberculosis brought on by the practice." Papa leaned back against the far cabinet, arms crossed.

"What about diseases that can't be survived without vaccination? Like rabies?"

She cleared her throat and both men turned toward her. "The waiting room is empty. I thought I'd go home and see if I can help Mama with the lunch preparations."

Maxwell hopped down from the table. "I'll walk down to the café."

"Nonsense. You're welcome to eat with Hattie and me. The wife always makes plenty."

"I don't want to wear out my welcome."

Hattie let them argue as she preceded them into the hall. She turned to lock the front door of the clinic and then met the two men on the back stoop. Maxwell took her arm momentarily to guide her down the step, quickly moving away once she'd gained her footing below. A polite gesture her father often seemed to forget.

"What's your opinion on vaccinations?"

Frazzled by the simple touch of his hand, it took moments for Hattie to realize Maxwell was speaking to her.

She knew her papa's opinion; he disagreed with vaccinations. He truly believed what he'd been telling Maxwell inside, that many times they resulted in other complications for the patients.

"Hattie hasn't had a formal education," her papa interjected.

Not unless he counted the many texts from his library that she had read and reread. Certainly she'd never taken a formal lecture, but she knew much about the human body from her hands-on experience. Did Papa even notice?

But Maxwell had asked for her opinion. It raised him in her estimation.

She phrased her answer carefully. "I can concede your point. Rabies vaccinations could save a life when nothing else can. But is it necessary to vaccinate children against smallpox if there has been no recent outbreak?"

"The vaccination won't do any good if the child

contracts the disease," he argued softly. His green eyes were alight with interest and intelligence, the way they had been the other night when he'd talked about his university classes.

She turned her face away to look at the opposite side of the street.

She couldn't afford the distraction he presented. Even if he did invite her into the conversation as if she was an equal participant. Even if he was handsome and intelligent and the only person of the male variety who had interested her in a long time. Most of the others were intimidated by her. But not Maxwell, it seemed.

She needed to stay focused. Her future in the medical profession demanded it.

The man was a distraction, even in Sunday worship service.

"It's a lovely day for a picnic," Mama said as Hattie attempted to avert her face from Maxwell White and his family. They did indeed take up an entire pew. She'd been aware of Maxwell sitting kitty-corner behind her since he'd come in. And when they'd sung hymns, his strong baritone rang out and sent chills down her spine.

It had taken all of her effort to concentrate on the preacher's sermon.

And now several young ladies Hattie recognized from town were tittering nearby. She distinctly heard the whispered words *doctor* and *back in town*. Were they already setting their caps for the young medical student?

It shouldn't bother her. In fact, if Maxwell began

paying court to one of the pretty young ladies in town, he might have less time to devote to her father's clinic.

But something about it rankled, and she didn't want to dwell on why it bothered her.

"Are you still joining Emily Castlerock and her husband for the meal?" Mama asked, bringing Hattie out of her embarrassing thoughts. "Will any other gentlemen be joining you? Single gentlemen?"

"Yes to the first, and no to the second, Mama." Hattie scooped up the small basket with the cake she'd baked and settled it over her forearm. Part of her wished she could better attend to her mama's expectations, but she'd been dreaming of being a doctor and working with papa as a true partner for so long that she didn't dare to try to court, as well. She'd never heard of a man who wanted a doctor for a wife.

Mama sighed. "Your father and I may go ahead and return home. He's overtired from his workload this week and will be better off resting this afternoon instead of socializing."

"Fine. I can walk home." Bear Creek was small enough that she needn't worry. The saloons weren't open on Sundays, and she should be safe enough. "Will you remind Papa that I'd like to speak to him tonight?" Hattie's stomach swooped as she said the words. If everything went as planned, she might be able to secure her papa's agreement tonight.

Her mother nodded idly. "Perhaps some young man will offer to escort you home. I can hope, can't I?" The last part was whispered as Mama turned away to find Papa in the crowded aisle.

"Hattie!"

She spotted Emily's effusive wave over the heads

of several people and edged her way toward the outside door to meet up with her friend.

She joined Emily just before the door, and they swept outside together, linking arms, with Hattie's basket on the outside.

"Sam is already spreading the blanket. I asked him to find a bit of shade." Emily gave a chagrined smile, her free hand absently going to her gently burgeoning belly. "It seems I can never get cool enough anymore."

Hattie chuckled. "It will pass in time."

"I hope so. Er...I hope you don't mind that Sam invited a friend to join us. And it looks like Oscar and Sarah White have settled their blanket next to ours, as well."

Hattie had been idly scanning the picnic area outside the church, but now her eyes went right to the large oak near the back of the church, where Sam Castlerock stood with Maxwell and another man she vaguely recognized as Maxwell's older brother. Next to the quilt beneath the tree, another blanket had been spread and a woman a few years older than Hattie unloaded a picnic blanket, a swaddled infant on the blanket next to her.

She almost turned back to find her parents and return home with them. But she wasn't a coward. She could endure one lunch with the man she found so disarming. And if Mama heard about it later, perhaps she would be happy, as well. She asked after Maxwell nearly every day, as if sensing the interest Hattie needed to deny.

"Afternoon, Miss Hattie." Sam greeted her with a smile. He turned the same on his wife, but the expression became intimate and warm.

Hattie looked away. Right into Maxwell's face.

"Hattie." He nodded, tipping his hat but not removing it.

Either he'd spent some time in the sun without his hat between when she'd seen him Friday and this moment, or he was blushing slightly.

It seemed coincidental that Sam and Emily had innocently invited Maxwell to join the picnic Hattie had previously agreed to. But a deeper question was, had Maxwell put them up to it? Did he have some motive to do so? To attempt to get in her good graces?

She didn't know, and he didn't speak.

The awkward moment was broken when a small girl of about three ran up and clung to Maxwell's leg. "Unca Max!"

He bent and scooped up the young girl, bouncing her in his arms before settling her on his hip.

"Who's this?" Hattie asked, grateful for something to draw her attention from the uncomfortable thought that Emily might've set her up.

"My niece Velma. Her two older sisters are around somewhere. Probably running around with Breanna."

The girl's glossy dark fall of hair, darkly tanned skin and deep coffee-colored eyes were a contrast to the woman on the nearby blanket, who had a fair complexion and blond hair, and Maxwell's brother, who had brown hair but fair skin, as well. And…she had two older sisters?

Hattie darted a confused glance at Maxwell's brother, scrutinizing his face as he knelt to help his wife.

"The girls are adopted," Maxwell explained quietly, as if he'd sensed her questions without her having to ask.

"That's right." She remembered now, a little embarrassed that it had taken his reminder to jog her memory. "I suppose I've been spending too much time with Papa in the clinic and not enough socializing. I don't know that I've officially met your brother."

Introductions were made and bodies found seats, and Hattie found herself sandwiched between the two couples on their respective blankets, far too close to Maxwell, who balanced the toddler on his knee.

"I'll take Velma," Sarah said, but Maxwell shook his head.

"She's fine where she is. Not bothering me."

As she settled her skirts, Hattie's gaze was drawn behind Maxwell to the small white dog crouching half-hidden in the green grass, the little creature he'd brought to supper.

"Still following you around, I see," she said.

He glanced over his shoulder, then turned a chagrined smile back on Hattie. "Can't seem to shake him, no matter if I'm out rustling up the horses or at the barn or the bunkhouse."

The dog's tail swished through the grass.

"At least he is polite," she said, smiling a little in return.

Hattie attempted to focus on Emily and the food being served, but couldn't help being aware of the man next to her, his quiet voice conversing with the tot and her excited chatter in response.

He was good with Velma. It probably shouldn't be a surprise, with how many siblings he had.

"Has my friend been a pain underfoot in the clinic?" Sam asked as he passed her a filled plate.

Maxwell's head didn't come up, but she had the sense he was listening.

"Maxwell and I haven't had much of a chance to work together." Hattie considered stuffing the whole biscuit in her mouth to avoid having to answer further. Unfortunately, her mother would be mortified by such a lack of manners. "Papa seems content with his help." And content to stick Hattie with the administrative tasks and cleaning.

But she couldn't be satisfied with the way things were. Not yet.

He was going to kill his brother and Sam.

Maxwell thought he'd kept his attraction to Hattie under his hat, but somehow Oscar must've found out and orchestrated the picnic lunch with Hattie in attendance. He couldn't imagine their wives putting them up to it, so it *must've* been the two men who had conspired against him.

He knew his brother probably had his best interests at heart. One of Oscar's first interactions with Sarah had been at a picnic for a town fund-raiser, so no doubt he thought the situation perfect for Maxwell to charm Hattie. But Maxwell's discomfort at Oscar and Sam's maneuvering choked him up and made it nearly impossible for him to speak.

It reminded him of the time eight years ago when Penny had invited Emily to sit with their family at a barn raising and he'd been humiliated by his youngest brother, Seb.

In fact, it might behoove him to keep an eye out for

the boys. Penny had long since corralled their most devious impulses, but he wouldn't put it past one of his brothers—or even Breanna—to play a prank in hopes of embarrassing him.

And he was already embarrassed enough.

"Hattie. Oh, Hattie!"

He looked up to find a gaggle of beruffled young women descending on them. He choked on the bite of cake he'd been chewing. Coughing, eyes watering, he blinked several times, then took a drink of his sweet tea.

Finally breathing freely, he looked up to find two young women speaking with Hattie, who had risen to join them. Only two, not the large group he'd initially thought. And feared.

He knew his ma had hoped that being away at university would build his confidence, remove some of his shyness around the opposite sex. And it had, up until Elizabeth, the girl he'd planned to marry, had broken things off with him. And that had come after another young lady had found him wanting, as well. His birth ma had told him up until he was eleven that no woman would ever want him. And after those rejections at college, it seemed she was right.

Safer to assume he would never marry. So he'd fallen back into his old habits of avoidance and quiet. He was just as tongue-tied now as he'd been at sixteen.

"Can we join you for a moment?" Two of Hattie's friends folded themselves onto the very edge of the blanket and darted glances at Maxwell from beneath their eyelashes.

"Have you met Maxwell White?" Hattie asked. "He's a medical student back in town for the summer." She suspected they already knew it, but pretended ignorance of their intention in joining the group. "My friends, Annabelle and Corrine."

Interestingly, he was even more pink than he'd been before.

He doffed his hat and reached out to shake their hands, turning the tot on his knee over to Oscar.

The girls twittered and preened beneath his notice.

"Where have you been in school?" asked Annabelle.

"Denver."

"Oh, Denver. I've only ever visited Cheyenne."

He nodded, shifting his legs on the blanket. His boot knocked into Hattie's shoe and he cleared his throat. He didn't say more.

"And do you find the lectures diverting?"

"Yes."

Annabelle appeared crestfallen at his lack of conversation, lips forming a small, attractive pout.

"We missed you at the poetry club reading last night," Corrine said to Hattie.

Maxwell's head came up, but then he looked away, hand flexing on his knee.

"I couldn't make it." Hattie had been worried her nerves would act up after a busy Saturday on her feet at the clinic.

"What's the poetry club?" asked Sam.

Maxwell shot a glare at his friend. Had Sam seen Maxwell's interest, as Hattie had, or was he simply making conversation?

"It's an opportunity for some of the young people

in town to get together," Annabelle explained. "We have a poetry reading and refreshments and time to chat."

"You should come next time." Corrine directed her statement at Maxwell, though he was looking down at his hands.

"It was Wanda's brainchild." Corrine went on when Maxwell didn't respond. She pointed over her shoulder and Hattie's gaze followed.

The grocer's daughter met Hattie's gaze with a glare. While they weren't rivals, the other girl hadn't particularly liked Hattie since her family had arrived in town.

After a few more polite exchanges, through which Maxwell was noticeably quiet, the other two girls left.

Hattie actually heard a soft sigh escape the man beside her.

She shouldn't even care that he was awkward but couldn't help herself from noticing the color high in his cheeks. He kept his face downturned, and his hat brim hid most of his expression. Probably Annabelle and Corrine hadn't even noticed. But Hattie had.

Her heart thumped with compassion. She knew what it was like to be a little different than everyone else. To not quite fit in.

But what kept this fit, handsome young man from doing so? There was something deeper behind his reticence to talk to the young women. She was almost sure of it.

His brother captured his attention with a quiet comment Hattie couldn't make out.

She was still idly wondering about it a few moments

later when two boys of about six ran up. The white dog darted away, barely escaping being stepped on.

"Maxwell—" one of them gasped.

The man scooped the child onto his knee, where the toddler had been shortly before. "What's the matter?" He was completely unruffled by the boy's upset.

"Bobby cut his hand," the boy panted, "and I told him you was a doctor…and could help."

Maxwell sat the first boy beside him and motioned Bobby onto the blanket.

"I'm not a doctor. Yet." She had to admire the determination in his voice—it mirrored her own. "But let's take a look."

The boy held out a grubby hand, palm up. Too dirty to see much. Typical of a little boy.

Anticipating what he would need, Hattie already had her handkerchief out. She wetted it in the Mason jar of water she'd been drinking from and passed it to Maxwell, ignoring the jolt she felt when her fingers brushed his palm.

"Thanks," he murmured. To the boy, he said, "Have you met Miss Hattie? She's Doc Powell's nurse. This is my brother Walt and his friend Bobby."

Both boys turned to her with wide eyes. She admired the way he'd distracted them as he worked to wipe the grime off the boy's palm.

"I'm not really a nurse," Hattie said softly.

"Might as well be," Maxwell returned as he handed her back the now-soiled handkerchief. "You've got enough experience. You helped save the man who'd been shot."

She fidgeted with her skirt. Wished his words

didn't affect her, but they sent a bolt of pleasure through her.

"What do you think, Nurse Hattie?" he asked, extending the boy's hand for her to see. There was a thin scratch on the surface, with only a few beads of blood. Nothing that would require stitches or even much of a bandage. And yet Maxwell treated it seriously, not downplaying his brother's concern for his friend.

"Hmm." She pretended to consider it, and their eyes met momentarily. She was stunned again at the intense green of Maxwell's eyes and had to look away. "I think a bandage is the best course of treatment. It will keep the wound clean. But I've used my handkerchief."

"Here," said Emily, passing a clean, white cloth from Hattie's other side.

Emily's eyes shone with interest, and Hattie was suddenly reminded that she and Maxwell were not alone with the boys. A glance at Oscar and Sarah's blanket revealed they were watching the exchange, as well.

"Thanks," Hattie muttered to her friend.

Emily's knowing gaze sent a shaft of discomfort through Hattie. Whatever her friend was thinking, she wasn't interested in the cowboy medical student. No matter how good he was with kids. Or how handsome he was.

She wasn't interested. She couldn't afford to be, couldn't afford to lose sight of her goals. Being a doctor was too important to her.

Perhaps she needed to go back to some of her father's texts. If she could prove she could diagnose some of the injuries and sickness they were bound to see in the coming days, her father would have to see things Hattie's way.

She could only hope.

Chapter Four

"The swelling appears to be minor...."

Hattie turned her back to stifle the grin that wanted to escape. If Annabelle's ankle was swollen at all, Hattie couldn't see it. Several days after the church picnic, it was clear her friend had manufactured the injury simply to have an excuse to see the cowboy doctor. And she hadn't been the first. Wanda had been one of the first patients yesterday morning, sporting a small burn she'd sustained in the kitchen. Something Hattie's own mother could've attended to.

"Does this hurt?" Maxwell asked.

"Not—not too badly."

Hattie turned back to the tableau in front of her. Her father was in the surgery next door, talking to a farmer who had a cancerous mass in his upper stomach. Hattie would much rather be in on that discussion, listening to her father speak on the merits and dangers of surgery to remove the mass. Especially after papa had put off their discussion about her schooling again.

But her father had insisted she accompany Maxwell into this sham appointment of Annabelle's for propriety's sake.

The young woman sat with shoe off and skirt demurely covering all of her leg except her ankle, which she had supposedly twisted.

Her fluttery-lashed gaze locked on Maxwell's face made Hattie a bit nauseous.

To his merit, he was completely focused on the other girl's supposed injury and seemed oblivious to her interest in him. It was so different from his manner outside of the clinic that Hattie was surprised, to say the least.

He rotated the ankle, his strong fingers closing over the joint. Hattie knew he would be able to tell if anything felt out of place, though she sincerely doubted there was anything wrong.

Finally making some internal determination, he released the ankle with a nod. "You can put your... your stocking and shoe back on now." It was the first time he'd seemed disconcerted during the interview. He turned his back as if to allow Annabelle privacy.

Observing the speed with which the other girl was able to do up the hooks on her stylish shoe, Hattie knew there was nothing seriously wrong. She moved to her friend's side and offered an elbow to help the other girl down from the examination table.

Hattie gave her friend a reproving glance, at which the other girl flushed delicately. However, Annabelle quickly returned her brown-eyed gaze to the doctor in training. "What should I do?"

"Rest. Try to stay off of the ankle as much as you can. If it starts paining you, elevate it. It should be all right in a few days. Maybe a couple of weeks at the outside. If it gets worse, come back and Doc Powell can look at it."

Annabelle looked up into his face, giving her widest smile as they both turned toward the hallway. Hattie followed them a few steps as they moved to the empty waiting room and paused near the door.

"Thank you so much for your kind attention," Annabelle gushed.

Hattie couldn't see his face, but the back of Maxwell's neck was turning red. "I was just…ah…doing my job. Or, well…what I hope will be my job—that is, after I'm able to return to my schooling. And finish."

Annabelle pretended not to notice his evident nervousness. "Will you have time for a luncheon break tomorrow? I know my mother would love you to come share the noon meal with us—and thank you for your help today."

"Well, I don't know—"

Papa and the farmer joined them from the back room, forestalling Annabelle from pushing Maxwell into the invitation. She took her leave as the farmer did, with one last, regretful glance.

Hattie glanced out the window and smiled. Her friend wasn't limping at all as she crossed the street toward her mother's dress shop.

"Everything all right with Miss Perkins?" Papa asked Maxwell as they turned and walked back down the hall to the examining room.

"Probably a minor turned ankle." Maxwell said. Did he really not know?

Hattie snorted as she bent to straighten a basket of extra linens kept behind the desk in the corner of the waiting room.

"Hattie?" Papa asked. "Do you have something to add?"

She shook out the top linen to refold it. "Only that I don't believe Annabelle twisted her ankle at all."

"Are you saying Maxwell's diagnosis was incorrect?" Papa challenged her. "On what basis?"

"There was no bruising, no discoloration like there should've been if there was a real injury."

Maxwell's sharp green gaze landed on her. Considering her. Actively listening to her, in contrast to her papa, who had already turned away.

"The young lady claimed to be in pain," Maxwell said.

Hattie motioned to her father. "How often have you told me that sometimes patients will give false information or not tell the whole story? That a doctor has to read between the lines?"

"But why would she do that?" Maxwell asked, seeming genuinely perplexed.

"To get your attention," Hattie informed him. "She's sweet on you."

"What?" Maxwell sputtered. His face mottled with color.

"Hmm. Well, perhaps it was good that you were involved in the examination, Hattie."

"Sir, I don't— Why would she— That can't be right," Maxwell said. He turned to Hattie, as if for clarification. "You must be mistaken."

"I don't think so." She fluttered her hand in his direction but didn't look directly at him. "A handsome man such as yourself…even at Sunday's picnic the young ladies were eyeing you."

Now his face was almost purple. He clutched the

back of his neck with one hand. A nervous gesture or an unconscious one?

Papa patted him on the shoulder. "I'm afraid a single young man like yourself in a profession like ours will be chased by mamas and daughters alike."

Maxwell's face was on fire.

Hattie thinks I'm handsome.

He should probably be irritated that she'd challenged his diagnosis—although her observations seemed correct—but the thought that throbbed in the forefront of his brain was that Hattie found him pleasing to the eye.

He stuffed his hands in his pockets, not knowing what to do with them or what he really felt, still stuck on that one thought until Doc Powell said, "I've noticed your bedside manner when you are with some of the young ladies needs...shall we say, some work."

Now humiliation raced through him for another reason. Maxwell knew his manners tended to be awkward when he didn't know a lady well. In a clinical situation he was usually fine, but put him in a social situation and he didn't know what to say or do.

"You're an intelligent young man," the doctor said. "But if you can't speak to your patients, you will have trouble throughout your career."

Maxwell barely heard the compliment in the doctor's words, but the criticism hit home. He nodded. And was relieved to hear the jingle of a harness outside the front of the clinic. "I'll see if that's a new patient." And get some air. He needed to think. Plan.

Figure out a way to talk to ladies without sounding like a blithering idiot.

Out in the fresh spring air, he took a deep breath.

"Maxwell!" a female voice called out and he flinched. Then realized who it was.

"Ma. What're you doing here?"

His pa rounded the back of the wagon. "I had to come into town to talk to the banker, and your ma insisted on coming along to have a visit with you." The older man settled one forearm on the wagon railing.

Maxwell met Penny at the wagon bench and swung her down, noting that for an expectant mother nearing her time, she didn't carry much extra weight. A benefit to being an active homesteader's wife.

She reached up and bussed Maxwell's cheek. "I'm not so cumbersome that I can't come into town for a visit. Since you're either busy at home or busy at the doctor's office, it seems like this is my only choice." She slid one hand through his arm. They waved to Jonas, who headed down the street, leaving his son to take care of his very pregnant wife. The implied trust swelled Maxwell's chest.

"Maxwell—" Hattie stuck her head out the clinic door. "Oh, hello."

"Have you met my ma?" he asked, proud to turn to the side with Penny on his arm.

"Yes, of course. How are you today, Mrs. White? Are you here for an examination?"

"Hmm. Well, I wanted to sneak Maxwell away for lunch if he was available. Perhaps I should speak to the doctor before we return home."

"Fine. I'll tell Papa." Hattie's smile dimmed when she included Maxwell in her gaze. His heart dipped. She might think he was handsome—so she said—but she didn't like him much.

It shouldn't come as a surprise. How often had his birth ma told him how worthless he was? That no woman would ever love him?

Penny had. With her support, he'd learned to read, and her encouragement—and Oscar's—had put him on the road to medical school. She loved him as his own mother hadn't been able to. He couldn't ask for more than that, could he?

"How have you been feeling?" he asked, making an effort to turn his morose thoughts just as he guided his ma toward the little café on Main Street. "Not overdoing it?"

She laughed. "You sound like Jonas. He caught me on the bottom rung of the ladder in the barn and about had a conniption—"

"What were you doing climbing the ladder?"

"I wasn't." She nudged him with her elbow. "Breanna was in the hayloft, where we've stored some things for the new baby, fetching them for me. I was waiting patiently at the bottom—"

"Mmm-hmm." He raised one brow at his ma, knowing her penchant for impatience.

She laughed again. He'd missed her so much when he'd been gone. Missed her ready smile and the love she gave so freely to the family around her.

They ducked into the café and found a table. After they'd ordered the daily special, Penny laid one hand over her bulging belly and turned her quizzical gaze on him.

"And how are things going at the clinic? I know your plans for medical school haven't exactly come to fruition, but do you feel you can learn something working with Doctor Powell?"

As he thought about the doctor's criticism—albeit a deserved one—Maxwell's unease must've shown in his face. Penny leaned forward. "What? Did something happen?"

"Nothing bad." He stumbled over the words. "It's just…" How did he even phrase what had taken place this morning? "A young lady came into the clinic, but the nurse—I mean, the doctor's daughter—thought she was feigning her complaint. So she could…er—invite me for lunch." His neck heated just saying the words.

Penny's eyes lit up. "Who was it?"

He really didn't need his ma getting any romantic ideas. He shook his head. "Doesn't matter. It's not just this morning. Sometimes I have trouble…conversing easily with…" He shrugged.

She seemed to know. "Young ladies of a marriageable age? Still? Did my lessons before you left for university fall on deaf ears?"

He wrinkled his nose at the humor in her tone. Crossed his arms over his chest, although he knew she wasn't laughing at his plight. She would never do something so hurtful. He'd seen her nearly come to blows with an old schoolteacher over Breanna's education and knew how fiercely she cared for each of her children, both adopted and natural.

"Do you remember when I first came to know your family?" She brushed an escaped lock of her auburn hair off her cheek. "And you asked me for help talking to Emily—now Emily Castlerock?"

"Of course." He shifted in his seat, instinctively knowing what she was going to say.

"Just be yourself. You've got no trouble relating to

any of your brothers or sisters, or even young women who have become your friends. Don't worry so much about it."

He remembered when she'd said the same to him at age sixteen. He'd had trouble believing her then. And he'd never told her specifically what had happened with Elizabeth or the other college girl. That his being himself hadn't been enough to hold either young woman's interest, much less her love. He still couldn't quite believe Penny's words.

And apparently, she wasn't finished yet. "You are a charming young man with such potential. It's no wonder some of the young ladies in Bear Creek are noticing your fine qualities."

He shifted again.

He didn't plan on marriage for his future. Couldn't. He'd been surprised when Jonas had accepted him into his large family, and even more so when Penny had come to love him. He held no illusions of finding love, the kind of true love that made a strong marriage, not after the childhood he'd had. But what about friendship?

"What about…if there's someone who doesn't particularly like me…but I'd like to be her friend. What should I do?"

For a moment, a fierce light shone in his ma's eyes. "My advice is the same. Be yourself."

He'd been trying. Working to find natural ways to include Hattie in his conversations with the doctor. And she still didn't seem to like him.

He didn't think he'd done anything to offend her.

Couldn't think of anything he hadn't already done to earn her trust.

How could he believe what Penny said, that he was enough as himself, when it obviously wasn't true?

Hattie attended Mrs. White after she and Maxwell returned from their noon meal and his mother had spoken to the doctor.

"Thank you," Mrs. White said as Hattie helped her off of the examination table. "My balance isn't what it used to be."

The older woman looked at Hattie. "I know we haven't met other than once or twice, but Maxwell only has kind things to say about you."

Hattie half turned away, embarrassment staining her cheeks. She fiddled with the bow on her full-length apron.

"I'd like to ask a favor—from one woman to another, you understand."

Now Hattie's head came up.

"My son hasn't always had the easiest time. He probably won't thank me for saying so, but he's been a bit discouraged since he had to return home for the summer. If there is any way you could…smooth the way for him in your father's clinic, I would be grateful."

Hattie inhaled deeply. How dare this woman come in and ask for favors for her son—when he already had so many advantages? Being born a male, for one. He'd been allowed to pursue his education, had been given the opportunity she desperately wanted.

Penny's brow creased. She seemed to realize Hattie had stiffened.

"I don't mean to offend or ask more than I should," the older woman said in a quieter voice, putting one hand on Hattie's arm when Hattie would have turned away. "I only want things…not to be so hard for him."

While Hattie could understand a mother's concern, to a point, this particular woman asked too much. Hattie smiled wanly. "I'm certain we'll rub along just fine." As long as he stayed out of her way, she would stay out of his.

"I also wanted to say, I think it's admirable that you help your father in his work," Penny said, just before she left. Hattie heard her speak to Maxwell in the front vestibule before things went silent.

Hattie was left to ponder her words. Had Maxwell really said positive things about Hattie, when she hadn't been particularly kind to him? She'd been a part of the conversation with her papa earlier and knew she could perhaps make things easier for Maxwell with her friends and acquaintances as they came to the clinic. But why should she? She didn't owe the cowboy anything.

Her roiling thoughts didn't last long. She had reorganized the examination room and was moving toward the waiting area when a screaming woman burst through the outer door.

Maxwell bumped Hattie's shoulder as he joined her. "What—"

"He's choking! Please help!" the mother shrieked. She held out a limp, white-faced toddler.

When Maxwell didn't respond, Hattie took the small boy into her arms. "Where's Papa?" she demanded of Maxwell.

"He stepped out to check on someone—said he wouldn't take long."

Even if Papa would only be gone a matter of minutes, any delay would be too late for this child. The toddler's lips were turning blue. He gasped for breath but found none.

Hattie sank to the floor, heedless of dirtying her dress, and positioned the child facedown across her knees.

"Do something!" the mother cried.

"I am." Hattie pounded the boy between his shoulder blades. Again. Again.

Nothing happened. The boy remained still, draped over her lap, and a jolt of fear surged through her.

She felt it when Maxwell knelt beside her. Would he attempt to yank the child from her, to try something else, thinking she didn't know what she was doing?

He didn't. He only placed one hand in support of her back and said, "C'mon, Hattie."

Her open palm thudded against the little back once more, and this time the child hacked and a small object pinged against the wooden floor.

The boy gasped and squirmed. Hattie helped him to turn over and immediately noted the color blooming into his cheeks, his chest expanding with breath. And the boy began sobbing, reaching for his mother.

Weak-kneed now that the moment was over, Hattie attempted to lift him in trembling arms. Maxwell was there to help him get into his mother's embrace. The mother was now crying as well, tears streaking down her cheeks.

Shaken, Hattie attempted to push off the floor. Maxwell's hand came beneath her elbow and steadied her, remaining even after she'd managed to find her feet.

"You saved his life," the mother said through her tears, clutching the now-quieting child to her shoulder.

Maxwell bent. When he rose, he held up the obstruction in his palm. "A marble, looks like."

"From my older boy's things," the mother explained. "I've told him time and again to keep them put up when the baby is on the floor—" She dissolved into tears again.

A glance at Maxwell revealed he appeared flummoxed as to how to deal with the woman. Hattie rolled her eyes in his direction and moved forward to offer a comforting embrace. "It's all right now. Look at him—he's just fine."

Indeed, the baby was reaching for Maxwell. Or possibly the marble. Bright-eyed and alert, he didn't seem to know the danger he'd just escaped.

"He wouldn't have been fine without you," the mother said. "How can I ever thank you?"

Hattie only smiled. She was still shaken, but at least her trembling had stopped. "I was only doing what needed to be done."

She felt Maxwell's gaze on her but couldn't meet it. She escorted the mother and son outdoors, attempting to catch her breath. A feeling of elation and *rightness* stole over her. Hattie wanted to do more things like that, saving that child's life. And she could do more, as a doctor.

If only Papa had been here to see.

Regardless, the event made her more determined than ever to speak to her papa. She'd saved a boy's life today. And she wanted to do so again in the future— by being a doctor.

* * *

Hours later, Maxwell stood in the clinic's hallway, debating between taking his leave of Hattie or stepping into the examination room to help her tidy up. He could guess which course of action she would prefer he take.

The doctor had already left on a late house call, and they were alone in the quiet building. Afternoon sunlight slanted in the window.

Penny's advice and the doctor's urging to find a way to be more comfortable with the opposite sex both rang in his head. He wanted Hattie for a friend, even if nothing more would ever come of it. How many rejections did it take for a man to realize he wouldn't make a good husband for anyone? And why did knowing Hattie rub against that thought like an annoying blister?

His heart thudded painfully. Should he be polite or make himself scarce?

The manners Penny had drilled into him and his brothers won out.

He cleared his throat so she would hear him come into the room. She looked over her shoulder from where she knelt near the cupboard on the far wall, scrubbing the lower front of the cabinet.

He went to the table and gathered up the soiled linens, putting them in a canvas bag laid alongside, as he'd seen her do once before. He guessed Hattie or her mother laundered the bandages and other linens at their home.

"You don't have to stay," she said.

"I know."

Without turning his head, he saw her scrub the

cabinet even harder than before. "Papa likely won't notice you've helped clean up in here." Meaning she wouldn't tell her father.

"I'm not doing it for your father. I agreed to work here to learn—and that includes helping out in the clinic. And I'd like to help you." He stuffed the last of the linens into the sack and went out the door, face burning. He deposited the canvas bag near the back door, where he would offer to take it home for her. If she would let him.

She didn't glance up when he returned and wordlessly took the scrub bucket from her and began wiping down the countertop.

She turned her back and set about unfolding a new sheet across the table for the next morning's first patient.

"Most men would consider this women's work."

He considered his words, considered what one thing he might be able to say to change her mind about him. "Maybe I'm not like most men."

Hattie slipped out of the clinic, throwing the bag of dirty linens over her shoulder.

Not only had Maxwell stayed late the past few nights, talking to her father and ruining her opportunity to start the conversation about medical school, but now he intruded into her usual time of settling things in the clinic. After talking with his mother earlier, Hattie was feeling distinctly guilty.

She needed to escape, wanted to go home and have some time to herself, get her bearings again.

She was starting to like the man. Against everything—his presence in her space, his influence with her father, her worries that she wouldn't be able to convince her father about medical school—she liked Maxwell White.

She needed to get away from him.

She heard the clinic door open and snap closed behind her. Papa had given the man a key so he could lock up. She kept going, hurrying her pace a bit.

He called after her, "Hattie. Hattie, wait!"

The alley wasn't long, but two men stumbled into the mouth of it, blocking her path to the street beyond. By their wobbly stances, they were obviously intoxicated, though it was early in the evening for them to be in such a state. Hattie's mother had warned her about rowdy cowboys, which by the looks of these men's worn shirts and chaps-covered trousers, had been a fair warning.

"Well, lookee here," one of them slurred. "Found us a pretty lady."

The other tried to doff his Stetson but ended up knocking it from his head. It took him two tries to pick it up.

"Excuse me." She didn't waste time looking behind to see if Maxwell had followed her. No doubt her manner had put him off. She quickly pushed past the men onto the street. There wasn't much foot traffic, with it being the end of the business day. But it was still broad daylight. Surely they wouldn't pester her, even if they were inebriated.

She set her feet toward home, but a rough hand on her shoulder spun her around and she dropped the linens.

"Hold on there, missy."

"Let go!" She struggled to get away from the man's

surprisingly strong grip. She got tangled in the bundle she'd dropped and lost her footing, quickly finding herself sitting down in the street.

The men laughed, looming over her. Throat dry, she couldn't find her voice to call out for help. Fear sliced through her.

Was there no one on the street to come to her assistance?

"That's enough, fellas."

A bolt of relief flared through her even as she recognized the voice. Maxwell.

The men turned to face him as he came up the alley behind, but they remained between Hattie and her would-be rescuer.

"Aw, now. We're just having a bit of fun. Nothing to concern you."

"Anything to do with Miss Powell concerns me."

Hattie's heart thudded at the blatant overexaggeration. With the way she'd treated Maxwell, he would be in the right to turn and walk away.

One of the men looked back at her, squinting. "Powell? This the doctor's daughter? One of the other hands was telling me all about her—how she was a pretty li'l thing but as high-strung as a rattler about to strike. That true, sweetheart?" The man shot her a leering look.

Maxwell pushed his way between the two men and knelt over her. "As I said before, that's enough." He was smart enough to glance over his shoulder as he helped her to her feet, but she knew it was still risky for him to turn his back on the men.

The warmth of his hand over her elbow was a momentary comfort. He gave her a gentle push down the street, away from the men. But she turned back, unable to just leave him to fend for himself against the two goons.

"Now, hold on, mister. You ain't got no right to interfere—"

"As a gentleman, I have enough—" Maxwell started, but the man interrupted.

"You sayin' we ain't gentlemen?"

"That an insult?" The men's voices overlapped each other this time.

Before she could blink, one of them swung at Maxwell, clipping his shoulder.

Hattie shrieked.

The other man threw a punch, his fist connecting with Maxwell's cheek. But Maxwell recovered, shoving his shoulder into one man's chest and ducking a second punch from the other.

"Stop!" Hattie cried out as Maxwell took a kick to the stomach and went to his knees.

"Get outta here," he ordered her, eyes like fire.

Unable to commit to running down to the sheriff's office, Hattie was relieved when a man with a tin badge thundered up the street to them.

He reined in his horse and roared, "What's going on here?"

Instantly, the two drunks stopped fighting, leaving Maxwell on his knees on the packed-dirt street, a trickle of blood flowing down his cheek.

Across the street, a door opened and one of the shopkeepers stepped out onto the boardwalk. "I saw the whole thing!" he shouted.

Then why hadn't the man come outside to help?

Hattie wondered. She rushed to Maxwell's side, taking his arm in preparation to help him to his feet.

He squinted up at her. "You all right?"

How could he even ask that, when he'd been the one in the fistfight?

Beneath her hand, the muscles of his arm flexed as he stood. He hadn't really needed her assistance. But part of her needed to hang on to him—to make sure he was in one piece.

The emotion frightened her, and she quickly let him go, bending to scoop up the laundry bag and the few items that had spilled out of it. He took it out of her shaking hands before she could protest.

Somehow he knew. He grasped her wrist, holding her still, until she looked up at him.

She couldn't meet his gaze. Her eyes flickered instead to the trickle of blood on his cheekbone. "We should go back to the clinic and patch you up."

His eyes remained on her for a long, silent moment. He wiped his cheek with the back of his other hand and barely glanced at the red stain that came away. "This is nothing. I've had worse tussling with my brothers."

She breathed deeply. "It would make me feel better. I don't want my mother to see me like this. I could use a few minutes to compose myself."

He watched her carefully. Then he nodded and turned to speak to the lawman in low tones. Remnants of fear still snaked through her, making her tremble deeply inside.

Then he was at her side, hand beneath her elbow, guiding her down the boardwalk instead of back through the alley.

"The leather-goods worker across the street saw the men accost you. The sheriff's deputy is taking those two down to the jail. There wasn't any question they'd both had a bit too much to drink."

He'd never strung so many words together, to her at least, at one time, but he kept up a steady stream of commentary as he ushered her carefully down the street.

"Didn't know you'd left the building until I came outside after you. I was going to offer to escort you home but you were already halfway down the alley. Then I saw those men...."

They reached the front door of the clinic, and she drew the brass key from her skirt pocket. She was relieved that her hand didn't shake as she turned the key in the lock. Of course, she would have to tell her mama and papa about the incident, but if she was able to compose herself first, then perhaps she could downplay her foolishness.

She locked the door behind them and he followed her into the first exam room, silent now.

"Sit down and I'll clean your cheek." She pointed to a hard-backed chair near the far wall. She moved to throw open the curtain so the last of the afternoon light would prevent the need for lighting a lamp.

Maxwell perched on the edge of the chair, acutely aware that they were alone in the silent building—and that Hattie's focus was on him. He probably should've just taken her home, but he understood her need for a few moments to herself. He just hoped he could be in her presence without making an utter fool of himself.

When Hattie approached with a damp rag, he swallowed hard. She stepped into the shaft of sunlight and it turned her hair gold, including the wisps now curling around her cheeks—they hadn't been loose when she'd left the clinic, and a renewed surge of anger went through him at the thought of what those two thugs might've done to her.

Gently, she touched beneath his chin and turned his face to the side.

The damp cloth moved over his skin, but what he noticed most was the light brush of her fingertips that followed. He closed his eyes against the sensation. Tried to forget the slice of fear that had cut through him when he'd seen her fall to the ground. Why had she rushed off alone?

"It's not terrible. A little scrape." Her voice remained matter-of-fact, as if she was totally unconcerned with touching him.

He knew it was just a scrape. But he wasn't going to risk her moving away by saying so. The cheek barely stung at all. However, his stomach muscles ached from the fluke kick one of the men had given him. In a few days, that would wear off, as well.

He'd wanted to do so much more to the two bullies but hadn't been able to with Hattie nearby and the urge to protect her still so strong in him.

"I'll put a little ointment on it, regardless." She turned to the cabinet, giving him a reprieve from her close presence, her womanly scent. He took a deep breath.

"I'm a bit surprised you came to my rescue," she said with her back still turned. "I haven't exactly had the most welcoming attitude toward you. I probably owe you an apology."

He shifted his feet, uneasy with her words, her acknowledgment that there was something between them—but not in the way he wanted. He shifted his legs again, out of her way, when she moved close.

He was glad to turn his face and focus out the window as he said, "I'm sorry if I make you uncomfortable. But I really need this experience with your father." He wouldn't apologize for that. Being a doctor was his life's mission.

"It's not that." Even though they were conversing, her total focus seemed to be on her task as she brushed medicine across his cheekbone. "You might say I'm a little protective of my working relationship with my father. A bit reluctant to let anyone in, I suppose."

He could understand that, given that her mother didn't seem to approve. But he also had the sense there was something else she held back, something more that meant she didn't want him in the clinic. He was surprised by how much he wanted her to trust him with it. But she stayed silent. Disappointed, he remained quiet, too.

She leaned back and wiped her fingers with the damp rag, then surprised him by reaching down and scooping up his hand from where it rested on his knee. She wiped away the small dried patch of blood from his knuckles, then turned his hand and wiped across his palm, as well.

He had the strongest urge to curl his fingers around her hand, to clasp it, to hold just that one part of her close, even for a moment. He resisted, afraid of what her reaction would be.

He flexed his hand as she moved away. He watched

as she moved to the cabinet and used a small hand mirror to attempt to fix her hair, finally giving up and removing some pins so that her chestnut locks fell loose. He swallowed hard as his eyes followed her every movement.

Now was his chance to ask what he'd been building up to before she'd sneaked out the back of the clinic. He'd been thinking about it all afternoon, since the doctor's challenge and his ma's visit. Hattie seemed more settled now, less shaken than she'd been right after the attack. She seemed a bit more open, maybe because of their shared experience.

So he stopped thinking and just asked.

"I was wondering if…you'd consider helping me with something. After what your father said, I need to…to figure out a way to talk to gals our age better. I was thinking, if you'd give me some advice… maybe help me through a couple of interactions with your friends, then start some conversations, help me get to know them…"

She had turned in the middle of his request and stood staring at him, mouth slightly open. Surprised or dismayed?

He tried to backpedal. "It's all right if you don't want to. I just thought since we were already spending some time together here in the clinic—"

"All right," she said softly, interrupting him.

He went silent. Afraid she could hear his heart thundering in his ears.

"I suppose I owe you, after what happened this afternoon." She appraised him with those vivid eyes. "There's a poetry-club meeting early next week. I can't remember which evening—Monday or Tuesday. If you'll escort me, I'll give you some pointers on talking to the other girls."

He nodded, pulse still pounding frantically. She'd agreed to help him—why did he wonder what he'd gotten himself into?

Chapter Five

Maxwell stood just outside the doctor's front door, shoring up his courage to knock. He was really doing this. Escorting Hattie to the poetry-club reading.

Behind him, voices conversed, and a low laugh sounded. He couldn't resist looking over his shoulder to see if one of his brothers was laughing at him. Oscar had reluctantly agreed when Maxwell had asked if he would attend, too. Then some of his other brothers had found out about it, and Davy, Ricky and Matty had somehow ended up in the wagon as well, spiffed and shined in their Sunday best. Edgar, the jokester who was notorious for being wary of women, was absent.

No one in the wagon seemed to be paying him any attention; his brothers were listening avidly to something Sarah was saying. Then Matty looked up and shot him a rakish grin.

All Maxwell could think about was the moment, years ago when Seb had blurted out to Emily that Maxwell couldn't read, humiliating him in front of the girl he'd been interested in at the time. Had he made a mistake in requesting his brothers' presence?

He never should've asked Oscar and his wife to go, but he was afraid he would run out of things to talk about with Hattie on his own.

His hand shook as he raised it to rap on the door.

Hattie's mother answered, a smile on her lips. "Hello, Maxwell. Come in. Hattie's just gathering a light shawl."

He followed Mrs. Powell into the foyer. He heard the doctor's voice from somewhere deeper in the house but couldn't make out the man's words. Hattie's mother seemed preoccupied, glancing over her shoulder instead of making conversation with Maxwell.

"Is everything all right? Hattie okay?" he asked, concern instantly cinching his chest tight. Had something happened between the time he'd left the office to get cleaned up and now? Had her condition, whatever it was, worsened?

"I'm fine." Hattie's voice turned his head, and he swallowed hard.

She wore a dress of dark pink that complemented her complexion. Her chestnut hair was done up fancier than it had been earlier, with several wisps clinging to the line of her neck. She was beautiful. But her eyes were shadowed.

"What's the matter?" he asked, coming closer. He wanted to reach out and touch her elbow, reassure her in some way, but he didn't dare.

She shook her head wordlessly, and at that moment the doctor came in from the hallway.

"Oh, good, Maxwell. You're here. Can you come into the parlor for a moment? Hattie, you, too."

She glanced at Maxwell, a wordless fear in her eyes, and this time he allowed himself to clasp her elbow as they followed the doctor into the sitting room. The older man didn't motion them to sit, though. Doc looked worried, with his bushy white brows down low over his eyes.

"Papa?" Hattie prompted him.

"Oh, yes. The doctor from Pear Grove just rang me up again. What he suspected was cholera has gone from two cases to an outbreak. In fact, he's down with it himself. He's asked for assistance, and I feel I have to go."

Maxwell's spirits sank. Without the doctor here, he wouldn't have the benefit of training with the man. Would he lose a week of patient care? A month? And worse—what about the people of Bear Creek who needed help?

"At this point, I don't know how long I'll be gone. And I'm conflicted about leaving my patients here without care."

Maxwell strove to control his disappointment. Working with Doc Powell hadn't been in his plans when he'd returned to Bear Creek, but it had eased his frustrations in not being able to return to medical school.

"Maxwell, do you think your brother can survive without you training those horses? At least for a while?"

Doc's words brought Maxwell's eyes up and stopped his whirling thoughts.

The other man was bent over his desk, rifling through a drawer.

"I thought that if the two of you could work together, perhaps you could take on the minor cases in the office. Can your brother spare you?"

Everything in Maxwell stilled as the doctor's words registered. His hand beneath Hattie's elbow, he realized she'd frozen, as well. Was she as surprised as he was by her pa's request?

He nodded. Oscar would have to rely on one of the other brothers to help him break the horses for a few days. It wouldn't be long, sounded like.

"Since last week, you've both shown better cooperation in the clinic. If you can work together, I believe the people of Bear Creek will be better off than not having anyone to help them."

The older man went silent, obviously waiting for an answer.

Hattie worked to contain her rioting emotions, to remain as still as possible, not to show the excitement that thrilled her. Here was her chance to prove her real worth to her father. All she had to do was agree to work with Maxwell while her papa was gone.

She would do anything to reach her dreams of becoming a doctor. Even that.

"Of course, Papa." She glanced quickly at Maxwell. Would he agree?

He met her eyes and nodded gravely, apparently as serious about the responsibility as she was. Her heart thrilled.

"Any life-threatening injuries or illnesses you'll need to send on to the doctor in Calvin. Hopefully, there won't be many of those cases until I return."

Hattie nodded, her mind spinning ahead. She would need to keep a journal, a record of all the treatments she administered while her father was gone. To prove what she'd done.

"With Hattie's longtime assistance to me, she'll be familiar with some of the chronic cases. Maxwell, you've proven yourself in the last couple days. If you work together, you should be able to help the people of Bear Creek."

Her mind went to Mrs. Fishbourne, one of the older ladies in town who suffered from rheumatism and came in often for treatment. Hattie would have to hope that there would be some new cases that she could diagnose, in hopes of impressing her father.

"I know you children are off to a social event, so I won't keep you. I've got to pack—the train leaves first thing in the morning. If I think of anything important, I'll leave a note for you, Hattie, and you can share it with Maxwell."

She blinked. In her rising excitement, she'd forgotten about the poetry reading. She would much rather stay home to make plans for working in the clinic, but she *had* promised to help Maxwell. She couldn't go back on it now.

She followed the cowboy doctor into the foyer, tucking the ends of her shawl around her upper arms.

With a quick buss on her mother's cheek and a squeeze of the older woman's shoulders—she could see the worry in her mother's eyes, no doubt over her father's impending trip—they scooted out the front door. She would have to comfort her mother later. Her father practiced more preventative cleanliness than many. She had faith he would be all right even in the midst of an occurrence of cholera. They had to trust to his training and trust God to prevent the outbreak from spreading further.

As she stepped over the threshold, Maxwell's hand came to her elbow again, enclosing her with warmth. She looked up to find his eyes resting on her, something unreadable in their depths. The moment stretched between them, until the sound of voices broke the connection.

Hattie looked up to find a passel of people bundled in the wagon that awaited them, and she hesitated on the stoop.

Maxwell cleared his throat. "I forgot to mention that some of my brothers decided to join us."

Well, that was a surprise but not totally unwelcome. Maybe they would ease the sudden tension that had sprung up between them after their talk with her father.

The wagon's tailgate was down. "Do you mind riding back here? It isn't far." Maxwell seemed so apologetic that she felt a pang of pity for his discomfort.

He gently boosted her into the back of the wagon, where two young men sat watching curiously. She couldn't help but be aware of his strong, wide hands at her waist. Her legs dangled off the back of the wagon and she shifted her skirts around them.

"All right?" he asked quietly.

She barely eked out a nod.

"Good evening, Hattie!" Sarah welcomed her with a smile from the wagon's bench seat.

"Hello," Hattie responded.

The wagon dipped as Maxwell climbed up beside her. His thigh brushed hers, and when he settled, they were hip to hip. She was aware of his warmth, his height. Where their legs and shoulders touched, sparks zinged along her traitorous nerves. There was no hint of numbness or fatigue tonight—she felt everything connected to the man beside her.

A soft slap of the reins from the front set the wagon in motion. Fortunately it was only a few blocks to the tearoom, where the rest of the young people would be gathered.

"Hullo," said another voice, and there was another shift in the bodies in the wagon. Hattie half turned to find one of the young men had extended a freckled hand to her. The freckles were a dominant feature, flowing all the way up into his face, where dancing blue eyes examined her. He had a mop of red hair, as well.

"These reprobates are some of my other brothers. Davy—" through Maxwell's introduction, the redhead pumped her hand enthusiastically "—and Matty. And that far one is Ricky."

Matty had blond hair and brown eyes and mischief in his quicksilver grin; Ricky was a darker blond with gray eyes. Both were slightly younger than the others, perhaps in their late teens.

"I'm Hattie," she offered. "I didn't know Maxwell had so many brothers interested in poetry."

Davy coughed, but Matty's smile spelled his orneriness. "You could say we're more interested in the gals interested in poetry. Ain't that right, Maxwell?"

Maxwell's hand on the wagon's side flexed.

"You might actually learn something about wooing women, Matty," Sarah chimed from the front of the wagon. "Women like romantic things like poetry."

"I don't need no help with my wooin'," the teen

retorted. "What, did Oscar quote you rhymes when y'all was courtin'?"

A hearty baritone laugh broke out from the front of the wagon. "*That* must be what I did wrong, why I messed up my original proposal."

Hattie heard a *thwack* as if the man's wife had thumped his arm with the back of her hand, and his chuckles ceased. Hattie glanced over her shoulder to see the couple sharing a deep, intimate look. There must be a story there—Oscar had said *original proposal.* Did that mean he'd had to propose marriage to Sarah more than once? How curious.

"I took a poetry class at the normal school," Sarah went on, ignoring her husband and his younger brother's cutting up as if it hadn't happened. "It was one of my favorite courses. Maxwell, did you have to study poetry while you were at college?"

"Um...yes." Hattie thought for a moment that was his entire contribution to Sarah's attempt to draw him into the conversation. Then came a hesitant, "I don't want to court anyone...just make some friends."

The wagon slowed as they neared the tearoom, and Maxwell hopped off before it had even come to a complete stop.

There were several people out on the boardwalk, including Corrine and Wanda. Annabelle must be inside. Hattie waved when the girls glanced in the direction of the Whites' wagon. They seemed to barely see her, their gaze immediately going to Maxwell.

He didn't notice, coming to Hattie and gently taking her waist to set her on the ground. Behind her, the younger brothers clambered over the side of the wagon as Oscar helped his wife from the bench seat.

Maxwell rubbed the back of his neck, glancing around awkwardly, as if he didn't know what to do next. She took his arm and turned him toward the tearoom.

"Did you enjoy your poetry class?" she asked quietly, wanting to ease his nervousness.

"Hmm?" He looked down at her.

"The poetry course. Did you enjoy it? A subject like that would at least be a conversation starter if you're hoping to make some new friends of the female persuasion tonight."

He looked over at his brothers. Was he afraid of their censure if he said yes?

"Yes, I enjoyed it," he finally responded in a low voice. "How should I...? What should I say about it?"

"Just bring it into conversation naturally," she said, squeezing his arm lightly. The others were descending, greeting Maxwell's family, and Hattie couldn't help but notice that Corrine's gaze was on the cowboy doctor. "You're thinking too much, worrying too much. Just let the conversation go naturally where it goes."

"Will you stay with me? By my side?"

His words sent a thrill of sensation through her. Before she could agree or disagree, the group surrounded them, greetings and conversations flowing. Wanda shot Hattie an envious look when Maxwell kept her arm practically clamped to his side.

Hattie wanted to take the girl aside and tell her there was nothing to be envious of...but she couldn't quite make herself do it.

There was a part of her—a very small part—that was happy, proud to be at his side.

* * *

Maxwell had never been so glad as he was when the poetry-reading portion of the evening began. Chairs had been arranged in rows as if in a classroom setting, and somehow Hattie guided him toward the back and one side.

He hadn't even known this many young single people resided in Bear Creek. He recognized a few faces from his school days, but more had moved into the area and some had left, moved away. He'd met so many young ladies tonight he couldn't keep their names straight. Even Sam and Emily had shown up.

His face felt permanently hot, and the collar of his white Sunday shirt choked him.

Hattie had kept her word and stayed tucked close to his side. Almost as if they were courting. Even with her gentle prompting and guiding the conversations, he felt awkward and unsure.

This situation was infinitely uncomfortable for him. When Hattie had suggested the event, he'd agreed because of his enjoyment of poetry—not thinking about just how overwhelming it would be. He should've suggested something more private, perhaps a lunch with one or two of her close friends. Not this mass of chattering, flirting, fluttering young women.

Why was he able to talk to Hattie so easily—or, if not easily, then at least not as awkwardly as with the other girls? Was it really their shared interest in medicine, or was there something else between them?

But once the gal in charge began the reading, he was able to relax a little. Some of the tension left his shoulders, until Hattie shifted in her chair and her skirt brushed his calf. In the small room, they were pressed so close together that he couldn't help but be aware of her closeness. She smelled like peaches and something else sweet, and he knew he still had to smell of horse after working all day with Oscar. He'd dunked his head in the stream and cleaned up as best he could before they'd come into town, but he *was* a working cowboy.

Ricky had disappeared, but Matty and Davy stood at the back of the room, not taking seats. He'd been surprised how they'd gotten on with the others and realized that his brothers had grown up some while he'd been gone to college and medical school. Davy seemed to be looking through the crowd, but Maxwell couldn't guess who he was looking for. Did his brother have a sweetheart? Max had been so caught up in his own plans that he hadn't noticed if the boy did.

And Matty had spoken to every single girl in the room already, his charm full-on. Even though he was younger than many of the young ladies, he had a way to make them smile.

Maxwell tried not to be jealous of his brother's easy manner with his acquaintances.

Or of his best friend's love match, either. When Sam and Emily settled in chairs directly in front of him and Hattie, and Sam tucked his wife close to his side with an arm around her shoulders, Maxwell looked down at his feet.

He couldn't expect to find love, not with his past.

The gal up at the front of the room was reading something of Elizabeth Barrett Browning's. Maxwell knew some of her love poems, but she wasn't particularly a favorite of his. Until one of the phrases being quoted made him think of the woman beside him.

He had his private notebook tucked in his pocket and itched to take it out and mark down a stanza of what he'd just heard. He didn't dare risk it. He tried to commit the phrase to memory, instead, so he could jot it down as soon as he escaped to the bunkhouse tonight.

After a short reading, refreshments were served, and the young people began mingling again.

Hattie seemed lost in thought at his side as they lingered near the rear of the room.

"You all right?"

His question seemed to stir her from her thoughts. She nodded, expression serious. "I was just thinking about what we might need to do in the office tomorrow. Are you certain your brother will be able to spare you?"

"Yeah. I'll talk to him on the way back to my pa's place tonight. He'll understand—probably be glad to get me out from underfoot for a while."

Thinking about what they might face in the office made him realize he should probably let Hattie turn in early so she could be rested up for the day. He still didn't know what illness plagued her, hadn't seen any specific symptoms, but if he could ease things for her throughout the day, he would.

"Should we— Can I escort you home? I mean, we could walk, and I'll meet my brothers back here to head out to the ranch."

She agreed, and he told Oscar he'd walk Hattie home and come back. His older brother waggled his eyebrows but, to Maxwell's relief, made no other protest or comment.

On the boardwalk, Hattie slipped her hand through the crook of his arm, and he nearly lost his footing.

Aware of the noise coming from the saloon one street over, he turned them in the opposite direction, which he hoped would keep them out of the way of any carousing cowboys. It was dark, and he'd hate to face a repeat of what had happened in the street days before. And the longer walk would give him at least a few more moments of Hattie's company.

"So, what was your favorite class in college?" Was it his imagination, or did Hattie sound particularly wistful when she asked the question?

He couldn't admit that he'd loved the poetry more than anything else. "Probably some of the literature courses."

"You like to read? I'm sure your primary-school teachers appreciated a student like you."

His face burned in the dark, remembering his teenage embarrassment in front of Emily about his education or lack thereof. "I didn't have much of an education before my ma got ahold of me. She actually taught me to read when I was sixteen." Would Hattie think less of him for that admission? He hadn't meant to admit to it, but the words had just burst out on their own.

Looking down on her in the moonlight, he found himself talking about a subject that was usually painful for him, but somehow the words flowed easily tonight. "My birth ma didn't care much about me— didn't let me go to school or anything like that. She died when I was pretty young, then I was on my own, trying to survive, and school was low on the list when my belly was empty."

Hattie didn't look up at him, watching where she was stepping as they moved down off the boardwalk to a more residential side street. But he had the sense she was listening intently.

"By the time Jonas took me in, I was older—a teenager—and too ashamed to admit I couldn't do the lessons. Until Penny got ahold of me, that is."

He was watching her, but Hattie's gaze didn't stray in his direction as they neared her house.

"My mother kept me home from school on the days when my condition would act up," she said. "I never knew what to tell the other children and had to work extremely hard to keep up on my own. It was hard... not quite fitting in."

He really wanted to ask more about her health complaint, but he couldn't find the words. Instead, he said, "And yet, you've found a way to work through it now, working with your pa."

He hoped that she would take the opening to tell him more about what plagued her, but all she said was "The same way you've overcome your childhood to get an education, I suppose. A strong will."

As they reached the porch steps, he tried to think of the best way to phrase what he wanted to ask. "Is there anything you need in the next few days—anything I can do to help so you won't overtax yourself?" An idea sparked and he blurted it out before he thought. "I could bring your rolling chair to the office and if you got overtired or needed to rest awhile it would be there for you."

She went stiff at his side, withdrew her hand from his arm. Had he blundered by mentioning the chair?

"I'll be fine." By her quick, blunt words he knew that he had.

"Hattie—"

"I'm certainly capable of knowing if I need to sit down and rest for a few moments. My condition won't hamper you in any way."

She cut her eyes to him, and the coolness in the blue depths stunned him.

"Hattie, wait—"

"I think we've said enough to each other tonight. Good night." She slipped inside and the door clicked shut behind her.

He'd thought they'd shared something, talking about their pasts, but obviously, it hadn't been enough to build a camaraderie. He was beginning to think such a thing might be impossible between them.

Hattie stood just inside the front door, shaken by what she'd shared—something she'd never told another soul. But now Maxwell knew. She guessed he hadn't meant any harm bringing up her medical condition—she'd almost forgotten that he knew about it, though he didn't know the details. They'd had such an enjoyable evening. Though he was shy with the other women at the poetry reading, he'd been conversational with her, asking questions and even sharing things of a personal nature.

And then he'd shared something, and she'd shared something, and suddenly it seemed they'd gone from being mere acquaintances, working together for a purpose, to almost…friends. She didn't have room in her life for a friendship with Maxwell. She needed to be at her best while Papa was gone and then move forward with her plans.

No matter if she'd thought there had been a connection between herself and Maxwell tonight. She needed to keep her focus on her real aim—medical school. And forget about the polite, quiet cowboy with an ear for poetry.

Maxwell was trying to figure out how things had gone so wrong when he returned to the wagon. By the rumble of voices still coming from inside the tearoom, he knew most folks were still visiting.

He elected to stay out in the dark, alone.

He hadn't meant to offend Hattie by questioning her about the medical condition. But she was so prickly about it....

A feminine giggle brought his head up, jolting him out of his thoughts. Something moved in the shadows around the corner of the building. Make that some*one*. A young woman dragged a young man by the hand, saying, "We can find some privacy over at the—"

Her companion interrupted her by drawing her in for a kiss. Maxwell started to avert his eyes, but a shaft of light fell on the man—

"Ricky?"

Folks started pouring out of the tearoom as his younger brother broke away from the girl.

Oscar and Sarah were among the first outside and they seemed to understand the situation instantly. Oscar clapped a hand on Ricky's shoulder and Sarah pulled the girl aside, effectively separating them.

They headed home quickly, Oscar reading Ricky the riot act while the younger boy grumbled.

"Y'all won't tell Pa, will ya?" Ricky asked as they neared the homestead.

Maxwell shrugged.

"Aw, just 'cause you can't woo your nursie don't mean you have to ruin my fun," Ricky taunted.

"It's not your brothers' job to cover for you," Sarah admonished. "You are responsible for your own actions."

"Says the schoolteacher."

Oscar started to take up for his wife, and Maxwell ignored his brothers' arguing.

Was it so obvious to everyone that he had trouble relating to Hattie? And that he desperately wanted to win her as a friend?

Should he give up on her? It might make things difficult as they worked together.

He wished he knew the right thing to do.

Chapter Six

Maxwell had tossed and turned all night, unable to shake the remembrance of the shadows in Hattie's eyes when he'd left her. Of the connection they'd shared, even briefly, before she'd rushed inside. He wanted to be her friend, knew it could never be more than that, but he almost…craved her friendship. Had he ruined everything by talking about some of the things he was ashamed of in his past?

The sun was only a hint of silver on the horizon when he crossed from the bunkhouse to the barn, intent on saddling his mount and getting to town. His ma would probably fuss at him for missing breakfast, but he had a powerful urge to see Hattie, to find out if what he'd said last night would affect her manner this morning.

The sound of whistling turned his head. Seb sauntered into the barn, scrubbing his eyes. His whistling broke off under a huge yawn.

"What're you doing up?" his youngest brother asked, voice cracking.

"Going to town. The doctor had to leave for a

while, and he asked me and his daughter to watch over the clinic." Oscar had understood and even been proud of his brother last night when Maxwell had informed him of the change on their way back out to Pa's ranch in the wagon.

Maxwell buckled the last strap, tugging on the stirrup to ensure it was secure. He paused, letting out a long breath. Would Hattie be happy to see him, or upset?

Seb lounged against a nearby stall. "What'sa matter? Thought you liked the doctor's girl."

Maxwell ignored the insinuation, knowing that if he admitted his attraction to Hattie that every single brother would know by breakfast. "She's a friend. At least I think we're friends. I might've offended her last night after the poetry reading. I just don't…" *know how to talk to her.*

Seb snorted, and it was all the impetus Maxwell needed to put his foot in the stirrup and mount up. Face hot, he wheeled the horse toward the barn door.

"Remember how we left those wildflowers for Ma when she and Pa were courtin'?" Seb asked casually as Maxwell walked his horse past the younger boy.

Maxwell didn't respond, only sent his brother a wave as he left the barn. No doubt his brothers would tease him mercilessly tonight, but maybe there was no helping it. He'd missed the camaraderie while he'd been away at medical school, but he could certainly do without their constant teasing about his romantic life. Or lack thereof.

He'd gotten to the edge of his pa's property before he slowed his horse. Could Seb be right? Would wildflowers sooth Hattie's feelings? Or make a fool out of him?

Would she think he meant more than just an apology by the gesture? He didn't want to overstep his bounds, especially since they needed to work together.

He got off the horse anyway and began gathering a colorful collection of flowers. Then he realized he didn't have anything to tie them up with. He turned his Stetson upside down and put the flowers inside. Remounting, he settled the hat upside down in front of him. He'd be all right as long as no one saw him riding into town with a lap full of flowers. Then he'd never live it down.

He'd thought he might beat Hattie to the clinic, but by the time he'd stabled his horse at the livery for the day, gathered up his handful of wildflowers and made his way down the boardwalk to the clinic, he found the front door unlocked. Soft rustling from the examination room told him Hattie was preparing for the day.

"Good morning," he called out.

Her reply was muffled, but at least she'd answered. He clutched the wildflowers in his now-sweating hand and went looking for her. She was opening the curtains, looking pert and fine in a dark blue dress covered by a white apron, her hair tucked behind her head in a bun.

He nearly choked on the words, but forced them out. "I wanted to apologize if I offended you last night. I was only trying to help. I know you'll do a good job while your pa is gone."

She turned and he stuck out his hand, the multihued flowers bobbing as he did so. Her eyes widened minutely, and she hesitated. Then, finally, she reached out and took the flowers from him.

"Thank you," she murmured, averting her face. "I think there's an extra pitcher in the supply room."

She ducked past him, scurrying from the room.

What had her reaction meant? Did it mean she forgave him for his blunder last night? He wished he could read her better, wished that this awkwardness between them would disappear.

Hattie hid in the supply room, momentarily unable to do anything but stare down at the clutch of flowers in her grasp. The bright blues, yellows and purples blurred together momentarily until she blinked.

He'd brought her flowers.

It was a small gesture, but no one had ever done something like that for her before. Blood rushed to her ears, and her spine tingled—and she still had to work with the man all day.

She was intensely aware of him as they stood shoulder to shoulder to treat a child with a deep, racking cough.

Aware of his steady manner as they disinfected and stitched a nasty cut for the butcher.

And when Mrs. Fishbourne had arrived complaining that her rheumatism was acting up, she'd been amazed by his patient, quiet manner in reassuring her. Hattie had seen the older woman just about every other day since her papa had set up practice in Bear Creek, and found it hard to bear the long-winded Mrs. Fishbourne, whom she suspected was lonely and wanted conversation more than she actually experienced pain.

Now Corrine was the only person left in the waiting room.

Hattie escorted her friend to the examination room. "I'm afraid Papa is out of town, but Maxwell and I are handling the clinic until he returns."

Corrine smiled warmly at Maxwell as she climbed onto the examination table. Hattie's statement didn't seem to surprise her one bit. Did her friend have an agenda in coming to the clinic?

"I'm sorry to hear about your papa, but glad that you're...*both* here. Wasn't the poetry reading last night divine?"

"Browning is all right," agreed Maxwell as he remained near the counter at the far wall.

Hattie tried to see him through the other girl's eyes, his lanky, tall bearing, his quiet manner. Strong hands.

He wasn't bad to look at.

And he seemed a bit more at ease with Corrine this morning, at least offering the one comment on the poet. Part of Hattie didn't particularly like the idea of Corrine chasing the cowboy.

"What seems to be the problem?" Hattie asked the other girl briskly.

"I've been experiencing a headache for the past few days. It hasn't gotten any better."

Hattie narrowed her eyes at her friend. Corrine hadn't mentioned anything when they'd chatted last night at the poetry reading. Was this another ploy to get Maxwell's attention, like Annabelle's "injured" ankle had been?

"Is there anything specific you've noticed that has brought on the headaches? Being out in the sunlight? Working on a certain project? Attempting to see long distances?"

Hattie watched her friend's face as she considered Maxwell's questions. When Corrine's eyes darted to one side, Hattie was sure she wasn't telling the full truth. "Not that I've noticed. But it has been persistent over several days."

Maxwell moved closer to Corrine and examined her eyes, asking her to follow his finger back and forth several times. He touched her forehead with the back of his hand. "Not feverish." Took her pulse.

He glanced back at Hattie once, brows furrowed. Had his mind followed the path hers had taken? Was he wondering if the girl's complaint was genuine?

Hattie shrugged and ticked her head toward the door, asking him silently to exit the room.

"Excuse me a moment." He quickly backed out into the hall.

Hattie asked what Papa would've. "When was your last woman's time?"

The other girl flushed slightly, eyes averted. "I don't see how that's relevant."

"Sometimes that can cause headaches, or if there's a chance you might be carrying a child, that could be a cause, as well—"

"Hattie!" Corrine cried, with a quick glance at the door Maxwell had departed from. "How could you even ask such a thing?"

Hattie crossed her arms over her middle. "It's a valid question. Papa would've asked."

"Nothing like that," the other girl muttered, with

another glance at the doorway. Then her eyes seemed to swing around the room and stop on the small pitcher holding the wildflowers Maxwell had brought Hattie this morning.

When Corrine glanced back at Hattie, it was with raised brows, but before she could say anything, Maxwell pushed back inside. "Everything all right, ladies?"

"Hmm, yes," said Corrine, still with eyes narrowed at Hattie. "Can you give me something to ease the pain or not?"

Maxwell took three small envelopes from the corner cabinet, a simple powdered form of pain relief. "This should help for now. If the headaches continue or get worse, you should consult Doc Powell when he returns."

He went over the instructions for mixing the powder with her.

"Will you be at the next poetry reading?" Corrine asked, looking up at Maxwell from beneath long eyelashes.

Hattie felt slightly ill. She was gratified—and she probably shouldn't have been—when Maxwell glanced at her briefly. "Perhaps."

Hattie waited near the door for her friend to join her. Corrine's eyes flicked back to the pitcher and flowers before joining Hattie and sweeping from the room.

In the hallway, Corrine gripped Hattie's arm almost painfully. "Is there something going on between you two?" she whispered.

Hattie glanced behind to ensure Maxwell hadn't followed them out the exam room door. "Absolutely not."

"Then do you have another suitor?" the other girl continued.

Hattie wasn't close enough with Corrine for the question to be appropriate—it was entirely too nosy, but Hattie gave a tight-lipped "No" in response anyway.

"Then what—" Her friend seemed to think better of continuing her questioning, but her narrowed eyes on Hattie made her feel as if Corrine could see through her feeble defenses.

"If you aren't interested in Maxwell, why don't you tell him so and give the rest of us a fighting chance?"

Heat rose in Hattie's cheeks. Her friend had it all wrong. She and Maxwell weren't even *friends*. They were only working together.

"If you aren't smart enough to snatch up a man like that…" Corrine let the words trail off and then flounced through the hall and out of the clinic, closing the door behind her.

"We're working together, and that's all," Hattie repeated softly to herself after her friend had gone.

She lingered in the hallway longer than she probably should've, trying to get her rioting thoughts and heartbeat under control.

Friendship was all that could ever be between them. She had plans, goals, a future mapped out for herself.

Even if a tiny part of her registered disappointment way down deep in her gut.

Maxwell suspected that something had passed between Hattie and her friend. Hattie had been close-lipped when she'd returned from escorting the other girl out of the clinic, but before he'd decided whether or not to ask about it, the afternoon had gotten away from them.

One of the last patients to come in was the man who had been shot on the first day Maxwell had arrived back in town. He looked hale and hearty, if a little pale. He was standing on his own two feet, though, so that was a good sign. The woman Maxwell recognized from that day came in right behind him.

Hattie greeted them both with a smile from behind the desk in the front corner. "Mr. Spencer. How are you feeling?"

"Fine." The man scowled at the woman beside him.

"He isn't," she said. "He's in a lot of pain. We're hoping to see the doctor."

"I'm sorry." Hattie's brows drew together in concern.

Maxwell took a step closer as she continued.

"There's been an outbreak of cholera nearby, and Papa went to help the doctor over in Pear Grove. He won't be back for several days, at least. This is Mr. White, a medical student home for the summer. He and I are watching over Papa's patients. Would you mind if we examined you?"

The man shot a disgruntled look at his wife. "The doc ain't even here."

Maxwell cleared his throat, hoping he wasn't stepping on Hattie's toes, but he couldn't remain silent. "If there are still internal injuries present, they could become life-threatening if they aren't treated."

Now the man's assessing eyes rested on him, as if taking Maxwell's measure. Finally, Spencer relented, nodding once.

Hattie ushered him into the examination room, asking him to unbutton his shirt and lie back flat on the table.

"I don't like it," Hattie said in a low voice moments later as they conferred in the hallway while the man and his wife remained in the examination room. "He's too tender. And did you hear him groan—he tried to stifle it—when he was lying down on the table?"

"You'd probably be tender, too, if you'd had a surgery like that," Maxwell reminded her. He'd only seen the crisscross of healing scars on the man's side—Hattie had been there with Doc Powell in that surgery and seen the man's inner workings—but surely it would take a good long time to heal that much damage.

"Did his skin feel warm to you? Too hot. I think he might have internal bleeding."

Maxwell wished there was a way to be sure. "There was no discoloration, though. No swelling."

"There doesn't have to be. If the blood swells so much that it mottles the skin, many times it's too late to save the patient—he could bleed to death."

Her emphatic words were underscored by the passion in her expression. It was obvious she had the patient's best interests at heart. They stood so close in the hallway that Maxwell felt the brush of her breath against his chin.

"But what if we're wrong? What if the tenderness is just part of the healing process? The initial surgery was dangerous enough—infection could set in if he goes under the knife again. And if there wasn't anything wrong…"

They would be responsible.

Hattie's eyes flashed. "I've seen my share of surgeries working with my papa. Not everyone survives, but if there's something wrong, it needs to be addressed."

She swung away, pushing through the door before Maxwell could say anything else.

He followed. Saw her shoulders draw up and drop, as if she'd taken a deep breath to fortify herself.

The man was buttoning his shirt and looked up from the table.

"Mr. Spencer, I'll be frank. I'm concerned about the lingering tenderness you're feeling. I'm sorry that my papa isn't here, but my best recommendation is for you to get on a train this afternoon and head down to the town of Calvin and have a physician examine you. If there is still internal bleeding, your life could be in danger."

The man barely acknowledged her words, instead looking to Maxwell. "What do you think?"

"I'm not a doctor—yet," Maxwell hedged. He couldn't fully agree with Hattie's diagnosis, but neither could he disagree. Again, he wished there was a way to be sure.

"Neither is she," the man said. He didn't outright sneer at Hattie, but it was clear he didn't think much of the doctor's daughter's worries.

"What if she's right?" his wife asked. "What if there is something wrong inside you?"

The man shot a disbelieving look at Maxwell, as if to say *Women!* "What if she's wrong? We ain't got money to waste on train tickets when there's nothing ailing me."

"I can't say for sure that nothing is wrong," Maxwell insisted. "Internal injuries can be very tricky."

Hattie sent a look at him over her shoulder, her meaning clear. She wanted him to persuade the man to her way of thinking. But he still couldn't be certain. He looked away and heard her quiet huff.

"I really think it would be best for you to see a doctor—just in case."

The man ignored Hattie and stood from the examination table, straightening his shirt. He left the room without waiting or saying goodbye. It was the first time Maxwell had seen Hattie not escort a patient back to the front waiting room. Maxwell saw the worried look his wife turned in Hattie's direction as she slowly followed her husband.

Hattie's lips were pinched and white as she turned toward the cabinet, straightening an already-neat pile of bandages. She didn't look directly at Maxwell.

"You couldn't have agreed with me?" she demanded.

"How can you be sure of your diagnosis?" he countered.

"I would rather be safe than sorry, wouldn't you?"

"But—"

"If he dies, it's your fault," she said fiercely, before turning and banging out of the room.

She wasn't happy with him, but how could Maxwell have done differently? He hadn't seen the initial wound; she'd done multiple surgeries assisting her father. Should he have deferred to her, even if he was unsure?

He didn't know. At the moment he felt as if he didn't know anything anymore.

* * *

"I'm having doubts," Maxwell said to his bowl of potpie. He sat in Sam and Emily's small kitchen at their scarred kitchen table.

The events of the afternoon kept replaying in his mind. Had Hattie been right? She'd pushed him, but what if...

"About what?" Emily asked. "Hattie Powell? She might be a little touchy, but she has a good heart. She and I have been friends since the doctor moved to town."

Familiar heat prickled beneath Maxwell's cheeks. He liked Hattie. But whatever progress he'd made on their friendship had likely been erased when he hadn't agreed with her diagnosis. But that hadn't been what he'd meant by his words.

He shook his head. "About being a doctor. I can't talk to women—not well, anyway—and I don't know if I trust myself to diagnose patients correctly. How can I be a doctor when I can't be sure what's wrong with someone?"

He couldn't forget Hattie's concerns about the man with the gunshot wound. The more he thought about it, the more he wondered if she was right. Had there been a mass beneath the man's scar tissue? Had the skin been hot to the touch? The man hadn't wanted to believe Hattie's concerns, but what if she was right? Maxwell hadn't backed her up.

His two friends considered him in silence. Sam was the first to break it.

"But your education isn't finished yet," Sam pointed out. "That will probably help in knowing what's ailing people."

"Yes, but—"

"And having some experience will help, too, don't you think?" Emily asked. "If you can find someone experienced to work with, like you're doing with Doc Powell, you'll gain a practical education in diagnosing illnesses. With more time, won't it be easier for you?"

Her words had a ring of truth. Wasn't he questioning himself because he didn't have the doc's guidance to rely on?

"You're too hard on yourself." Sam clapped a hand on his shoulder. "No one expects you to be a doctor yet—you've still got schooling to go, and like Emily said, with practice under your belt, you'll gain confidence in yourself. Didn't you feel the same when you first went to college?"

Were his friends right? He *had* doubted his abilities when he'd first enrolled in college, until he'd begun to get grades back on the work he'd turned in. Then he'd begun to believe in himself, believe that perhaps he *could* achieve his dream of being a doctor.

"Sam!" a female voice cried from outside, startling all three occupants of the table.

Silverware rattled and plates clinked as both men started to rise from the table. Before they could push back their chairs fully, the door burst open and Hattie swept in, skirts swirling around her. "Sam, I need help! I need—" her wild gaze swept the front room and finally came to rest on the three of them, motionless around the table "—Max," she finished.

His heart thrummed once, so intensely it was almost painful.

Her eyes locked with his, and she seemed to steady herself, even as she panted, as if she'd run all the way from town to the Castlerocks' homestead just outside of town. Judging by the roses in her cheeks, Maxwell deduced she might've.

He extricated himself from the kitchen chair and went to her. She immediately grabbed his hand.

"Mr. Spencer is worse. His wife sent for me at home—I've been to their house and there's blood pooling beneath the skin now. He's feverish and hallucinating and—"

She gasped for breath, and Maxwell finished for her, a bolt of fear slicing through him. "He needs surgery immediately."

Her wide eyes and manner communicated that her panic matched his. "There's not time to send for the doctor in Calvin."

"Then you'll have to do it." Maxwell took both her hands in his, his intention to offer comfort. He'd seen the scars. Knew Hattie had helped her pa with the initial surgery. She could do it.

Her eyes widened slightly as he looked down into her face, trying to project his confidence in her.

"I'll assist you."

She still didn't say anything, and he could feel her trembling beneath the clasp of his hands. Finally, she spoke.

"Sam, can you help us get him back to the clinic? The Spencers' home isn't far, and I'd feel better working with Papa's supplies nearby."

Sam was already pulling on his boots by the door.

"My horse is saddled in the barn." Maxwell towed Hattie with him toward the door.

Emily stood near the table, seemingly calm even though her supper had been interrupted. "Is there anything I can do?" she called after them. "Anything you need for the clinic?"

Hattie simply shook her head, but Maxwell looked over his shoulder to his friend. "Pray."

After a wild flight on foot out to her friends' home and a quick ride back to the clinic, clinging to Maxwell's broad shoulders, Hattie slid from the horse. Breathless, she directed Maxwell to the Spencers' home, where he would meet Sam to bring the injured man to the clinic. She went inside to prep the surgery.

By rote she wiped down the surgery table with carbolic solution, arranged the multiple lanterns around the operating table, and laid out the scalpels and other surgical instruments on the small side table, just as she would for Papa. She donned a large white apron that had also been boiled to sterilize it and laid one out on the counter for Maxwell when he arrived.

It seemed the men were only gone moments before she heard footsteps and a low voice say "Watch his shoulders!"

"On the table, please," she directed them from where she stood vigorously scrubbing her hands beneath the water pump. She was glad her back was turned—her hands shook badly beneath the running water. Was she really going to do this? Really going to perform surgery on one of her father's patients? What if…?

But what choice did she have? She couldn't leave the man to die.

Spencer gave a low moan as they gently laid him out on the table. Hattie took a steadying breath and looked at the patient. His face was mottled with sweat, pinched with pain. She took a clean cloth from the nearby counter and mopped his brow. He seemed to slip in and out of consciousness even as she watched.

"You'll have to instruct me," Maxwell said.

"Sam, can you steady our patient on the table for a moment?"

The second cowboy nodded and kept his hands on Spencer's shoulders.

Looking to Maxwell, hoping he couldn't read the panic swelling in her chest through her expression, she whispered, "Wash up first. Soap all the way to your elbows. There's an apron for you on the counter."

She half expected him to balk at wearing the apron—something a woman might wear—but he didn't. Perhaps he'd seen his professors wearing them, or perhaps he just wanted to preserve his clothing.

Sam helped her remove the man's clothing and then she covered his lower body with a sheet. Then she realized the clothes had contaminated her clean hands and she would need to wash up again. Papa would have known to undress the man first. She'd known but had been preoccupied.

She passed Maxwell as he tied the apron around his waist, shaking her head at her mistake.

"There's a sterilizing solution just there." She pointed over her shoulder to the counter. "Wet a rag with it and wipe down his torso."

When she rejoined Maxwell and Sam at the table, she did her best to clear her mind of her fears and the faint disappointment in the mistake she'd already made. There was no room for error here, no room for hesitation or self-recrimination. Only action.

Breathing a prayer, she took a rag from the small

side table and demonstrated to Maxwell how to apply the ether. He held it over Spencer's nose and mouth until the man was still on the table, and Hattie nodded.

The scalpel was cold and heavy in her hand as she wielded it just above the swelling on the man's upper left side.

"If y'all don't need me, I'm going to wait out front." Sam's face had turned suspiciously white.

She nodded, and his footsteps retreated.

One deep breath.

She made the first cut. Blood welled, and for a second she was terrified.

Maxwell must've observed at least one surgery in his time at medical school, because he blotted the oozing redness with a clean towel. The motion of his large, callused hands doing the task she normally would've done shocked her from her frozen state.

It was different, standing on her papa's side of the operating table. But not impossible. It couldn't be.

"How did you know I would be at Sam and Emily's house for supper?" Maxwell asked. His attention was on both the patient and on Hattie, awaiting further instruction.

Finding her focus, she leaned forward into her task, answering him only absently. "I didn't. I thought you'd gone home, but I knew Sam would be the best person to be able to find you quickly."

She didn't mention the intense relief that had flashed through her when she'd seen him sitting at Sam and Emily's dining table. What was it about the cowboy that steadied her?

"It was God's providence that you were there," she

said instead. "Any more delay would've been dangerous to our patient."

She asked him to move one of the lamps closer,
and he complied immediately. She could sense his
avid interest as he assisted her, but she only halfway
registered it.

"How old were you when you first assisted your
pa in a surgery?" he asked next as he handed her a
clamp before she could even ask.

"Fourteen. My mother was furious. She'd tried
to keep me out of Papa's practice, but his usual as-
sistant was gone, or sick, I don't remember, and he
didn't want to perform the surgery alone. I itched to
prove myself, and I did. We saved that patient's life."

She bit her lip as her tool slipped, but then gasped
as she recovered it and saw a large swelling that she
would've missed otherwise. She moved to examine
it closer and dimly registered the press of Maxwell's
shoulder against hers as he leaned over the patient,
too.

"Has your mother never helped your father as a
nurse?"

Hattie's lips twitched, but she was concentrating
too hard to outright laugh. "Mama can't stand the
sight of blood. She's more than content to keep up
the house and take care of Papa's needs. I think she
wished for a bigger family."

She knew her parents had wanted a son. If they'd
had one, would Hattie be the doting daughter her
mama wanted? Some of her bitterness over what
she couldn't be for her papa, and the life her mama
wanted to confine her to, must've leaked into her
voice because Maxwell hesitated slightly at her side.

"You don't want a family of your own?"

Now it was her turn to hesitate. Their murmured conversation was nearing dangerous territory. "Someday. Perhaps."

If she ever met a man who could appreciate her ambitions. And if that man was content to help raise their family so she could practice medicine. Both of those scenarios seemed unlikely.

For a brief second, she allowed her gaze to slide to the steady, broad hands of the man working beside her. His quick support tonight was in direct contrast to his manner earlier in the day—because he felt guilty for not supporting her or because of the urgent need to save the man beneath their hands?

If Maxwell respected her...was there any chance the handsome cowboy could be her match?

A sudden welling of blood from the wound ended their conversation for the moment. Hattie blinked aside the turmoil of her rushing thoughts, forcing herself only to focus on the patient. If she could save this man, how could her father refuse to let her attend medical school?

Chapter Seven

It was well into the wee hours of the night when Hattie closed up Mr. Spencer.

Maxwell watched her put in the last stitches and then drop the needle on the smaller table beside them. She flexed both hands, still covered in blood, and he saw her begin to tremble.

She'd held up amazingly. Been stoic. Calm. Until now.

He was no more comfortable than his pa or brothers with a woman's sensitive emotions, but he went to her without thinking, taking her in his arms. She tucked her head beneath his chin, and she just…fit.

He closed his eyes tightly, aware of the tickle of her hair at his collar, the womanly scent of her even beneath the antiseptic smells that surrounded them. Holding her just felt right.

It was also a reminder that she wasn't really his. *No woman will love you* came that insidious voice from his past. Hattie was everything he would never have.

Her entire body shook, and he pushed away his own turmoil. Was her medical condition affecting her, or, after performing the surgery, were her nerves simply wearing thin at this point?

"Are you all right?" he asked, the words muffled in the crown of her hair. She hadn't rested once since they'd begun the operation.

"Just exhausted." Her mumbled words were hot on his chest through his shirt.

Above her head, he could see that, while Spencer remained pale, the man's breathing had eased.

"You did it." He meant to say the words into her ear, but when he tilted his head down, the scruff on his chin caught in her hair, and he had to raise his hand to brush it away.

She slipped out of his hold, and he ached with wanting her back in his arms. He fisted his hands at his sides.

"We did it," she said, turning her back to him and going to the sink. "I don't know how you always knew what I needed, but you did. Whether it was a cotton swab or you asking questions to keep me from being terror-stricken."

He'd never sensed that she'd been close. She'd seemed as calm and unruffled as he imagined her pa would've been.

"We make a good team." He dared to say the words, dared to hope that, after this, they wouldn't have to return to the cool politeness they'd shared in the clinic before.

She looked over her shoulder, and their eyes met and held. She nodded slightly, and he experienced a moment of joy. Oh, she would likely never be attracted to him as he was to her, but if they could be *friends,* what more could he ask?

He piled the soiled cloths and linens they'd used near the back counter, then changed places with her at the sink to wash his own hands. When he was done, she stood at the patient's side, lifting the man's eyelids.

"Time will tell," she said softly. "If he makes it through the night…"

"He will."

She was still shaking. She had to be tired, after they had worked in the clinic all day—it wouldn't be long until dawn.

"I can stay with him while you get a few hours' rest," Maxwell told her.

He received the protest he'd expected. "I should stay." But her words were more a sigh than anything else.

"I'll come get you if there's any change," he promised. He took her elbow and gently ushered her to the front room, where Sam was sleeping upright in a chair, head back against the wall, snoring.

He shook his friend awake and urged Sam to escort her home and then get some sleep himself, then Maxwell returned to keep vigil over the still-anesthetized man. Sitting on the cot in the corner of the room, he rubbed a hand through his hair.

Had holding Hattie been a mistake? She'd felt so right in his arms…but he couldn't expect anything from her.

How often had his birth mother told him he'd never have someone? He hadn't wanted to believe her, but when the first girl he'd tried to court at college had rejected him and then Elizabeth had broken things off, it had seemed to prove the woman right. He couldn't trust his emotions, his desire to be close to Hattie. Couldn't stand it if he got closer to her and she broke his heart, too.

Hattie woke to bright sunlight—marking the time as much later than she'd asked her mama to wake her in the note she'd left downstairs. When Hattie had been called out of the house at suppertime, Mama hadn't had time to make a protest, but Hattie hadn't wanted her to worry.

But neither did she want Maxwell to be stuck with a clinic full of patients by himself.

She hurriedly donned one of the dresses she reserved for working in the clinic and met Mama in the kitchen, where she found her pounding on bread dough.

"Why didn't you wake me? It's late." Hattie went to the bread basket, then the cold case, and began assembling ingredients for a thick sandwich that she could eat on her way to the clinic.

"I thought you needed your rest, dear. You didn't come in until late. Very late." Mama didn't even look up from her work. Maybe on purpose.

"I'm not an invalid, Mama. I know my limits."

Mama only hummed while pressing the heel of her hand into the dough before her.

"I do," Hattie mumbled as she broke off a piece of bread and popped it into her mouth. She was ravenous.

Why couldn't Mama see past Hattie's disease? That Hattie was capable of not only helping in the clinic but being a physician herself? It wasn't as if the condition prevented her from having an active life. She just had to be careful.

Hattie blinked away the familiar train of thought. She and Mama hadn't seen eye to eye for years, and it was up to Hattie to bring Papa to her side—so he could help convince Mama.

"Did Maxwell send over a note or anything this morning?" she asked.

"No, dear."

Would Maxwell have eaten anything? She couldn't know, and she was much later getting to the clinic than she'd wanted to be. Perhaps Emily had sent over something for him, but it wouldn't hurt to make a kind gesture, not after his help with Mr. Spencer.

Hattie started a second sandwich for him, setting out a large cloth napkin to wrap it in.

Maxwell had been proud of her accomplishments last night. He'd understood that her fatigue hadn't prevented her from doing what was needed.

"There was some apple pie left from supper last night," Mama said. "Since you missed it. Perhaps your Maxwell would like a slice, if you're taking him a sandwich, as well."

Hattie let the comment about her skipping dessert slide. "He's not 'my' anything, Mama."

"Maybe not yet. But that's a good idea, bringing him food. Men think with their stomachs sometimes. It won't hurt for him to see you have a feminine side, as well."

Hattie barely resisted the urge to express her annoyance at her mother's assumptions. It wasn't as if she strutted around the clinic in men's clothing or acted inappropriately. Nursing was not an uncommon vocation for a woman.

For now, she wouldn't protest her mama's misconceptions. Hattie wouldn't risk Mama pulling her away from helping at the practice while Papa was gone, not when Bear Creek needed her. And not when this could be her chance to prove herself to Papa.

She slipped out of the kitchen moments later, unable to bear more of her mama's overprotective mothering. Would Mama's disappointment be worse after Hattie left for medical school? Providing she could win Papa to her side…

Determined to focus on last night's success, rather than her slightly frustrating morning, she put on a smile for Maxwell as she climbed the steps to the clinic, finding he hadn't left the office-closed sign on the door as she'd expected. Inside, the waiting room was dim and empty, but she could hear his voice coming from somewhere in the back.

Had their patient wakened?

She tightened her hold on the basket of food she'd brought from home and slipped back into the hallway. The exam room door was partially open, and as she passed she heard Maxwell speaking to someone inside.

She left his food in the supply room and slipped into the operating room. Mr. Spencer remained on the table. She put the back of her hand against his forehead, where he felt slightly warm to her touch. But that was to be expected. A slight fever would burn off any infection that had managed to remain in the open wound during the surgery.

Behind her, footsteps sounded. She looked over

her shoulder to see Maxwell poke his head inside. "Thought I heard you come in. What's that basket in the other room? Did you bring me breakfast? I thought I smelled something good."

The moment hung between them. They both knew that everything had changed last night when they'd worked together so closely—saved a man's life together.

"I did. You brought me flowers," she explained. She smiled, and perhaps it was a bit tremulous, but the warmth in his eyes eclipsed her trembling.

He looked exhausted, with shadows beneath his eyes, but when he joined her in the room, he radiated positive energy. Handsome, tall, a pillar of solid strength. He'd gone from rival to friend. She never would've been able to accomplish the surgery last night without him.

"He woke earlier for a bit," Maxwell said. "He was coherent and said the pain had abated some."

"I almost can't believe we did it."

"You were amazing." His quiet words thrilled her. Maxwell believed in her. Why couldn't Papa?

"How come you aren't a doctor—or attending medical school—yourself?"

His words stunned her. How could he have guessed her most closely held dream? And then she realized he didn't know; he was waiting expectantly for an answer. If she told him, would he say something to Papa, get in the way of her plans?

"Doc?" an urgent voice said from the front room, saving her from answering.

She and Maxwell moved together through the hallway to find a man supporting his teenage son. The teen was white-faced and clutching his stomach.

"Bring him back this way." Hattie ushered the man into the exam room, where Maxwell helped settle him on the table.

Hattie hurriedly tied on an apron.

"I'm afraid the doctor isn't here. What's wrong?" Maxwell asked as the teen groaned, attempting to curl into himself.

"He started complaining of a stomachache this morning. I thought maybe it was something he ate— or he was trying to get out of his chores. You know how kids do."

"And it's gotten worse?" Hattie moved to press gently on the boy's abdomen. As she did, he leaned forward and vomited, splattering the floor and the bottom of her apron. The vomit was speckled with blood.

Hattie and Maxwell shared a concerned look.

The father stammered, "I'm sorry—real sorry."

"Don't worry. It'll clean." Hattie tried to reassure him. "Are you sure the pains didn't start in the night?" she asked the boy. "Or last night, even?"

He shook his head, sweat breaking out on his brow. She touched his face and he was burning up. "Just this morning."

"Did you eat anything unusual? Anything that might've been spoiled? Anything from the woods or outdoors?"

The teen shook his head, looking even more pallid than a moment before.

"All right. Lie back down." She ticked her head to the side, a silent gesture to Maxwell that she wanted to speak to him in the hall. "I'm going to fetch a basin and talk to Mr. White for a moment."

Maxwell followed her into the supply room, where she rustled around beneath the cabinet for the basin usually kept there.

"I'm worried," she said. "A simple virus or something he'd eaten shouldn't have had such a fast onset or be showing so violently. And he was burning up—a high fever."

She found the basin tucked in the very back of the cabinet and pulled it out. She hesitated momentarily, sitting on her heels before gathering the courage to turn to Maxwell. What if he discounted her opinion again, as he'd done with Mr. Spencer?

He reached out one hand to take the basin and the other to help her to her feet. "Are you thinking it's possible the cholera has spread from Pear Grove to Bear Creek?"

"It's certainly possible. But is it probable?" she asked herself.

"The boy could be an isolated case. Or something else entirely."

She glanced at Maxwell as she rinsed the basin quickly. He only seemed to be working through his thoughts aloud, not questioning her. "It certainly wouldn't be prudent to start a panic in town if it *isn't* cholera."

"Should we try telephoning your pa?"

"Perhaps. What if we kept the boy here for observation for a bit first, see if there is any improvement on his own?"

Maxwell nodded, accepting her suggestion. "I'll go tell the boy's pa."

By later that afternoon, Hattie's suspicions had become reality. They'd received four more patients with symptoms of violent stomach pain, including Annabelle and a small boy, Bobby, Walt's friend from the church picnic. Hattie was especially concerned about the boy, since he was so young.

"We've used up all the cots," she murmured to Maxwell as they passed each other in the hallway. She had an armful of soiled linens to take to the storeroom, while he carried a pitcher of water.

"I want to send Sam to ride for my brothers. There's enough of them to start spreading the word in town and the surrounding areas to boil all water and cook all food before it's consumed and how to best help anybody else who comes down with this. Like you said, we're already running out of room for more patients."

"It's a good idea." She fought back a yawn. After their late night and now an influx of severely ill patients, her energy was flagging.

Maxwell had gotten even less sleep than she had, but only concern showed in his expression as he looked down at her. "Should you rest for a while? You were on your feet for hours last night."

He touched her arm lightly, reassuring, supporting her.

"I'll be all right." She would have to be. Her nervous condition had been quiet for months, even though she'd had to take precautions on the day Maxwell came to dinner. And if Bear Creek was experiencing cases of cholera, she would be needed.

The gravity of his expression didn't lighten, but this time she knew it for what it was—genuine concern and not Maxwell trying to edge her out of her place in Papa's clinic.

"I will tell you if I need to rest for a bit," she said. It would have to be enough for now, because there was too much to do. "Let me put these out." She held up the soiled linens in her arms. "Wash up, and I'll take over for you with the water, and you can go find Sam."

He nodded.

She'd turned for the storeroom but then turned back when a worrisome thought came.

"And…"

He stopped, looking back at her with his intense green eyes.

"Make sure to tell Emily about the precautions. She's already worried enough about the baby…."

A flicker of emotion passed over his face, as if this was the first time he'd thought about the possibility of his friends becoming sick. He nodded gravely, and they parted ways.

By nightfall, they'd been forced to relocate the patients—a dozen now—to the church, utilizing the pews, cots from the clinic and even pallets on the floor.

They'd left Mr. Spencer at the clinic, calling for his wife to watch over him and have him moved home when he could bear it. It was too dangerous to have him around the cholera patients—he was already weak and perhaps too susceptible to another disease, though they'd kept him carefully separate from the other patients.

Maxwell lingered over Bobby, attempting to dribble a bit of water through his blue-tinged lips. The boy was the same age as Walt. Six years old. And one of the worst off. If only he and Hattie could fight this disease for Bobby. Maxwell was extremely worried about the severity of the kid's symptoms—weak breath, thready pulse, chilled extremities.

He was frightened for the tyke's life. While the other patients suffered and fought, including the boy's mother and father, this little helpless child had somehow touched him. Was it because of Walt? Or because the boy seemed so much more fragile than the men and women, and the one teen, who had been brought in for care?

In the past hours, his prayers had changed from coherent thoughts to a nearly wordless plea: *Don't take him!*

Sam had sensed his upset earlier when Maxwell had asked his friend to ride for Jonas's place. Maxwell had said more in his message to them than he'd told Hattie. While he'd asked his brothers to ride and spread the word on how to prevent the disease and care for the people who contracted it, he'd also urged his mother and the younger children to stay home, stay away from the danger in town and take every precaution for themselves.

Maybe it was selfish, but he couldn't bear the thought of losing any member of his family.

"C'mon," he whispered as he attempted to drip another teaspoon of water into the little boy's mouth. Most of it dribbled from his lips and down his jaw. "You've got to drink."

A soft touch on his shoulder startled him.

Hattie.

Somehow, she must've seen the desperation swamping him, because her fingers tightened and she didn't release him immediately.

"You should take a break. Go outside for a moment," she said softly. "Mrs. Potter and I will watch over the patients for a bit." She motioned over her shoulder to where another, older woman tended a man on one of the cots. The woman had refused to leave her husband, and Hattie had recruited her to help them nurse the rest of those afflicted.

"I can't," Maxwell said tightly. "He isn't any better." He tucked the blanket more tightly around the small, still form.

"You must." Hattie pressed on his shoulder until he was forced to shift in the uncomfortable wooden chair he'd pulled close to the cot.

Stubbornly, he remained in his seat. Hattie locked eyes with him. Stared him down, willing him to get up out of the chair. Behind her inflexibility, he could see the same desperation he shared.

"Mama came by," Hattie said.

He was surprised. He hadn't seen Mrs. Powell come into the sanctuary.

"She stayed outside in the yard," Hattie went on. "But she said she'd finally reached Papa."

For a moment, a ray of hope lit inside Maxwell. "Is he coming?"

"Not yet."

And was doused. Was it any use, after all? Could anyone other than God save Bobby now?

"He mentioned that he'd had some success with giving certain patients milk."

She held up a small mug held in her other hand,

one he hadn't noticed until now. He moved to take it from her, but she drew it back against her side, still careful not to spill it.

"Stubborn," he half-growled.

She only raised her brows at him. Against everything, against the pain tightening his chest, one corner of his mouth lifted.

Finally, he stood, registering the stiffness in his muscles. How long had he lingered with Bobby? Should he have been making rounds of the others?

"The other patients?" he asked as Hattie brushed past him.

She mock glared at him. "Go outside. Give yourself five minutes to settle. And then come back."

Standing under the stars with his hands stuffed in his pockets, he tried to breathe deeply, but it felt as though a loaded wagon sat on his chest. He'd missed the expansive sky when he'd been at school in Denver. Somehow the gas lamps and constant busyness of the city muted the stars, and he'd often wished to be home beneath the wide-open sky he remembered.

But tonight he felt none of the peace he usually did being out in the vast Wyoming dark.

Around him, the town was completely silent. Not even any sounds of the saloons or rowdy cowboys— he could only guess that everyone had heard about what was happening and had done their best to attempt to keep from getting sick themselves.

He felt very alone.

In Denver, when loneliness threatened to overtake him, he would often take long walks around the city. Right now, he didn't want to stray too far from Hattie or the patients, in case they needed him, so he looped around the church building, attempting to stir his blood, remove the morbid thoughts and worries from his head. Once, twice, three times.

It didn't help.

He stood it for as long as he could bear, then returned inside to find Hattie's eyes alight. "I think he's a bit better," Hattie whispered. "Does his pulse seem stronger?"

Maxwell didn't hesitate; he knelt at the boy's bedside and reached to touch his throat and see for himself. He thought Hattie was right.

But the fight wasn't over. They'd only just begun.

Chapter Eight

The next day, they lost their first patient. Hattie stood beside Maxwell as a woman from town faded away. Maxwell remained stoic and silent. Detached.

Or so she thought, until she turned and saw the fire burning in his eyes, the desperation that she'd only barely admitted to feeling herself.

She watched as he threw himself into caring for the remaining patients, spending time at each bedside, urging them with his actions and his voice to *live*.

She'd been so wrong about him.

He was more than a cowboy. More than a medical student. He was a man of honor, of conviction. A sensitive soul. It was so obvious he cared about saving each person they treated. How could she guard her heart, keep her distance from a man like this, when they had to work so closely together?

Although they'd taken turns getting a few hours' rest during the darkest part of night, they were both exhausted and dragging. Hattie prayed that her nervous condition would continue to remain dormant.

It was late afternoon when Hattie paused across

from Maxwell, who was again lingering beside Bobby. This time he wore a puzzled expression, his brows drawn across his forehead.

"What is it?"

"I think he…moved," he whispered hoarsely.

And then the boy's head twitched on the pillow. His small, freckled face scrunched and a croaky whisper came. "Firsty…"

Bobby was thirsty.

Maxwell's hand shook as he raised a glass of boiled and cooled water; he dipped a teaspoon into the water and fed it to the boy, who swallowed on his own for the first time since he'd been brought to them.

Hattie's first reaction was to tell the boy's mother, who was in and out of consciousness in a cot to one side, but when Maxwell looked up at Hattie, the fierce emotion on his face barely registered because she couldn't see past the tears standing in his eyes.

He stood without a word and rushed outside, boots pounding on the wood floor. Hattie brushed her fingers across the child's head. He was perhaps a bit cooler, although still feverish. He'd apparently fallen back asleep, though his breathing, too, seemed more even than it had before. Hattie told Mrs. Potter that she would return shortly and went after Maxwell.

She found him around the corner, behind the church building. He was leaning against the building, his head thrust into the crook of his arm.

Hattie's heart thudded. Should she turn around? Go back inside? She hated intruding on his private moment….

He must've heard her somehow, because he turned his head slightly. There was no sign of tears, other than the red rims around his eyes, but those green eyes were brimming with emotion.

Gone were any thoughts of turning away now.

She moved toward him, and he captured her in his arms, holding her tightly, fiercely. She let her arms come around his shoulders; her palms rested against the nape of his neck, fingers brushing his hair.

He trembled against her.

Gone were any thoughts of her plans, medical school, her papa. The walls between them had been demolished. Gone was her carefully maintained distance. All that was left was his heart—his joy, the man himself.

When she finally stepped away, they both kept their faces averted. Was he as nervous as she about the connection sparking between them?

"I'll relieve Mrs. Potter." He thrust a hand through his dark hair.

"I'll check our water supply." She hung back, allowed him to disappear inside the church.

Where did things between them go now? To a deeper friendship? To something more?

She didn't know. She only knew that the way she thought about Maxwell had changed. There was so much more to the man than she'd known. And she found she wanted to be even closer—know even more about him.

It had just gone dark when Hattie's left leg faltered as she moved between two cots. She gripped the back of the chair she'd been heading for to steady herself before dropping into it.

No. It couldn't be. Not now.

A glance over to the cot where she'd finally convinced Maxwell to sleep for a few hours revealed he hadn't heard the drag of her shoe or the slight scrape of the chair legs against the floor. He slept soundly, one arm thrown above his head. And Mrs. Potter was engrossed with a patient across the room and hadn't seemed to notice Hattie's stumble.

She flexed the leg before her, pointing her toes inside her shoe. Had it been a fluke? She was overtired after missing out on sleep for most of seventy-two hours. Anyone would be.

It could've been a misstep; perhaps her peripheral vision had wavered, and she'd misjudged the distance to the chair.

Or was her condition flaring up? If her symptoms manifested in weak nerves now, she wouldn't be much use to Maxwell.

If it was a minor event, she might have some weakness but be able to handle most of her duties.

If it was a major episode, Hattie would lose function, be rendered useless.

Could she bear it? If Papa found out, her arguments for medical school would be nullified.... She couldn't even think about what her mama would insist on—possibly that Hattie not leave the house again until Papa arrived back in town. Why did this have to happen now?

And what would Maxwell think? Hot tears scalded beneath her eyelids. She blinked them away furiously. Even though they'd been close this afternoon, she hated for him to see weakness in her.

Perhaps if she limited her standing and walking

for a bit, she could prevent a full episode from coming on.

She would use the wooden chair to help her move between patients and then sit carefully near each one, giving herself ample time to get them water and cooling rags. If someone cried out or became worse, Hattie could always rouse Maxwell or call for Mrs. Potter.

Over the next hour, moving between patients grew more and more difficult. Hattie finally resigned herself to wake Maxwell.

She'd walked several steps toward his cot when she stumbled, this time falling all the way to the floor, catching herself with her hands just beside where he slept.

The noise was enough that he stirred.

She pushed to her knees with difficulty as he sat up in the cot, shoving one hand through his tousled dark curls. His cheeks were flushed with sleep, his eyes drowsy and curious. His shirt had become rumpled and the blanket tangled around him.

"Hattie? You all right? How long has it been?" His last question dissolved in a yawn. He moved his hand from his hair to rub his face. His sock-clad feet met the floor.

If she weren't so upset, she might be discomfited by the intimacy.

"Not long. I—"

She swallowed the words. If she could only get up off the floor on her own, maybe it wouldn't be so humiliating to ask for his help....

"Hattie?" Concerned now, he reached for her.

"I'm not all right. I need your help." She whispered the difficult words, but he barely acknowledged them as his strong hands closed over her shoulders. To her humiliation, a tear slipped down her cheek.

"Did you trip? Scrape your hands?" He drew her up easily, changing their places as he settled her on the bed, still warm from his body, and knelt before her. Her leg was so weak she had to manipulate it with her hands in order to adjust it into place on the cot.

"It's my nerves. I have…I have a condition very much like multiple sclerosis," she admitted, keeping her face turned down to her lap. She hadn't wanted him to think less of her, but how could he not, now that she'd said the words aloud? "And I've been in a period of remission for several months, but just now… the nerves have gone. I can barely move my left leg. And…" She held up her hands that trembled uncontrollably, though she still didn't look at him.

"Hattie…" he breathed.

His fingers came to her jaw, just a gentle touch to nudge her face up. She found it too difficult to meet his eyes.

"I can't believe you or your father didn't tell me. I've been letting you work yourself into the ground for three days. If I'd known…"

Now her chin came all the way up—quickly—and her lips firmed. "I'm not an invalid."

And she immediately saw the way the right side of his mouth had turned upward, just the slightest bit. Had he said what he had to provoke her…purposely? To shake her out of her despondency?

He closed her hands in his, and although her trembling didn't stop—likely wouldn't for several minutes or longer—the warmth of his touch chased away her shame and brought back the shared emotion of earlier. This time, she held his gaze.

"What can I do for you?" he asked.

Tears welled again at his easy acceptance. He could've been angry that she hadn't told him all of it before this point, before she needed his help in a large way.

"I've been several weeks without any symptoms," she told him. "Perhaps the exhaustion has something to do with it. Maybe if I can get a few hours of sleep…"

"And if that doesn't help, then we'll deal with it in the morning." He sounded so sure, as if dealing with her condition were easy. As if he'd already accepted it. "Do you want me to take you home? Maybe if you slept in your own bed, you'd rest more comfortably."

She shook her head. "I'd rather stay."

Again came that half smile, the quirk at one corner of his mouth. "How did I know you were going to say that?"

She told him about the last patient she'd seen, and he told her not to worry, that he and Mrs. Potter could take care of things through the night. When her trembling fingers wouldn't let her take off her shoes, once again his large, warm hands enclosed hers. He tucked her hands into her lap and then unlaced the shoes himself, nimble fingers moving quickly over the task. Where another man might've used the chance to admire her ankles, or worse, Maxwell simply tucked her shoes beneath the cot and spread his hands on his thighs as he boosted himself into a crouch.

"Is there anything else you need?"

Breathless with an emotion she didn't want to

name, all she could do was shake her head. He stood, and she tucked her legs beneath the covers, lying down on the cot.

She knew she should try to sleep, but after his tender ministrations, Hattie felt wide-awake, nerves jangling. She lay with her face to the room, cheek on top of her hands, watching Maxwell through slitted eyes. He moved among the patients quietly, steadily. The same way he did everything, she was coming to realize.

He'd handled the news of her condition with remarkable aplomb, looking for ways to take action without overstepping his bounds. He hadn't acted as if having an affliction similar to multiple sclerosis changed his view of her—he'd only asked what she'd needed to get through tonight.

Although Hattie's mother wanted her to court and find a husband, she couldn't imagine another man of her acquaintance being so accepting upon finding out that Hattie had a degenerative disease. It was one of the reasons she'd held herself distant when men attempted to make conversation with her—that and her dreams of becoming a doctor in her own right.

All of a sudden, Mama's pushing her in Maxwell's direction didn't seem so bad.

Was it because Maxwell had seen her working, first alongside her papa and then with him? He had to know she was capable, even if her nerves limited her usefulness on the rare occasion.

She didn't know. All she knew was that somehow…Maxwell hadn't made her feel like less of a person when he'd found out. He'd even teased her.

She thought perhaps…perhaps he still saw her as an equal.

When she finally fell off to sleep, a small smile curved her lips.

Maxwell moved as quietly as he could through the rows of cots and pallets, toting the large pot of boiled water that had been brought for their use this morning. He settled it on the makeshift worktable he and Hattie had set up—was it just yesterday?—and turned to assess the room, where most of the patients slept quietly.

They'd taken on two additional cases in the night, but the sickness seemed to have slowed. He would have to thank his brothers for their quick response in spreading the word—surely it had had something to do with keeping more people from coming down with the dreaded cholera. Or maybe it just hadn't hit as hard here as it had in Pear Grove. He didn't know.

He'd sent Mrs. Potter home for a few hours of rest and was the only one awake in the building, for the moment. He knew the disease would take several more days to pass for these people—if they could keep them hydrated enough to survive. Certainly no one, not even little Bobby, who was much improved, was out of the woods yet.

But he'd found a kernel of hope when the boy had spoken.

He was a little embarrassed that Hattie had witnessed his emotional reaction. He would never live it down if any of his brothers found out that he'd been brought to tears by a little child, but Hattie's reaction had been just as powerful as his.

He'd held her, they'd held each other—and the closeness they'd shared frightened him in light of his past.

Thoughts of his colleague brought his gaze down to where she rested close by.

Dawn's light barely lit the windows of the church building, but it was enough for him to see her profile as she slept. She looked more peaceful than he'd ever seen her. And with good reason. Was sleep the only time she felt that way? Now he knew how big her struggles really were. Not only did she have to fight to do what she loved—against her mother's wishes, against the prejudice of others like Mr. Spencer—but she also had to overcome a debilitating medical condition. He couldn't imagine what she went through each day, yet she gave her all in the clinic.

His admiration for her knew no bounds. But admiration had nothing to do with how beautiful she looked right at this moment. Her hair had loosened from its pins and curled around her jaw. Her lashes were a shadowy smudge against her cheeks, and he could barely make out the light dusting of freckles across the slope of her pert nose.

His fingers itched for his poetry journal, which was currently stowed in his saddlebags back at the clinic. He would love to capture a verse about how she looked just at this very moment. With all that had been going on, with the doctor being gone and then this outbreak of cholera, he'd barely had time to think about his poetry or the journal. Until now.

He was a little afraid his feelings for her were growing beyond friendship.

And after both women he'd cared for had deserted

him before he'd even made it to medical school, he knew that it wasn't entirely realistic for Hattie to return his feelings. He needed to find a way to protect his heart, to stifle his admiration from growing into something it shouldn't.

She hummed softly and shifted. Before he could look away, her eyes fluttered open, and he was caught by the welcome in the blue depths, warmer than he'd ever seen before.

She blinked and he quickly turned away, hands shaking, to ladle some of the prepared water into a sterilized Mason jar.

"Good—" He had to clear his throat when his voice threatened to crack like Seb's. "Good morning," he offered quietly.

Behind him, he heard soft movements, blankets stirring and Hattie's soft "Morning."

He dared a look over his shoulder to see her sitting up in the cot, attempting to twist her hair back into place. She had several pins pinched between her lips.

The near darkness and their hushed voices gave the moment a peculiar intimacy—what it might be like to be married to Hattie, readying for their day.

And again, the look in her eyes—soft, warm…

He turned back to the table, squeezing his eyes closed, trying to erase the image from his vision, but instead searing it into his memory. Whether she felt the link between them or not, he had to find a way to get his rioting imagination in check. They were working together. Saving patients' lives. That was it. He couldn't expect more.

He cleared his throat again. He hoped she would think his voice was rusty from whispering to the patients all night and not attribute it to the real cause—how she unsettled him. "How are you feeling?"

The soft swish of fabric and movement at his elbow was his only warning of her presence as she joined him before the table. "Better."

She extended her hands, and he saw the tremors were gone. She seemed steady on her feet, but he carefully kept his eyes from straying to her face, half afraid her bright-eyed gaze would unman him further.

"Steady enough to perform surgery."

He sensed more than saw her smile. "One of us should check on Mr. Spencer this morning."

"Your ma was here a little bit ago. She said his wife got help and moved him home. Your ma didn't know for sure but thought he was awake and talking."

Her hands gripped the table. "Did you tell her—about last night? About my nerves?" The tremor in her voice betrayed what she wanted the answer to be.

"Didn't see any reason to. She only asked if you were getting rest, and since you were asleep, I told her you were."

"Thank you…" she breathed. "Sometimes it seems she doesn't see me as an adult yet—capable of knowing my own limitations. I'd rather not have to fight with her to stay and help today. Not with so many who need us…"

He scratched the back of his neck, knowing he needed to put some distance between them. "If you don't mind, I'll check on Mr. Spencer and then bunk down at the clinic for a bit. I'll be back by lunchtime."

She made a noise in the affirmative and turned to look over the room full of patients. "Is there anything I should know about?"

He shook his head. "Two more people arrived real early, about the same condition as the others. No one seems particularly worse, or better for that matter. I think we're in for a siege."

When she only nodded, mind obviously on what tasks she would start with, he headed for the door. Her soft words stopped him.

"I'm sorry you had to take the burden of work last night. It…it wasn't fair to you. My condition is worse when I overextend myself, and the last couple of days…"

He fought and won against the urge to go to her. Better to hold himself distant than risk getting hurt one more time.

"I should've told you sooner, made a better effort to rest. I won't let it happen again."

Her chin tipped up in the way he was coming to recognize, and he plopped his Stetson on his head, hoping it would shield the grin he couldn't suppress. He couldn't *not* encourage her. "Hattie, you're something. That's all I got to say."

Chapter Nine

"Here's some milk that Mrs. Fishbourne just dropped off." Hattie passed the full jug to Maxwell, who nodded and took it from her, not giving her a verbal reply as he turned to take it to the table along the back wall.

His reserved manner unnerved her. Ever since he'd returned from his rest around lunchtime, he'd seemed quieter, more hesitant around her, although he'd worked hard all afternoon with hydrating the patients and changing linens.

Oh, he was as professional as he'd ever been, but the easy, more conversational manner he'd shown, the warm smiles he'd shared with her last night had disappeared.

He was putting distance between them. After the emotional moments yesterday following Bobby's small improvement and his understanding of her condition, she'd expected something different.

Could his manner be attributed to the exhaustion and strain they were both under? Or had she done something this morning to offend him? Could it be because she hadn't wanted her mama to know that she'd had to ask for help?

Her parents believed her condition meant she shouldn't be a doctor. Did Maxwell now think the same way?

Evening was falling and Maxwell stood outside the church, leaning back against the building with his hands pressed over his eyes.

He'd woken from a few hours of broken sleep more convinced than ever that he should pull back from Hattie. But keeping his distance from her all afternoon hadn't been easy, and seeing the confusion in her eyes as the afternoon wore on made him feel like a heel.

Wasn't it better to hold himself back, to keep what had happened with both of the girls he'd cared about in Denver from happening again? He'd thought his feelings for them had been reciprocated, but both women had found him lacking. With Elizabeth, it had hurt even more because he'd believed he had loved her enough to want marriage. But when they'd spoken of future plans and Maxwell had revealed he wanted to move back to Bear Creek or a similar small town, she had quickly broken things off.

He knew the need for doctors in small towns. Before Doc Powell's arrival, Bear Creek had been without a doctor for several years after the previous doc had retired. Maxwell had seen folks suffering firsthand without proper medical care.

He'd thought if Elizabeth really loved him, she would be willing to go with him, even to a small town. But she hadn't loved him enough. Just as his birth ma had told him over and over again. With his record of women leaving him, how could he doubt it was true?

He knew better than to think that Hattie could develop true feelings for him. So wasn't it better to guard his heart and keep from feeling the awful things he had when Elizabeth had left him?

What if the things he felt for Hattie, what she was willing to share with him, weren't real anyway, just emotions forced by their proximity?

The sound of a wagon creaking and a horse's soft blow brought him upright and out of his morose thoughts. Was someone bringing another patient?

But it was a familiar pair on the seat of the wagon. Jonas and Penny.

"Ma? Pa? What're you doing here? Is it one of the kids?" Maxwell's heart pounded, his thoughts immediately going to Ida and Walt. He pushed off the wall and bolted forward, reaching out for the wagon bed.

"No, no," Penny reassured him. "We just came to check on you. And from the shadows under your eyes, it's a good thing we did."

"Didn't Sam deliver my message for you to stay on the homestead? Stay safe?" His heart still thudded painfully, thinking of the danger his parents had put themselves in by coming to town. What if they came in contact with the cholera and got sick themselves?

"Of course he delivered it, but you know your ma…." Jonas said. It was clear from his voice he didn't fully agree with her decision to come to town. He set the brake on the wagon and climbed down while Maxwell went to Penny's side and raised his arms.

"I was afraid she'd try to hitch the horses herself if I didn't bring her to see you."

Penny wrinkled her nose at her husband's words—they were obviously only half in jest. Once on her feet, she reached up and smoothed Maxwell's hair from his forehead. He'd left his Stetson inside the church and had forgotten to grab it before he'd come outdoors. He wished he had the slight protection it might offer in keeping Penny from reading his eyes—she always seemed to know when he was most discouraged.

"How are things?" she asked.

Jonas rounded the wagon and came close to clap Maxwell on the shoulder.

At his parents' show of support, Maxwell felt the emotions he'd been suppressing for the past days expand in his chest. He shook his head, unable to express the despair he'd felt when the one patient had slipped away from him and Hattie, or the exhaustion that seemed a part of his marrow from days and nights of working.

Somehow, they knew. Both put their arms around him, supporting him. Loving him.

It was their love that had given him courage to go to college and further to medical school, and it was that same love that held him up now.

Finally, after a few moments, he was able to clear his throat of emotion and speak. "Hattie—Miss Powell and I are both tired, working day and night. We've been blessed that we've only lost one patient. Cholera is an awful thing."

"I'm real proud of you, son," Jonas said, hugging his shoulders before stepping back.

Penny still stood close, her arm wrapped around his waist and his around her back, her burgeoning belly between them.

"We brought some fresh milk. Heard that was helping some folks," Jonas said, moving to the back of the wagon, where a large container had been wedged in.

A small bark came from the back of the wagon and a white fur ball jumped to the ground.

"And a stowaway," Penny said.

Breanna's white dog lunged up and put its paws on Maxwell's knees, wiggling its whole body along with its tail in happy abandon. Maxwell couldn't suppress a chuckle.

"Breanna was worried about you being lonely. Walt and Ida overheard her, and the three of them cooked up the idea to send the pup along. If we need to take him home, we will, but the kids wanted you to see him."

Maxwell knelt for a moment, scratching the fur on the dog's ruff. "He'll be a welcome distraction for those who start to come out of it. It shouldn't be long for some of the folks."

With one final pat, Maxwell straightened and the dog moved to sniff his boots.

Maxwell directed Jonas inside, to where he could leave the milk. He could still feel Penny's gaze on him. And his pa was getting to be more perceptive; no doubt he'd sensed his wife had something to say to Maxwell.

"I was out in the bunkhouse, straightening up a bit—and missing you," Penny admitted as the door to the church building closed behind Jonas. "And this fell out from beneath your bunk." She held out a familiar small leather-covered book. His poetry journal.

He took it from her and tucked it in his breast pocket. "I thought I'd stowed it in my saddlebags." Had she looked into his most personal thoughts?

"I didn't read it," she said, seeming to understand his concern. "Once I saw what it was, I closed it up. But I thought perhaps you might not want your brothers to get ahold of it, either."

"Thanks." Relief sluiced through him. He trusted his ma more than anyone else—except maybe his pa—but these were his most personal thoughts and dreams, on paper. His ma's perceptiveness reminded him that she could be trusted. Her next words were still a surprise, though.

"I was wondering if…" She sighed. "At the risk of becoming as nosy as your brothers, I'll just ask. Has there been any resolution with Hattie? I know you were trying to befriend her…."

Maxwell leaned back against the wagon wheel, hand going to the back of his neck. "It's…complicated."

"Why?" His ma touched his arm gently.

"We've gotten…closer, I guess you'd say. Don't know how we couldn't, working together like we have been."

She nodded.

He swallowed. Considered what he should say, if anything. Must've considered a little too long, because she spoke again.

"Do your 'complications' have anything to do with the young lady you wrote about in your letters home and then suddenly stopped mentioning?"

She seemed to know what he couldn't say about Elizabeth. He looked off into the distance, squinting, because it was hard to meet her eyes, even knowing she wanted the best for him.

She squeezed his arm as the silence lengthened, as he couldn't tell her that Elizabeth hadn't really wanted him. And neither had his birth ma. She'd told him often enough.

"You can't be afraid to offer your heart," she said softly. "Whether that means friendship or something more. I think your father would tell you the same thing. I seem to remember a story about several of you boys convincing him to come after me when he was fearful of being vulnerable."

"Yes, but…" It hurt to be rejected.

Even though he was now thinking that maybe Elizabeth hadn't been right for him from the start. Not like Hattie could be. Maybe.

"Even if it isn't Miss Powell, there is someone out there for you. I believe it."

He was a little afraid he was already too attached to Hattie—he wanted her to be the woman for him.

"That's all I'll say for now," she whispered, putting her arms around his neck in one last hug.

Jonas stomped down the steps in front of the church, giving them ample warning he was on his way back.

"We know you're busy. We'll get outta your way, now that your ma's reassured you're alive and well. Take care of yourself," his pa said, clapping him on the shoulder once again. "And that gal in there."

Penny met Maxwell's eyes in a pointed gaze. "We love you."

She allowed Maxwell to help her back into the wagon, and then his parents were off.

He stood for a long moment after the wagon had gone, Penny's advice warring with everything his birth ma had said until he was thirteen years old.

Who was right? His birth ma had also said he'd never amount to anything, but because of Penny's pushing, he'd gotten into college—even graduated. He was still proving that he could be someone, could finish school and be a doctor. His family believed in him, even if he wasn't always sure himself.

But his ma had often told him that he was worthless, that he would never find a woman to love him.

She certainly hadn't loved him.

And neither had Elizabeth.

Could he trust in Penny's blind belief that there was a woman made for him? Was it possible that Hattie could develop feelings for him?

Could he risk opening his heart further...?

Dark had fallen and Hattie was supposed to be trying to sleep, but even though she was tucked into a cot at the back of the church sanctuary, she couldn't quiet her restless thoughts.

Two days had passed with minimal improvement in their patients—but at least no one else had died.

Being forced to work closely with Maxwell for the past several days had caused her to see him in an entirely new light. Would she have ever seen the real man behind the medical student if not for being forced into this situation with him? She doubted it.

She'd heard him whispering prayers over the patients when he thought no one was close enough to hear. He endured when her patience would've been tried, took time to ensure each person got the treatment they needed. Hiding behind his reserved manner was an intelligent and competent man.

It worried her a little. In her plans for medical school, she'd wanted to return to work with her father, but Maxwell was already more than halfway through his education. What if her father saw the potential in him and then had no room for her in his practice... if she could even convince him to allow her to go to medical school?

But she found she couldn't even begrudge Maxwell that. He wasn't her rival—not any longer. Working together so closely had changed her perspective on him. She could easily count him as a friend now.

Her eyes flicked over the silent, sleeping patients to where her surprising colleague sat at a chair pulled up to the table, partway across the room. Probably taking a well-deserved break. At his feet was the small white dog that she'd seen at the picnic; it had appeared at his side after his parents' visit. His dark head was bent over the desk, and his hand moved rapidly across a...journal? Yes, she could just hear the *scritch-scratch* of his pencil over the page.

He stopped writing, raising his pencil to gnaw on the end of it, brow scrunched in concentration.

His deep absorption in what he was doing allowed her to study him freely.

Her changing feelings wouldn't allow her to ignore him as a man any longer.

She'd recognized his strength and his height before but never looked beyond to make a study of his features. She considered his strong brow and the elegant line of his nose. She couldn't see his green eyes from this angle, but she couldn't forget his intensity when the patient had died or the tears she'd glimpsed when young Bobby had spoken.

He bent over his book again and the muscles of his shoulders bunched and stretched beneath the material of his shirt. He was a fine specimen indeed.

He glanced furtively at her, then back at his sketchbook. Then he froze.

Slowly, his head turned slightly and their eyes met. Surprise registered on his face. Had he just realized she was awake?

Color rushed into his face, and her curiosity went from mild to full-on. She sat up, heart drumming against her rib cage.

"Are you sketching me?" she demanded.

He shook his head slightly but that dark stain remained in his cheeks, belying his denial.

A hank of hair fell into her eyes but she shoved it aside, reaching out one hand toward him. "Let me see."

Again, he shook his head, this time with eyes slightly widened in panic. He tucked the book beneath his thigh as if he thought she would rush over and pluck it from his hands. His pencil clattered to the floor, startling the dog from its sleep; it raised its head. Were his quick actions a result of growing up with so many brothers?

"It's not a sketchbook."

"Then why are you turning red?"

Her words seemed to make the color in his face darker.

"It's just some writings…a journal."

"Then why don't you want to show it to me?"

A burst of air flew from his lips. "It's poetry, all right?" He rubbed a hand over the back of his neck, an endearing gesture she was coming to recognize.

"Your poetry?"

He hesitated, as if he didn't want to confirm what she already suspected. "Yes…my poetry. It's sorta… private."

She couldn't resist teasing him a bit more. "And are you writing about me?"

"I write about a lot of things…." he hedged. How interesting. It hadn't been an outright no.

"Are you any good?"

"No." Now he tucked the book into the breast pocket of his shirt. Hiding it, as if she would jump out of the cot and grab it from his hands. Somewhat in the way he held his emotions close…

She arranged the covers around her legs. Beneath, she was still fully dressed, although she'd gone home briefly to wash up earlier. If one of the patients needed something in the middle of the night, not having to struggle with dressing would expedite being able to help.

"How do you know?"

"I've read enough poetry to know."

"Ah. From your college courses."

He nodded. "And on my own. College introduced me to the subject, but I…found I liked it more than I expected."

"Hmm."

He darted a glance at her. "What does that mean?"

"It's just that I've never met a man who liked poetry. It makes you a bit of an enigma. You're a cowboy, a medical student on his way to becoming a doctor. And a poet." And she liked him more than she probably should.

He adjusted one of the water pitchers on the table, straightening it unnecessarily.

"We'd better keep this information hidden from the young ladies of town, or they'll be flocking even more to you."

He glared at her this time, and she laughed softly. It was true, though; this would be another thing for the young women to admire about him.

"No one else knows, except maybe my ma. And I'd like to keep it that way," he said.

"Hmm. I suppose your brothers might give you a hard time if they found out you were secretly a poet."

He shook his head. "To say the very least. I can just imagine them composing jesting verses to poke fun at me."

He shared a speaking glance with her, this time a small smile curling his lips.

One of the patients moaned and stirred, and Maxwell stood to go check on him. Hattie watched, relieved that the distance she'd felt this afternoon seemed to have disappeared with nightfall. Perhaps he'd just been tired earlier.

How intriguing that he liked poetry, wrote poetry. She was finding more and more to admire about the handsome cowboy.

She was curious. What had he written about her? Would they ever be close enough for him to share it with her? After the wavering emotions of the past day, she didn't know.

* * *

Hattie had lain down again when Maxwell made his way back to his chair in the corner, but her bright eyes met his gaze. She was still awake. His heart bucked in his chest.

He should probably feel anxious that she knew his secret, but somehow he didn't. He kind of liked that she knew something private about him.

All afternoon he'd thought about what Penny had told him. He didn't know if he could fully open his heart again, but remaining aloof with Hattie was too difficult. He would continue the friendship and try to keep his heart uninvolved.

He sat back down, aware she was watching him. Before she could ask something else to disconcert him, he spoke.

"You never did answer my question the other day, before we got interrupted."

"What?" she asked, propping her cheek on her bent elbow. He did his best to ignore the tousled hair falling around her ears and the pretty picture she made. Tried. Failed.

"Why aren't you on your way to becoming a doctor yourself?"

Her eyes darted to one side, and she shrugged. Would she refuse to answer?

"Your ma?" he prompted.

"She doesn't want me to work in the clinic in any capacity—helper, nurse, doctor. It's all the same to her."

"But she allows it. Surely she wants you to be happy."

She picked at the blanket before her. "She wants

me to be happy in her way—finding a husband and settling into a household and having babies."

"And you don't want that," he stated, so he could be sure he understood. He couldn't imagine not wanting to have a family. Although he wasn't sure it would ever happen for him, he desperately wanted a wife and family of his own. As much as he wanted to be a doctor.

"It's not that. I would like to have a family, eventually. If I could find a husband who supported me…"

"Supported you how…?" he asked when her voice trailed off, letting the question hang.

She hesitated for too long, and he again thought she wouldn't answer. Was her reticence because of the subject matter or because she was discussing it with *him?*

"In my desire to be a doctor," she whispered.

Ah. He'd guessed as much from her passion, her work at the clinic, even before her father had had to leave town. She was more than just a nurse or her father's helper.

"So, why aren't you in medical school? Surely your father has some connections. Is it the money?"

She shook her head slightly. "Papa has promised to consider letting me attend. But Mama…she worries because of my condition. And so far, he has been unwilling to overrule her wishes."

He examined her face for a long moment. "I wouldn't think you'd let that stop you."

Her chin came up, eyes flaming at him. "What is that supposed to mean?"

He held up his hands at the heat in her words. "Just that you've managed to work with your father for all these years. Your ma hasn't kept you from it, not really. Maybe she knows how important it is to you and she'd be more open to it now."

She considered his words with a tilt of her head and a far-off look in her eyes. "I was hoping if I could prove myself to Papa while he was gone, I might bring him around to seeing things my way. Then he might be more inclined to press my case to Mama."

"Have you already chosen a school, then, or are your plans more tentative than that?" he asked, because somehow he knew she had a plan.

Again, she picked at some small spot on the blanket. "I've been offered a tuition scholarship, contingent on passing an oral review with a committee. Later this month. Papa and Mama don't know—yet," she said. "I've been waiting for the right moment to bring it up—and I know I'm running out of time."

He could hear her frustration and tension in her voice, see the stiffness of her shoulders.

"I'm sorry. It must be hard to have to go against your parents' wishes," he said softly.

"Your parents have always supported you?" she asked.

"More like pushed me. Especially my ma—Penny, that is, not my birth ma. My birth ma wasn't real encouraging about…much of anything. She told me I wouldn't amount to much. But once Penny married Jonas and found out about me wanting to be a doctor, she did everything she could to make it happen for me."

He clamped his mouth shut against more words that were ready to follow. How was it that he found it so easy to speak to Hattie about a difficult subject, one he barely broached with his family and had hardly even spoken of with Sam, his best friend?

Hattie still played with the fold of the blanket. "You haven't asked me the one question I thought for certain you would."

He raised his brows at her, beckoning her to go on.

"I'm surprised you haven't mentioned my nervous condition as a hindrance to a career in medicine."

He raised his brows. "I don't see it like that," he admitted honestly. "It doesn't seem to be a limitation for you."

"But...the other night—"

He shrugged. "It isn't as if your father never gets sick or needs a day off, is it? I've seen my classmates nearly keel over from exhaustion during exams week. You seem to manage it fairly well."

Her eyes finally rose to meet his, and the gratefulness shining in their depths prompted him to look down and continue.

"And if you set up a practice with a partner, you would have someone to support you, in case you needed it."

The words were barely out of his mouth when he saw himself as Hattie's partner in his mind's eye. He swallowed and looked down, rubbed the edge of the table, hard, beneath his thumb. If they were married... if they worked together, day in and day out...

He blinked away the image, quickly. It was a dream, to be sure, a spur-of-the-moment thought and nothing more.

But he was shaking as he pushed up from the table and turned his face away, in case the emotion bursting through him showed on his face. "I should turn down the lamps—do one last check of the patients."

He found he loved talking to Hattie. But an intimate, late-night conversation wasn't exactly helping his plan to keep his distance from her.

Hattie watched Maxwell's abrupt departure, wondering momentarily if she'd said something wrong. He moved among the patients, tucking in a blanket here, touching someone's forehead there. Calm and confident as ever.

Had she imagined the pained look on his face just before he'd turned away?

She was still amazed at his sensitive soul. He wrote poetry. Who would've guessed behind his quiet cowboy demeanor that he hid the soul of a poet?

And he hadn't disparaged her dream of becoming a doctor—he'd actually sounded supportive in the things he'd said.

There were still some hidden depths to the cowboy. She found she wanted to know him—ease what hurt him.

She couldn't think of one other man of her acquaintance who would've encouraged her in her pursuit. Not even her father really understood her desire—and he was passionate about medicine and his patients.

Was it because they shared the same dream that Maxwell understood? Or was there something else between them that made him seem to know her better than anyone else?

She didn't know...but she *did* know she could trust Maxwell with her dreams.

It was that confidence that finally allowed her to ease off into sleep.

Chapter Ten

"Where—where am I?"

Hattie watched Maxwell lean over Annabelle Perkins where the young woman stirred on the cot.

"Easy, now." He supported the girl's shoulder and helped her sit up. "You're in the church, where we've been keeping an eye on everyone who came down with cholera. You're probably feeling pretty weak."

Hattie moved forward and passed Maxwell a mug of purified water. He shot her a grateful look over his shoulder before turning back to Annabelle.

The man one row over stirred and Hattie moved to check on him. After another day and a half of demanding patient care, several had woken. It was a good sign. And Hattie had had news that her father was expected back any day, which was further good news.

Hattie was close enough to notice when Annabelle raised a shaking hand to brush her hair out of her eyes after Maxwell had helped her take several sips of water. The other girl had a slight flush across her cheeks, one that Hattie suspected came from being in close proximity to the man, not from any remaining fever.

"Easy," Maxwell said again as he eased the girl back onto the pillow. "It'll take a while to get back your strength after fighting off a sickness like this."

"…wanted to go to the next poetry reading," Hattie heard the other girl say.

"The town council canceled all gatherings until after most folks have gotten past the cholera." Maxwell put Annabelle's glass of water on a small table nearby and straightened the blankets at the foot of her cot.

"Th-thank you for taking care of me all this time." Annabelle settled back onto the pillow weakly.

Hattie's head came up and she saw the girl give a trembling smile—still trying to impress Maxwell even while she was sick?

She couldn't see Maxwell's face from her vantage point, but the sides of his neck had turned pink. He must've recognized Annabelle's attempt at seeking attention.

"Hattie and I—" he motioned in Hattie's direction "—have certainly been busy with *all* the patients." He emphasized the words quietly, not in a hurtful way.

Annabelle's head swiveled and her eyes widened at the sight of all the cots and pallets. She'd been one of the first to arrive in the clutches of the sickness, Hattie remembered.

"You two have nursed all of us by yourselves?" the girl asked.

"We've had some other family members come in to help us," Maxwell told her.

The mention of family seemed to upset the other girl. "What about—my family?"

Maxwell patted her hand gently, something Hattie's papa might've done. It seemed to comfort the other girl, but Hattie was abruptly reminded of the other night, when Maxwell's large hands had enfolded hers, warming her and eradicating the sting of nerves flaring up. She cast her eyes down, willing herself to focus on the patient before her, but the man had slipped off into sleep again.

Another patient stirred, farther across the room, and Hattie moved to attend him, leaving Maxwell and Annabelle to their soft-spoken conversation, though her attention stayed on the couple.

Maxwell remained at the other girl's side, surprising Hattie. She cared for her patient, but when she was finished, she looked up to find Maxwell's dark head still bent over the spread of Annabelle's golden-blond hair on the pillow.

Hattie went hot and cold, and her stomach cramped. Pressing a hand against her midsection, she moved to a chair nearby and sank onto it, her knees going suddenly weak. Not in a nervous way, not with the way her heart was fluttering wildly.

Everyone they'd admitted as a cholera patient had claimed an onset of sudden stomach cramps before the more debilitating symptoms of the sickness had struck. Hattie had been so careful to sterilize her hands and everything she touched. Had she somehow contracted the disease regardless?

But just as soon as Maxwell stood up from Annabelle's bedside, the awful pain in her stomach subsided. She waved off his concerned glance and turned her face to the side.

Surely it wasn't... It couldn't be... Was she jealous of Annabelle? After nearly three years of avoiding her mama's attempts to push her to court with some-one—anyone—eligible, Hattie couldn't have devel-oped softer feelings for the man she worked with... could she?

But the closeness they'd developed—she'd told him her dreams when she hadn't yet told anyone else—couldn't be denied. Likewise, he was one of the few people in town who knew about her medi-cal condition.

Her mind quickly flew over his finer qualities. His kindness, his honor, his quiet confidence...

Certainly, he was someone she would be proud to consider a friend, but to be falling for him? Surely she wasn't.

Surely, surely not.

The doctor arrived later that evening, pushing into the church with a curious look around. Maxwell watched his gaze settle on Hattie and relax, watched her rush across the room and into her pa's arms. The two embraced tightly. Doc Powell's eyes rested on Maxwell, as if even from across the room he was taking the younger man's measure.

Maxwell nodded his hello and kept on spooning warm broth into little Bobby. Although the boy was far from the animated tyke he'd been at the church picnic, he had more color in his cheeks and the fever had subsided.

Maxwell was more aware of Hattie than anything

else—as usual—as she took her father on a short tour of the converted church sanctuary. Doc expressed his approval of their methods of keeping everything sanitary and finally ended up in Maxwell's vicinity.

"Maxwell. You look about as done in as I feel. How are you holding up?"

A glance at the heavy lines on the doctor's face showed the other man's exhaustion. Even his silver mustache seemed to droop.

"About the same as I usually do at the end of spring calving season," Maxwell said.

"Do you think you can oversee things here while I escort Hattie home for some rest? I see you two have done a fine job here, but I'd like her to lie down for a bit—and you can take the day off tomorrow. I'm sure you both have earned more of a break, but we'll look at things later, see how the patients are faring."

Maxwell raised his eyes to Hattie's face. A small frown line marred her forehead, and her mouth was set, but those were the only signs she wasn't happy with her father's directive. Maxwell schooled his face so the smile he felt forming wouldn't break through. Hattie wanted to stay. He knew it, and she seemed to see the knowledge in his face because she *did* smile at him, though she shook her head slightly. He guessed she would go along with what her father wanted for now, hoping to ease him into a conversation later about her medical-school plans.

"I'll be fine for a bit. Mrs. Potter is coming back soon with some more broth for the patients who can take it, anyway."

"Ah, good, good."

"You sure you don't need to rest a bit this evening,

too?" Maxwell asked. "You can spell me at midnight if you want to."

The doctor shook his head. "I'll return shortly."

Maxwell shrugged his acceptance.

Doc was only gone long enough to walk Hattie home and come back. When he stepped into the church, Maxwell thought he looked even more exhausted than before. Had he pretended to be less tired for Hattie's sake? Did the man really not understand how strong his daughter was?

With most of the patients settling for the night, the church was quiet. Maxwell knew these folks would have a road ahead of them to get back to normal—cholera was terribly hard on the human body. More sleep would help their bodies heal quicker.

"Hattie and I were planning on sending most of these folks home in the morning," Maxwell said as he joined the doctor at the back of the room.

"Good," the old man said absently as he looked over the room from where he stood.

"How did things go up in Pear Grove?" Maxwell asked, keeping his voice low so he wouldn't wake any of the patients.

The doc shook his head. "Not good. We lost too many." His voice told of the depth of his sorrow, though he continued to stare out over the quiet church.

Suddenly, Doc turned on Maxwell. "Hattie mentioned that John Spencer had internal bleeding. I suppose she brought it up before I found out from another source. I'd like to hear your opinion on what happened."

Maxwell met the older man's eyes steadily. "He came into the office complaining of soreness—actually, his wife pushed him to come. Hattie and I examined him. Hattie felt…" He shook his head, trying to think how best to phrase what he wanted to convey to the doctor. "Hattie advised him to seek attention from the nearest doctor, but I wasn't sure. I questioned myself—questioned the symptoms. If the both of us had listened to Hattie, she wouldn't have had to perform the surgery, but she saved his life later that night."

Maxwell knew his enthusiasm must be seeping into his voice, but he well remembered standing next to a calm and collected Hattie as she had worked on the patient that night. "She was amazing. She didn't hesitate to do what needed to be done. The man would've died without her intervention—and first thing he said when he came to was how he should've listened to her in the first place."

Words bubbled just beneath Maxwell's throat, the desire to urge the doctor to let her go to medical school, but he didn't want to overstep his bounds, especially since he doubted Hattie had had time to broach the subject with her father.

The doc was watching Maxwell's face almost uncomfortably closely, and Maxwell had a moment of fear that the other man would see his feelings for Hattie written plainly there, just as he'd written them in his poetry journal.

"And was there anything else that happened with Hattie while I was gone that I should know about?"

Feverish heat scorched Maxwell's neck, but he strove to ignore it. Although he and Hattie had spent time together, gotten to know each other in the quiet night hours, they'd done nothing wrong.

"If you're asking about Hattie's nervous condition, you should probably talk to her." He swallowed. "If you're asking about my…my intentions toward your daughter—" Maxwell had to stop to take a deep breath, clear his throat "—I've grown to admire Hattie. She's a fine woman. I'm a little afraid she's too good for me—I'm just a cowhand trying to make something of myself."

The doc's eyes didn't leave Maxwell. His continued scrutiny had Maxwell shifting his feet uncomfortably. "So, are you interested in my daughter or not?"

Maxwell's flush and silence must've said enough for the doctor to come to his own conclusion. He nodded to himself.

"And I'll also assume you haven't mentioned anything to Hattie?"

"No. We've had some conversations, but—no." He'd taken his ma's advice and tried not to distance himself from the lovely doctor's daughter, but he wouldn't dare admit that he actually admired her. Not without knowing if she could return his feelings. He wasn't that courageous.

"I will tell you that Hattie's got notions."

Maxwell assumed the doctor meant her desire to further her education, become a doctor. Doc couldn't know she'd already told him.

"But maybe if you expressed yourself—got her interested, you see—maybe she would…maybe she would change her mind. Think more about settling down."

It didn't take much for Maxwell to follow the doctor's train of thought. It sounded as if he was trying to find a way to keep his daughter in Bear Creek without having to outright forbid her to attend medical school. By keeping her interested in Maxwell.

The manipulation made Maxwell's mouth go dry as sand. He would never—*could* never do something like that to Hattie.

"I don't—" His voice cracked, and he cleared his throat. "Hattie's friendship means a lot to me and I wouldn't stand in the way of what she really wants to achieve." Didn't Doc Powell understand how much it meant to his daughter to be a doctor herself?

The doctor's narrowed gaze rested on him again. The moment was taut, rife with tension. Then finally something eased in the older man's posture. He turned and observed the room again.

"Well, in any case, I'm impressed at what the two of you managed to do while I was away. If you hadn't worked quickly and got the town involved, I know the casualties would've been much higher."

The man's praise was a contrast to his previous criticism of Maxwell with regard to working with women, but now Maxwell was unsure of the other man's motives. What if he was only encouraging Maxwell now to get him on his side?

Maxwell shrugged. "I followed Hattie's lead. She's got more practical experience than I do—and she's not afraid to speak her mind."

The older man sighed. "No, she's usually not."

The doctor sounded resigned, but Maxwell couldn't help liking that particular trait in Hattie. He didn't know enough about women to understand their hints or unspoken messages. Hattie's plainspoken manner was much easier for a rough cowboy like him.

What he'd really like right now was to talk with

his ma. Maybe Penny could shed some light on Maxwell's muddled feelings and general confusion. He was looking forward to heading home tomorrow, sleeping in his familiar bunk, spending time with the people who knew him best.

Hopefully, then he'd find a way to keep his heart from getting too involved with Hattie.

Several days later, Hattie peeked out of the curtains in the clinic's waiting room. Everything was quiet, empty for the moment. Maxwell was due in soon to work some afternoon hours, and her father had stepped out to grab a bite of lunch, leaving her to watch over the clinic until his return.

After all the chaos and work of the past weeks, the silence seemed out of place. Even the town itself seemed to hold its breath, not quite yet returned to the pace of usual business. All of the cholera patients had gone home, with her papa making frequent visits to ensure their continued improvement. But the clinic's usual steady stream of patients hadn't picked up yet.

It was as if everyone was waiting to see if the danger had truly passed.

Word had been spreading of the first Sunday worship service back in the church, this coming weekend, and Hattie looked forward to seeing her friends and acquaintances. And perhaps a bit more of Maxwell. It seemed they'd been scheduled for opposite hours in the clinic ever since their long hours together while Papa had been gone. She didn't know if Papa was trying to make up for the heavy burden of work they'd been under or if Maxwell had been needed at home, but she missed his quiet, steady presence. Her father's absentmindedness seemed to have increased since he'd returned from Pear Grove, and often Hattie found herself at a loss. Almost as if she were…lonely.

Which was silly. She'd always kept her own counsel. She had friends, including Emily, whom she counted as her best friend. She was busy with the daily work of the clinic.

But the fact remained that her thoughts traveled to the cowboy medical student far too often. Even more than she thought about her upcoming trip.

She still hadn't spoken to her papa about her plans, and time was becoming short—she was expected to meet with the scholarship committee in three weeks.

She heard the rear door open and close, and shook herself out of her musings.

"Papa? Is that you?" she called out, although she'd expected him to come up the boardwalk, the same way he'd left.

"No, ma'am." Maxwell peeked out from the hallway, raising his Stetson in one hand in a sort of wave. His hair was rumpled and in disarray, and his green eyes seemed to glow at her. "Afternoon, Hattie."

She returned his greeting and his smile, momentarily feeling feverish. Had the room warmed just from the opening of the back door to the heat outside? Or was it Maxwell's presence that made her feel overheated?

"Papa should be back shortly. He went to get some lunch."

He nodded and moved into the doorway, leaning one shoulder casually against the jamb. "How've you been? Feels like we haven't seen each other much since the cases of cholera were released."

"Fine. No nerves. Not even a hint of one."

His eyes warmed.

"And no emergency surgeries in the middle of the night, either?"

She laughed. "No. How did your family fare? Everyone all right?"

"Yes, thank the Lord. All my brothers are as ornery as ever, and Ma's exhausting herself trying to keep up with the younger ones. She's about ready to have this baby any day."

Hattie nodded. "Are you going to assist her?"

His head jerked back, expression changing from surprise to dismay. "I hadn't even thought of it— figured she'd be wanting your pa, if anyone."

"You don't want to?" She was unable to hold back a laugh at his obvious discomfort with the thought. "It would be hands-on experience you could take back to medical school with you."

"No! I mean—it's just fine with me if my ma's private affairs stay private."

Her quivering lips must've given away her urge to laugh and he mock glared at her, crossing his muscled arms over his chest. "What about you? Had a certain talk with your parents yet? You all packed to go?"

Her amusement faded quickly. "No. I've tried to bring it up a couple of times, but Mama keeps talking about how worried she was about Papa while he was gone—and how overworked she thought I was, as well. When she talks about it like that, I can't imagine how they will agree to let me go."

"The way I see it, you earned the right, between that surgery and working on all the cholera patients while your pa was gone."

Her face heated with that Maxwell-inspired fever again.

"You want me to talk to your pa?"

"No! No. Thank you. It's my future."

"So you're going to do it today?"

She breathed in.

Just then, the door opened, startling her and saving Hattie from having to answer. Papa came in, shaking dust off of his boots.

"Oh. Hello, Maxwell."

The younger man nodded a greeting.

"Hattie, no patients?"

"None yet." She smoothed her suddenly sweaty hands over the protective apron she wore, heart thudding in her ears.

"Why don't you go home and see if your mother needs any help with the supper preparations? Or enjoy this sunny afternoon out in the garden?"

Papa was already moving back into the hallway toward the examination rooms. As if he'd already dismissed her. He'd put her off so many times already, she couldn't stand it again.

Maxwell moved aside for Papa to pass through the hall and raised his brows at Hattie.

"I will in a moment. Papa, can I speak to you about something first?" She followed him down the hallway, passing Maxwell, who reached out and gave her hand a quick squeeze as she did so. Offering comfort. She soaked it up.

"What is it, dear?" Papa didn't even look up as he dug beneath one of the cabinets where he kept some of his journals for recording patient maladies.

Hattie stood in the doorway, waiting for him to

emerge from the cabinet. Waiting for his attention to turn to her, but he only kept mumbling with his head in the cupboard.

A glance back down the hall revealed Maxwell still standing in the front vestibule, watching her. He nodded to her, motioned with his hands that she should continue. She was embarrassed to think he might hear what she was getting ready to ask Papa, but less than she might've been because she knew he thought she could do it.

"Could you…could you look at me for a moment? It's rather important."

Papa finally stood, wrinkling his bushy white brows as he turned to her. "What is it?"

With his full attention on her, her courage wavered and she had to take a deep breath. "I'd like to talk about—" she faltered and then rushed on "—attending medical school in the fall."

"You want to *what?*"

"When we spoke earlier this spring, you promised to consider it," she reminded him. She kept her voice as even as possible. Didn't want him to see her as a hysterical female in this moment. "I've been offered a tuition scholarship, assuming I pass an oral interview—"

Papa's face had hardened into an unreadable mask and he shook his head. "You know your mother's feelings on you helping out in the clinic as it is."

"Papa, I'm old enough to make my own decisions—and I think I've proven myself in the last weeks, even the last years working at your side. This is what I really want." He had no idea how desperately true it was.

"But what about Maxwell? I think that young man fancies you."

Her eyes darted to the hallway door of their own accord. She hoped he was far enough away that he hadn't heard Papa's last words. She'd guessed he might have growing feelings for her, but she couldn't give up her dream for a *possibility*.

Noise from the front of the clinic interrupted them—footsteps, voices. She could clearly hear Maxwell greeting whoever had entered the clinic.

Her father was still shaking his head. "Your mother will never agree."

"But if you support me—"

"Hattie." The serious, final tone in his voice stopped her from arguing further. "We'll continue this conversation later. Why don't you head home for a bit?"

With that stinging dismissal, he brushed past her into the front of the clinic.

She sneaked out the back door, unable to face Maxwell and his optimism. Optimism that was apparently unwarranted.

Tears blurred her vision and she leaned against the back of the clinic, just outside the door.

How was it that Maxwell was the only one who understood her? Her own papa, a physician with a true passion for healing, couldn't believe that his daughter felt the same. Or if he knew it, he refused to go against her mother's wishes and allow Hattie to have the one thing she wanted most. How could he deny her, when she'd saved a man's life by performing surgery?

She sniffled and batted at her tears with the back of her hand.

What was she going to do now? If her father refused to see her side of things, how could she ever get her mother to agree? She'd been raised from an early age to respect her parents—did she have it within her to go against their wishes?

She was so confused.

And she ached to talk to Maxwell.

How had the man she hadn't wanted around in the first place crept into her heart? She considered him a true friend—he knew some things that she hadn't even shared with Emily. But this desire to run to him with her troubles was new. And a little frightening.

Could it be that the friendship she felt was deepening to something more...?

Chapter Eleven

Days later, Bear Creek was having its first church service since the outbreak, the first real chance the folks had to get together, and it seemed everyone in the whole town and surrounding area had come.

Maxwell stood at the back of the sanctuary, where the pews had been returned to their regular spots, scanning the crowd for Hattie. He saw the young woman Annabelle, who'd been one of the patients they'd treated. She smiled at him, and he nodded to her but didn't move from his post.

His brothers and parents moved around the crowd, greeting friends and hugging folks. His gaze kept landing on his brothers, and each one seemed to send him a teasing gesture, raised eyebrows or a wink, as if they knew he was looking for Hattie.

He'd barely seen her in the clinic since her pa had come back from Pear Grove. The doc had insisted Maxwell cut back on his days at the clinic to help Oscar with his horses, and it seemed as if they passed each other, often without being able to speak. Last week, they'd had a few moments to talk, but he hadn't discovered if she'd had any resolution to her conversation with her pa about medical school. Doc Powell had come into the clinic waiting room with compressed lips. Maxwell could guess things hadn't gone in Hattie's favor. But he wanted to know it from her, find out how she was doing. Encourage her.

He missed conversing with his friend. And that was what she'd become. It was different, talking with a woman versus with his brothers. He hadn't experienced exactly the same thing with Elizabeth, had still been slightly awkward with her, even up until they'd parted company. But something about passing a crisis with Hattie had changed things between them.

A waving hand caught his eye. Annabelle again. He didn't want to embolden her and had thought his manner in the church-turned-clinic was professional and that she wouldn't be encouraged by it. To his surprise, she now nodded toward another part of the sanctuary, a small, resigned smile on her lips.

And then he saw Hattie, passing between two folks near the front of the sanctuary, her hair pulled up in a fancy style. Was her dress new? The soft green accented the honey strands in her hair and made her eyes even bluer. His feet had taken him to her before he really knew what he was doing.

And she was looking up at him with a warm smile on her lips, in her eyes. He found himself as tongue-tied as ever.

"Hello," he managed to say.

Just then, the preacher stood up at the podium and began singing a hearty rendition of a favorite hymn, the usual signal for everyone to get into place at their pews. Maxwell craned his neck to see his family all crammed into a row at the back of the sanctuary. Should he walk back and join them? He was embarrassed for everyone to see that he'd made his way up front to talk to Hattie—and barely spoken to her! There were still folks standing in the aisle, so it would take some pushing for him to get back with his family.

She solved his dilemma for him by curving her hand around his arm and pulling him into the pew beside her. He nodded to the Powells on her other side.

As he stood shoulder to shoulder with her, heat scorched the back of his neck as he realized what all his brothers—and the rest of the folks in Bear Creek, likely—would think. That he was courting Hattie.

But some part of him didn't mind at all. Part of him wanted it to be true.

The song ended, and the preacher motioned everyone to take their seats.

As the crowd shuffled and settled into the pews, Hattie leaned close to Maxwell, so close that her words brushed his jaw with heat. "Mrs. Fishbourne asked for you yesterday when she came into the clinic."

He grinned, shaking his head. Somehow the woman, who had chronic complaints of rheumatism, had decided Maxwell was her favorite at the clinic and always asked to see him. He didn't mind the older lady's ramblings about her past, her now-deceased husband or her children, who had moved away. Part of him could sympathize with her loneliness and he always took the time to talk with her. At least it wasn't as uncomfortable as trying to converse with some of the younger ladies in town!

Hattie's teasing smile pushed the words from his

lips before he'd really intended to speak them. "My ma wants you to come for lunch—I'll drive you home later. If…if you want to."

Her sparkling blue eyes considered him even as the congregation began singing all around them. She gave a small nod, and his heart thundered so loudly he was surprised he could find his voice to join in the singing.

After worship services, Hattie found herself enfolded in the Whites' large, boisterous family, tucked in the back of the wagon behind Penny and Jonas on the bench seat and amid Sarah and her four, with Walt tucked up to her side and Ida perched on her knee.

She loved the busy feel of their family and having to keep up with multiple conversations at once.

Maxwell rode his horse just off to the side of the wagon, almost as if afraid to get too far away.

"And then—" Walt broke from his story to gasp a breath of air, in the manner of all little boys who couldn't get their words out fast enough "—Maxwell put a special bandage on the stuffed rabbit…"

Maxwell coughed, and Hattie shot him a grin. "I see I'm not the only one who treats the occasional animal, then."

The man in question looked off past his horse's ears, squinting a little beneath his Stetson. The hat shadowed his face, and she couldn't tell if he was blushing. She guessed he might be.

Ida patted her cheek, demanding Hattie's attention and distracting her from the handsome cowboy. "Maxwell fell. Horsey."

It seemed everyone wanted to talk about Maxwell

today. The first thing his mother had said was how proud they were that Maxwell had helped with the rash of cholera cases.

Hattie furrowed her brows, looking to the man not far from her side. "You fell? You didn't mention anything."

He rotated one shoulder. It could've been a shrug or even a twinge at the reminder of the injury.

"It wasn't anything bad—just a bruise. One of the colts threw me when I stepped into the saddle." Now she was sure he'd turned red. "Wasn't the first time and won't be the last."

"Maybe you should let her play doctor and do an examination when we get back to the house," one of Maxwell's brothers—she thought it was Ricky—called out, riding off quickly with a laugh when Maxwell stood up in his stirrups and reached for him.

She thought she heard Maxwell utter something under his breath, but she couldn't make out the words. "Sorry," he mumbled in her direction.

"I'll talk to him when we get home," Penny said.

Hattie had to stifle a grin when she caught Sarah's dancing eyes.

"They take a bit of getting used to," the other woman whispered. "But they love each other—regardless of all the pranks and teasing."

Hattie smiled conspiratorially. "I confess I always wanted a brother and sister." At least, she had before she'd found out her father had wanted a son instead of the daughter he'd gotten.

Penny shifted on the seat, and Hattie's attention was drawn to the pregnant woman. "Are you feeling all right?"

"Yes." The woman laughed. "Just at the stage where everything is uncomfortable."

"I couldn't get her to stay home," Jonas said over his shoulder.

"He did try," Penny admitted. "And Maxwell did, as well. But I couldn't miss the first service back."

Hattie nodded. She'd been so excited to see everyone but conscious of the empty seat in the Hall family's pew. Having Maxwell at her side during worship had eased her burden somewhat. She'd seen him glance at the family as well, a serious, considering look on his face. It was as if they shared the loss.

One of Maxwell's other brothers called to him, and he edged his horse farther away in response.

"You'll rest when we get home," Jonas told his wife, a no-nonsense tone in his voice. "The boys and I will get lunch on the table."

Hattie knew her curiosity must be showing on her face.

"I'm not much of a cook," Penny admitted, laughing at herself.

"Neither is our ma," the older of Sarah's girls, Cecelia, put in.

Sarah gasped in pretend outrage, then shrugged with a little self-deprecating laugh and hugged her daughter's shoulders. "It's true. I'm afraid our menfolk bear a bit more of the burden in the kitchen than they probably should."

"We make it work," Jonas said. "Our family might be different than some, but we're more than blessed."

Hattie swallowed and stared off at the mountains in the distance. Maxwell's adoptive father was more open with his emotions than hers was. His obvious love for his wife, even willingness to perform a task that some might think was solely a woman's domain, wasn't something Hattie had ever witnessed before. Was this where Maxwell had learned his compassion, his willingness to assist in cleaning up the clinic as a help to her?

Could the Whites' unconventional family be one of the reasons he was able to support her medical-school dreams?

He seemed more open today. Did she dare to ask him about his past?

"Have ya kissed her yet?" Matty asked from where he and Maxwell rubbed down their horses side by side in the barn.

"Shh!" Maxwell hissed, glancing over his shoulder. Hattie stood talking to Sarah just outside the barn door and didn't seem to have heard. "It isn't like that between us."

"He hasn't!" his brother called out over his shoulder to Davy and Seb, who were leading their horses into stalls farther in the barn.

"Told ya," Seb said with a smug tone.

Maxwell had to fight down the urge to slug his brothers—obviously they'd been talking among themselves about his relationship with Hattie.

"Well, we gotta rectify this situation," Davy said, coming back out of the stall. The spark in his eyes had Maxwell dropping the currycomb in a hurry.

"No, y'all—" he started, but two of his brothers had already gripped his arms and shoved him back farther into the barn, while Seb followed, closing in on him and blocking his view of the barn doors and his chance for escape.

"Leave off—he don't need no help. Needs to stay away from that gal," Edgar called out as he hefted the saddle from his animal.

The others ignored their pessimistic brother. Edgar shook his head and went back to his task.

Maxwell struggled against their hold, losing his hat in the scuffle. Fortunately they weren't being too rough, as none of them wanted to tell their ma why their Sunday clothes had a sudden hole in them. But he couldn't quite scramble away.

They shoved him into an empty stall, finally releasing him. He huffed in a breath, catching the wind that had been knocked out of him. He considered rushing the stall door, but with three of them blocking it, he couldn't see a way to escape. Maybe he could talk his way out of this.

"I'm not even sure she'd welcome my...kiss." He huffed the last word, rising on his toes to try to see past them, but he couldn't see outside of the barn to the woman in question. Hopefully, Sarah was still distracting her.

"Why not?" asked Matty. "She came to lunch with ya, didn't she?"

"As a *friend*," Maxwell emphasized.

"Y'all spent nearly a week together, and you're still calling her just a friend?" Davy asked incredulously.

"It wasn't as if we were courting!" Maxwell burst out. "Sitting around talking about the weather and gossiping and such. We were busy trying to take care of people who were very sick."

Although he couldn't discount the things he'd

learned about Hattie. He had several pages of poetry he'd scribbled about her, about her beauty, her bravery in overcoming her medical condition, her passion for what she wanted to achieve. He was thankful the book was well hidden in his bunk right at this moment.

"That might be true, but I saw her sneaking glances at you, riding out in the wagon with Ma and them," Seb put in. "She *does* like ya, and you need to get that kiss."

He couldn't believe this was happening, that his brothers had initiated this conversation with him. He couldn't admit that he'd never kissed anyone before—not even Emily or Elizabeth. They would never let him hear the end of it. But it boiled down to the fact that he didn't know how to go about kissing Hattie.

He wanted to.

The revelation wasn't new to him. Of course he'd thought about it in his bunk at night. He wanted to kiss her; he just couldn't figure out how to get to that point. He well remembered a situation from their teen years with his older brother stealing a kiss from the gal he liked—and it hadn't turned out well.

"Aw, he's thinking about it too much," Matty said, clearly disgusted. "He'll never do it. Why're we wasting our time?" The blond teen turned and slammed his way out of the barn.

The other two considered Maxwell for a long moment and then they shook their heads as well and turned.

That was it? They'd decided he just wasn't man enough to go through with it?

A sudden desire to prove them wrong puffed up his chest—until reason filtered in and he realized they must've cooked up the plan to muscle him into the stall and figured out what they'd say to get him to take their dare.

But now that the idea was planted, he couldn't stop thinking about it.

Hattie was a little relieved when Maxwell emerged from the barn behind several of his brothers.

He was sweaty, disheveled. And...blushing again? Had his brothers continued their teasing? Was she the root of it?

That thought pleased her more than it probably should.

"You all right?" he asked in a low voice as he came even with her, mashing his hat onto his head.

"Fine. You?"

He nodded, but a muscle ticked away in his jaw. What *had* his brothers said to him?

"I was thinking we might get the most peace corralling the little kids while my pa gets lunch on the table," he said, guiding her toward the unusually shaped dwelling across the yard—the home had obviously borne several additions to its structure.

She didn't miss how he allowed his brothers to outpace them.

"That would be nice for your mother—to let her get a bit of rest before the meal. I saw Ida follow her inside. Do you want me to fetch her?"

"If you don't mind. Why don't we meet in front of the house? There's a tree that offers some nice shade and a swing."

He whistled for Walt as she detoured into the house, blinking in the dim interior.

She found Penny and the toddler in the living room, the woman standing with one fist rubbing the small of her back, watching as the girl played on the rug with a dolly.

"Are you feeling all right?"

Penny waved off Hattie's concern with a smile. "I'm so glad you could join us today. I've heard Maxwell speak so highly of you, it's a pleasure to get to know you a bit better."

Hattie flushed at the compliment, remembering when Penny had come to the clinic that first time—and how much Hattie's views on her son had changed since then. "Maxwell sent me to fetch Ida so you can rest a bit."

"He is the most thoughtful of my sons," Penny said. "I'll say thank-you and not argue."

"Good!" Jonas called out from the kitchen. Hattie hadn't even been aware he was listening to them.

"Miss Ida, do you want to come swing?" Hattie held out her hand, and the toddler joined her moments later, giving Hattie a sticky palm to hold on to. The little girl's opposite thumb popped into her mouth.

Outside, Maxwell had Walt swinging wildly from the rope.

"Whee!" Ida cried as they got closer. "My turn!"

"Let's wait for a moment for your turn," Hattie said. She settled on the ground on the opposite side of the tree's trunk, spreading her skirt around her and perching the girl on her lap, wiggling the dolly she'd brought outside with her to distract the girl.

"I hope you don't swing her quite so high," Hattie admonished Maxwell when Walt whooped his enjoyment.

Maxwell laughed. "She's following in Breanna's bootsteps to be a little daredevil. Much to Ma's chagrin."

Hattie found herself smiling wistfully. What would it be like to be free to be a tomboy?

Behind the house and across the yard, muted laughter and male voices came from the corral. Hattie let her gaze flick over the other brothers, still holding Ida lightly in her lap to keep the girl out of the way of the swing. There was Breanna, wearing trousers and tucked up next to one of her older brothers on the corral rail.

The men clustered around the enclosure, several leaning on the railing, talking and tussling with each other. She'd met several of them through social events or spoken to them in passing or at church. They were certainly a handsome bunch, although they were all so different, thanks to their different heritages. But it was Maxwell who stirred her senses and had since his return to Bear Creek.

A glance at Maxwell revealed he was gazing off in that direction, too, though he kept up the momentum of Walt's swing. Did he want to be over there with his brothers? Or did his far-off gaze mean he was thinking of something else entirely?

The silence between them, punctuated by Walt's squeals and Ida's quiet play, was not uncomfortable in the least. There was something about being with Maxwell that calmed Hattie, anchored her. And she was starting to think he might feel the same.

"If you want to go join your brothers, I can watch the children for a bit," she offered.

His eyes careened to her, and this time he missed a push, causing Walt to howl, "Ma-ax!"

He caught up with the boy's swing but kept his gaze on Hattie. "I'm right where I want to be."

Her heart pounded at his words and the intensity in his gaze. Finally, *she* was the one who had to look away. She smiled down at Ida, who was gently rocking her dolly in her arms, an action she'd probably picked up from Sarah.

When Hattie looked back up, Maxwell was still looking at her, but his eyes had softened.

"You'll have to show me the horses you've been working with," she said. "I'm curious to see this animal that got the best of you."

"Don't let her ride Midnight, Max," Walt cautioned, voice and face serious even as he swung. "He's dangerous."

She and Maxwell shared a smile at the boy's protective words, but Maxwell was entirely serious when he answered the little tyke and assured him he wouldn't put Hattie on the "dangerous" horse.

The dinner bell pealed, and several of the group around the corral whooped, just as Walt had moments ago, and turned for the house. Walt jumped from the swing before Hattie could cry out, landing on his booted feet and running for the house. Ida pushed up and toddled after him, crying, "Wait!"

Maxwell came to Hattie with dancing eyes and outstretched hands. She put her palms in his, and he hoisted her upright. He didn't let her go, even when she stood close. She tipped her head back to be able to look into his face.

His intensity had returned. His green eyes smoldered down at her, and she suddenly couldn't breathe properly. Her legs went weak, and she swayed slightly toward him. Close enough that she could reach up and kiss him, if she wanted.

He linked their fingers together, still staring down into her face. "Hattie…"

Where had the reticent, shy man gone? This man… she had the wild thought that he wanted to kiss her.

"C'mon, Maxwell!" a male voice shouted, shattering the illusion of privacy.

With Maxwell between her and the house, she couldn't see his brothers or who had shouted, but it was a reminder that they weren't really alone, even if she'd gotten caught up in him, in the moment.

He looked over his shoulder and then back at her and sighed softly. The action drew her gaze to his lips. She'd been sure that he had been about to kiss her.

"There won't be any food left if we don't get down there," he murmured.

She nodded, raising a shaking hand to brush a stray strand of hair out of her eyes.

But suddenly, facing his family was the last thing she wanted to do. Would they all be able to see the flush in her cheeks?

Later, Maxwell dared to link his fingers with Hattie's as they walked from Jonas's original homestead down the valley toward Oscar's place. Behind them, the small white dog followed.

Hattie's eyes met his. There was a new awareness between them.

Before lunch, when he'd desperately wanted to kiss her, she hadn't backed away.

He couldn't have imagined it, could he?

Hattie looked behind and her head canted to one side. He followed her gaze to see the white mutt behind them.

"Still following you around, hmm?" she asked.

"Yes. I suppose if I ever get back to medical school, I'll have to arrange for lodgings for him," he teased. He wasn't used to this…this shared sense of humor, the joy of being with another person.

They shared a smile.

"You sure you don't want to ride?" he asked as they left the noisy family atmosphere behind and it became just the two of them again—as it had been under the big oak in front of the house.

"I'm sure. I'm not a very good rider."

The fact that she seemed to be content to meander along at his side meant they would spend more time together, so he had no complaints. It would give him a little longer to ponder the near kiss they'd almost shared and try to wrangle up his courage to try again.

"Did you think your mother seemed a little off during lunch?"

"You noticed, too? She kept shifting and getting up…."

They shared a look, almost the same thought. "You think the baby will come soon?" he asked, though he could guess the answer.

"Mmm-hmm. Maybe even tonight you'll have a new brother or sister."

She squeezed his hand; he loved feeling so connected to her. For once, his fears were pushed aside.

"After spending lunch with my family, you're

probably thinking we don't need any more faces around the table."

"Not at all." She half laughed the words and just being with her lifted his spirits. "I'll admit to being a little overwhelmed in the first few moments, but I kind of like your big family. Everyone fits." Her voice held a slightly wistful quality. She'd mentioned possibly wanting a family in the future—he assumed after her medical-school plans came to fruition—and the fact that she fit right into his as if she belonged made him hopeful.

He would never forget the sight of her across the table, squished between Seb and Breanna. It seemed each of his siblings did their best to embarrass Maxwell throughout the meal, but more than once he'd found himself grinning foolishly at Hattie, enjoying himself regardless.

"Did your parents want more children?"

She hesitated, and for a moment he thought she might not answer. When she did, her voice was softer, more serious than before. "I think my father wanted a son to carry on his practice. When I was a teenager, I overheard something to that effect, anyway. But they weren't able to have more children, for whatever reason." Her last words were matter-of-fact, as though she'd practiced saying them before. To convince herself?

Maxwell considered what to say. "I'm guessing he wasn't receptive to your plan to follow in his footsteps?"

She shook her head. The slight breeze had loosened some strands of hair at her temple and now swept them across her forehead. For a moment, he was distracted from the lingering sorrow in her eyes.

"Will you tell me what happened?" he asked.

"Nothing more than what you probably heard at the clinic. He said we'd talk about it later, but every time I've tried to speak to him alone, he claims to be busy or leaves the room."

She didn't try to hide her disappointment, and her trust in sharing such a sensitive topic with him pleased Maxwell.

"I'm sorry," he said. "I know your pa's approval is important to you."

She nodded slowly.

"What if— Have you ever thought that if you married, your husband might be agreeable to helping you get through medical school?"

He had no idea where the words came from. They surprised him as much as they must've surprised her; her head came up quickly at the same time the breeze gusted. She brushed several strands of hair from her eyes, but he could still read the slightly incredulous look on her face.

"Where do you suppose I would find such a man?"

Right in front of you. Afraid of revealing too much of his feelings for her, he could only shrug, tongue-tied.

She went on to shake her head, vigorously this time. "Every man of courting age I've ever spoken to has seemed to want the same things from a wife— someone to care for home and hearth and any little ones who come along. I've never met anyone who had the slightest interest in my ambitions—in fact, I believe you're the only man who even noticed I *had* ambitions."

He cleared his throat, but before he could find words, she asked, "What do you want from a wife?"

They were traversing dangerous territory. He pretended to be engrossed in watching their footing as they climbed the slight hill toward Oscar's place, if only to keep his face slightly averted and hope she couldn't read his discomfort. "I suppose…I suppose I'd like a partner. A match. Someone who would support me in my practice—in whatever form that might take." He couldn't help remembering the vivid flash he'd had of himself and Hattie working side by side in their own practice.

"But you do want a *family,* not just a wife," she clarified.

He flushed slightly.

"More than anything." It was his most closely held dream, after becoming a doctor. One that he hardly dared to believe he could have, after his upbringing with his mother's awful statements and then with what had happened with the two young ladies in college.

But somehow, being with Hattie ignited a spark of hope inside him. What if she was the one for him? What if Penny was right?

They crested a hill and more of the valley opened up before them, green and verdant. Oscar's herd spread across the grass, out to pasture for the day, each horse a healthy, vibrant color against the rich green of the swaying buffalo grass.

Hattie gasped softly and her grip on his hand tightened. "Oh, Maxwell, it's lovely."

"Mmm-hmm." But he knew what the horses looked like—he'd been spending day after day with them—and he couldn't tear his eyes away from her and the raw delight in her features. She shaded her eyes with her opposite hand, taking in both the animals and the scenery. His pa had chosen the homestead spot well, and Oscar's added land was picturesque, too.

"You want to meet some of them?" he asked.

Her quizzical gaze landed on him. "The horses?"

"Sure." He gave a shrill whistle, and several of the closest animals raised their heads or pricked their ears. One, a sorrel mare that he'd been working with regularly, broke into a trot and then walked up to them. Maxwell pulled out the carrot he'd snitched from the kitchen and broke it into several pieces, one of which he pressed into Hattie's palm.

"I'm not very good with— That is, it's very large," she whispered frantically as the mare approached. Hattie stepped back.

"Nothing to be scared of," he said. "She's a pretty gentle lady. Not the one Walt's been warning you about all afternoon."

He slid his arm around Hattie's waist, heart thundering, and kept her anchored at his side. Reaching out with a carrot in his own palm, he offered it to the mare, who ate it out of his hand almost before he could blink.

He chuckled, and the horse whickered softly, bobbing its head. It stepped forward, lowering its head and reaching toward Hattie, who pressed into his side. Blood rushed in his ears at her closeness.

"Put your hand out," he directed her.

When she hesitated, he used his free hand to cup

hers, helped her offer the horse the chunk of carrot. Once it was gone, Maxwell scratched beneath the animal's chin, waiting. Hattie took a breath and then tentatively raised her hand to touch the horse's forelock.

"That's it." Maxwell encouraged both horse and woman, keeping his voice low and soothing.

Hattie settled her palm against the mare's nose, inhaling but not moving away when the animal rubbed against her touch.

"You're not afraid of surgery, but a little old horse..." Maxwell teased.

"A patient can't trample me," she retorted. But her voice was soft, and she seemed interested in the animal. "She's beautiful."

With the carrot gone, the horse lost interest in them and instead turned to sniff the white dog, who was behaving remarkably calmly and lying in the grass nearby. The two animals touched noses briefly before the horse wandered off.

Maxwell and Hattie stood for several more minutes, watching the animals graze placidly. Did she realize she still huddled close to him? He couldn't concentrate on anything else, could barely catch his breath. Finally, he registered the slant of the afternoon sun.

"We should get back." But he wasn't in any hurry to return to the noise of his family or take Hattie back to her parents' place.

"But?" she asked intuitively, looking up at him.

He was drawn to her, as the mare had been drawn to his whistle, and found himself turning to face her.

"But...my brothers seem to think I should kiss

you, and this might be our last chance to be alone."
He didn't know where he got the courage to say the
words. Maybe he was dizzy from staring into her
eyes, making an examination of her golden eyelashes.
Or maybe his brothers' constant teasing had finally
gotten to him.

But she didn't back away, didn't recoil in horror.
Her eyes crinkled as her lips turned slightly upward.
"Hmm. Perhaps this is one of the rare times your
brothers might have the right idea."

He swallowed hard. A moment of panic flared
through him.

"I don't really know...how..." He raised a shaking
hand, touched her cheek lightly. Her skin was incred-
ibly soft, softer than anything he'd ever touched before. His fingertips slid gently against her jaw, and
his thumb brushed her cheekbone.

Her chin shifted slightly up, toward him. "You're
not afraid of a thousand-pound animal, but a little
kiss..." Her teasing whisper came from so close that
the warmth of her breath brushed his mouth.

And then she raised up, or he leaned down, and
their lips met. She tasted of sunshine and coffee. He
wanted her closer. His hand slid from her cheek to the
nape of her neck. Her hands came up and clutched his
sides, as if she wanted to be closer, too.

It could've been moments or minutes later when
they parted. He kept his hands at her waist, steadying them both. They both panted; her lips looked bee-
stung, her eyes soft and warm.

He wanted to do it all over again.

But a shout from behind had both of them turning away from the horses and back toward the house.

Seb was running toward them at an all-out gallop, his boots kicking up grass and dirt behind him. "Ma's havin' the baby!"

Chapter Twelve

The house slowly settled around the chaos of the baby's arrival until the infant actually made his entrance into the world, well into the night. The smaller children had been tucked into bed, and the older boys sent out to the bunkhouse, save Maxwell, who waited in the kitchen, keeping a pot of coffee warm.

Hattie had one of the brothers ride to town with a note informing her parents she wouldn't be home until the morning, providing that the baby was born. She'd actually tried to have Penny send for her papa, but the woman had said the first two births had gone fine and she preferred Hattie to assist. So that was what had happened.

Jonas and Hattie greeted the squirming, red-faced infant and introduced him to a tired but dreamy-eyed Penny.

Hattie watched the couple furtively as she cleaned up, changing the linens on the bed and such. Jonas knelt next to Penny's rocking chair, both of their heads bent over the small bundle Penny held.

Was this what Maxwell would be like as a father?

Tender, loving, gentle? She could imagine so. He gave so much to the patients he helped at the clinic. She thought he would be even more so with his own children.

While helping Penny with the baby, she'd only had snatched moments to reflect on what had happened between her and Maxwell out in the horse pasture earlier—or was it yesterday, now that it was so late?

His kiss had surprised her—at first. He'd been tentative, considering…overthinking things in the way she'd come to expect from him. Then their lips had met and she found he kissed with the same passion he threw himself into doctoring with.

Her toes had curled inside her Sunday boots. Even now, her hands trembled as she smoothed the bedspread, remembering the power behind his kiss.

A kiss she'd returned. She hadn't been able to stop herself from responding. She had gone from distrusting the man only a few weeks ago to friendship to… something deeper. Something she didn't dare define.

"Here we go." Hattie finished tucking a clean sheet and quilt over the feather-tick mattress. "Do you want me to wash up the baby while you get settled in? Then you can nurse, and after that you can both get some much-needed rest." Hattie had assisted her father enough to know what needed doing.

"Yes, thank you. I could sleep for a week."

Hattie moved to take the baby gently from Penny's arms, lips quirking. "I doubt you will, once this little one discovers where his food comes from."

They shared a smile. Hattie liked Maxwell's adoptive mother. She was kind, and her love for all the children was ever-present. While Hattie had had oc-

casion to wonder if her own mother even knew her
most precious dreams and wishes, Penny had practically pushed Maxwell into medical school, it seemed.

"We'll be right back."

She found Maxwell in the kitchen, his arms folded
on the long plank table and staring into the fire.

He roused when she entered, half rising from his
seat. Their eyes met, locked. She hadn't imagined his
intensity from earlier—it still burned like the coals
behind him in the hearth.

She looked down at the bundle in her arms,
cheeks warming. "Want to say hello to your new little brother? He needs a bit of washing up."

He came to her, peeking over her shoulder, so close
that she couldn't help but be aware of him. Especially
when the heat of his palm seared her lower back.
"He's got Penny's red hair. I heard him squalling for
a minute there—he must've gotten her lungs, as well."

She shifted—her feet were starting to hurt in the
Sunday shoes—and Maxwell moved. "I kept some
water heating on the back of the stove. D'you think
a large cooking pot would do for him?"

"It should be all right. We aren't going to dunk
him in or anything, just give him a good scrubbing."

Maxwell threw several towels and washcloths on
the table while Hattie deposited the small gown and
clean cloth diaper Penny had provided nearby.

"You doing okay?" Maxwell asked as he moved a
large cast-iron pot to the center of the table. He went
back to the stove for the warm water. "You've been
on your feet a long time. If you need to sit down, I'll
do what needs to be done."

Weeks ago, before she'd really known him, she

would've been offended by his query. But now, having discovered the real Maxwell, she knew he was only being sensitive to her needs.

"I'm fine. Still a little shaky from the adrenaline of delivering a healthy baby. You should've been in there with me." They shared a look, a remembrance of the conversation they'd had before about him not wanting to witness his adoptive mother giving birth.

He half grinned and half shrugged. "I'll have to wait for the next time."

After he'd poured an inch of water into the pot and checked it wasn't too hot, Maxwell settled at her elbow, one knee on the long bench beneath the table.

"Here, cup one hand behind his head," Hattie told him. "Just above the water. And the other beneath his rump. Hold tight—he'll be slippery once I get started."

Maxwell gasped softly when he took the baby's weight in his big hands. "He's a tiny one, isn't he? I don't remember Walt being this small, and I was away at college when Ida was born."

She looked at him sidelong. His concentration, the clear affection for this new scrap of life, touched her.

As they washed him, the baby let them know in no uncertain terms that he didn't appreciate being pulled out of his warm cocoon of linens and subjected to this indignity.

Several moments later, when Hattie had him clothed and swaddled tightly in a blanket, he was still fussing his discontent, but very softly. His eyes drooped and finally closed.

She looked up and had to release a giggle when

she noticed the sweat beaded on Maxwell's forehead. "Are *you* all right?" she teased.

"Yes. Just didn't expect him to be that unhappy about it…."

"Get used to it, mister medical student. Not all of your patients will be happy with the treatment you prescribe."

They shared a glance, the same connection as before. How was it they could read each other so easily now?

"Here, hold him a moment." Hattie pressed the baby into Maxwell's arms, turning away to remove the apron she'd borrowed from the kitchen earlier. Beneath, she'd donned one of Penny's older dresses, but she'd wear it home and carry her Sunday dress, which was neatly folded on the sofa, when she left in the morning.

When she looked back up, Maxwell was clutching the baby close, his chin tucked nearly to his chest as he looked down at him. The tender look on his face made her breath catch in her chest. He would be a fine father.

With the baby tucked into the crook of his elbow, he reached out for her with his other arm and drew her into his side, enveloping her with his warmth. His jaw brushed the top of her head, the day's scruff catching lightly on the fine hairs at her temple. Her pulse pounded at his nearness.

The baby's tiny rosebud mouth stretched wide in a silent yawn. Hattie's heart expanded. She glanced up at Maxwell to find that same intensity in his eyes as he glanced down on both her and the baby. He brushed a kiss against her forehead, naturally, as if he hadn't thought about the action at all.

"Thanks for helping my ma tonight."

Her stomach tightened into a small fist. Being here with Maxwell, close like this, made her want things she hadn't thought about since she'd been a small girl. What would it be like to be one of the warm, loving Whites? To be ensconced in the loud, overwhelming crowd that found it easy to show emotions, in contrast to her own family.

To have Maxwell at her side. To be loved by someone as decent, kind and honorable as he was. To have a family of her own.

The thought startled Hattie into pulling away. "I'd better get him back to his mama for some nourishment."

"And get some rest yourself, I hope," he said as he handed off the baby to her again.

"Yes. Hopefully, I won't wake Breanna when I crawl in next to her."

And she didn't.

It was Hattie who lay awake long after she'd returned the baby to Penny and given her a final check.

She couldn't forget Maxwell's kiss or the tenderness in his face when he'd looked down at both her and the baby.

She couldn't imagine her quiet cowboy showing the emotion he had if it wasn't genuine. How deeply did his feelings for her go?

What had she done, letting things grow between them so far?

She genuinely liked him, more than she'd ever liked any man. She respected him, and he respected her abilities, admired her for who she really was. He saw her.

He was the only man she could imagine marrying who would encourage her to practice medicine.

But he also wanted a family. Would he encourage her pursuits until the babies came? What then?

But the more dangerous thought, the question she couldn't shake was…what if she married him and she began wanting the little babe to hold in her arms?

Holding Penny's new son tonight had planted the thought, one that she hadn't considered for herself. She wanted to be a physician. Had wanted it almost half her life. Couldn't imagine being anything else.

Except possibly…a mother.

Could she give up her ambitions for a family? *Should* she?

Chapter Thirteen

The next morning, Maxwell stifled the urge to whistle as he guided the wagon toward Bear Creek, Hattie beside him on the bench seat. They shared a companionable silence, and he didn't want to disturb it.

He could fill several journals with verses on how full his heart felt right now. He'd managed to scribble several lines after he'd retired to the bunkhouse early this morning, before his candle had sputtered and he'd fallen into his bunk in a deep, dreamless sleep. He'd woken with more lines running through his head, but with his brothers up and about and Hattie no doubt overwhelmed inside the house with his pa and younger siblings, he hadn't dared to take the journal out again.

Hattie'd been quiet, pensive, almost the whole ride to town, but he supposed she was tired from staying up late helping his ma birth little Andrew.

He was almost sure she returned his growing feelings. He was hopeful. More than hopeful.

He wanted to make a declaration, but he didn't know if it was too soon. He definitely wanted to say something before she left for her scholarship interview in two weeks. He was pretty sure her pa could be won over to let her go to medical school. He had half a mind to speak to the man on Hattie's behalf. Maxwell didn't know what it would mean for a growing relationship between them—if she really did return his feelings—but Hattie needed to see her dreams through.

Maybe he should ask Oscar or Sam for advice on making his feelings known. Wouldn't that shock his brother and best friend, after they'd pushed him so hard in Hattie's direction?

He found himself grinning as the first of Bear Creek's buildings came into sight. The wagon creaked over a rut in the road and Hattie's shoulder jostled against him. She looked up at him, finally.

"What're you smiling about?"

There was no way he was admitting to the rabbit trail his thoughts had taken, so he blurted the first thing that came to his head.

"Just thinking how much I prefer seeing this little cluster of buildings than the outskirts of Denver." He nodded toward Bear Creek and she followed his gaze.

"You don't like Denver?"

"It's…different. Busier. More crowded." It reminded him of the bustle of Cheyenne, even though Denver was bigger. And remembering Cheyenne always made him remember his birth ma and scrapping on the streets before he'd met Jonas. He didn't like those memories.

"So, when you graduate medical school, will you seek out a practice in a small town, then?"

He hesitated, remembering how Elizabeth had left

him after he'd told her he wanted to practice in a small town. He hadn't heard any complaints from Hattie about living in Bear Creek with her parents, but what if she wanted to live in a bigger city?

"There's a lot of need in small towns," he hedged. And it was true. He'd seen it himself. "I guess it would depend on my...partner." He nearly choked on the word—he'd almost said *wife*. Although once it had been a fleeting image, a snatch of a dream, he was beginning to hope more and more that Hattie would be the one working beside him in his practice.

"What about you?" he asked. "Do you want to practice in a big city?"

She shrugged. "I don't know. I hadn't thought that far ahead—still trying to figure out how to get through medical school." She looked out over the prairie stretching around them. "I suppose there must be equal prejudice against women doctors in either place. Sometimes I consider that a larger city might offer more opportunities to help those who are more forward-thinking, but then perhaps a small town has more need—as you mentioned—and the people might be more likely to seek help from a woman if there were no other choices."

"I hadn't thought much about what you'd face setting up a practice."

She directed a wry smile at him. "You saw it yourself with Mr. Spencer. Of the two of us, he looked to you for advice. He barely even heard my recommendation."

"And yet you saved his life."

"Yes." She nodded gravely. "And that changed his mind, but what if we hadn't been able to save him?

He could've died because he didn't want a woman treating him."

"If you were able to work with someone—your father or a…husband—" he nearly swallowed the word but forced himself to go on "—maybe you could gain the trust of your patients that way."

She didn't look at him, kept looking outward. "Perhaps" came her quiet response.

Within minutes, they'd arrived at her parents' home. He wanted to see her again—soon—in a social way and cleared his throat nervously as he jumped down and helped her from the wagon.

"Can I…come courting?" It was early enough, there were no neighbors out, and he allowed his hands to remain loosely at her waist.

An adorable wrinkle appeared over the bridge of her nose, then smoothed just as quickly as it had come. "Come for supper on Friday."

He grinned, still soaring from the previous day and night, and dared to brush a kiss against her cheek.

She squeezed his shoulders briefly. "I'll see you at the clinic later."

If his steps were particularly jaunty as he rounded the wagon, he hoped she didn't notice as she went inside.

On Tuesday, Hattie excused herself from the men to have lunch with Emily, who'd been by the clinic twice already this week, demanding details about Hattie's excursion to the White homestead on Sunday.

And Hattie wanted a little space from Maxwell's nearly overwhelming presence in the clinic. Although he was still working with his brother part of the time and in the clinic part of the time, when he was there she couldn't ignore him.

He'd been kind and conscientious; the only real change in his behavior was in the warm glances he occasionally gave her—and one intense one she'd caught when he hadn't thought she'd been looking. He'd also left a pressed wildflower for her to find on the storeroom counter when she'd arrived this morning.

She'd spent several minutes daydreaming over the silly flower, twisting it in her fingers and remembering the previous bouquet he'd brought her. She'd been out of sorts and not ready when her papa had come into the room minutes later with a patient—the first time that had ever happened.

Maxwell was courting her.

And she liked the man. So why did she feel so muddled about things between them?

Because she hadn't spared one thought about medical school since their kiss. She'd missed a perfect opportunity to corner her papa in his office the evening before because she'd been caught up in thoughts about the cowboy.

What was wrong with her? She'd wanted to be a doctor for *so long*.

The walk to Emily and Sam's homestead took several minutes, but the waving grasses and the peaceful mountains in the distance didn't calm Hattie—on the contrary, she just kept remembering being out in that field with Maxwell and their kiss…and how he'd looked at her. As if she was precious to him.

Relieved when she arrived at her destination, and

hoping for a distraction, she knocked and then pushed inside as Emily called out for her to come in.

She found her friend humming tunelessly as she stirred something on the stovetop.

When Emily turned, her entire face was suffused with joy. "Tell me everything," she ordered, shooing Hattie into a kitchen chair with a wooden spoon.

So Hattie did. Or at least started to, as Emily served them both a hearty stew. Hattie had gotten to their kiss when Emily interrupted her.

"He really did it?" Her friend left the bowl before her forgotten and came around the table to hug Hattie's shoulders, squealing with joy. "Oh, Hattie, I'm so happy for you!"

"Well, thank you." But Hattie wasn't finished yet. She needed help sorting out her life.

"Just think…" Emily half turned away, going to the small window above her dry sink. "If you marry, you can file for a little homestead—there's one close that Sam has seen, with a little creek running through the property. We'll be neighbors. And Maxwell can work with your papa, already have a practice set up…"

"Yes, but—"

"And our children will grow up together, be the best of friends, just like you and I are close!"

Hattie couldn't tear her eyes from the other woman's hand resting gently on the bulge of her stomach. Remembered how Maxwell had looked holding his new baby brother. Wanted that for herself, too. So much that it surprised her.

Scared her.

She could see the future as Emily described it. See

herself in a kitchen, kids at her feet, welcoming Maxwell back from a day working in the clinic with Papa.

But could she really be happy with that future?

"But what about medical school?" Hattie asked.

"Oh, I wouldn't worry. I know Maxwell will finish. He is so determined." Emily didn't even seem to register Hattie's concerns, lost in a fanciful daydream. She smiled widely. "Hattie, you're so blessed. Maxwell is such a good man."

Unable to sit still a moment longer, unable to contain the conflicting emotions roiling through her, Hattie jumped out of her chair.

"I meant, what about medical school *for me,*" she blurted out. "What about my dreams? I want to be a doctor. I'm *meant* to be a doctor." She knew it, down deep inside. God had given her the desire, the skills.

Emily looked at her, surprise registering. She'd told Emily before about her dreams of being a doctor, but had the other woman gotten so caught up in a fantasy that she'd forgotten?

"But don't you want a—a family?"

That was the problem, one that hadn't gotten any clearer with Hattie's visit to her friend. She wanted to be a doctor. But she could also see herself as Maxwell's wife, raising a family alongside him.

Would she be willing to give up her dreams to do so?

The way her heart clattered whenever he was near, the way she'd started forgetting her duties to daydream about the man...

How could she trade one dream for another?

She shook her head tightly. "I don't know, Emily. I have to—I have to go."

And she ran out of her friend's house, leaving in a worse state than when she'd arrived.

By midday on Wednesday, Hattie's nerves sizzled with uneasy energy. She'd dropped several things, including an expensive vial of medication. The vision in her left eye was blurred. She'd thought Maxwell had caught her blinking repeatedly earlier that morning, trying to clear her vision, but the waiting room had been full and he'd had to help a different patient and only given her a concerned glance.

She guessed she was on the verge of an episode of nerves. One she could ill afford right now. She needed to talk to her parents about her medical-school plans, but if she was stuck in her wheeled chair, she could see her mother using her health as an excuse not to allow Hattie to go. And her papa would likely bow to Mama's wishes.

Could Hattie still leave without their approval? Did she dare?

And she'd found no resolution to her conflicted feelings about Maxwell.

She liked him so much that it frightened her. But she didn't know if there was room in her life for a man, even a man like Maxwell, someone willing to let her chase her dreams. She was half afraid that she'd fall so far in love with him that she'd be *willing* to give up her ambitions, and then where would she be?

She needed to focus on the here and now. Not on a romance. If she was truly on the verge of an episode, she needed to alert her father so he and Maxwell could make plans for the next few days.

And Friday evening, when Maxwell was coming to supper, loomed. It wasn't fair to lead him on if she couldn't commit to a relationship. Somehow, she had to decide before then what she should do.

Friday evening, Maxwell stood on Hattie's porch, hat in hand, trying to work up the courage to knock on the front door.

He'd been worried when she hadn't been in the clinic at her usual hour Thursday morning. Her pa had said she hadn't been feeling well. Maxwell guessed it was her nerves acting up. She'd been moving slowly and very deliberately in the clinic on Wednesday. Had she known something was about to happen with her condition? Why hadn't she mentioned it to him? He would've helped with extra chores around the clinic if needed.

He'd gone to try to see her late Thursday afternoon, after the clinic had closed, only to be turned away by her ma, who had said only that Hattie was resting. Hattie was the one who'd told him about her condition in the first place, but now it felt as though she was hiding from him.

Or maybe it was all in his head, because he was so nervous about seeing her tonight. He'd gotten the guts to stop by Sam and Emily's earlier in the week. His best friend had clapped him on the shoulder when he'd admitted he had strong feelings for Hattie and didn't know quite how to go about expressing them. Sam had advised him to just tell her everything.

Maxwell didn't know if he had the guts to do that yet. But Hattie was so special…he had to try.

Unwilling to delay any longer, he rapped on the door. Then he wiped his sweating palm on his trousers.

Hattie's ma answered with a smile and invited him in.

"How's Hattie?" he asked, stepping into the front hall. "I didn't know if I should still come tonight...."

After leaving the clinic, he'd changed into his white Sunday shirt and a tie that Sam had pressed on him, but that now felt as though it was choking him.

Mrs. Powell bustled back toward the kitchen. "See for yourself. She's in the parlor."

But she wasn't. The room was empty, and a sinking feeling swamped his chest. He'd been so anxious to see her, he hadn't thought about much else. Didn't Hattie want to see him? Was it because of her condition or something else?

He turned on the heel of his boot to head back to the kitchen and find her mother but paused when he saw a shadow move from another hallway, the same one that led to the back porch.

He took a step in that direction. The movement carried him far enough to see Hattie in her wheeled chair, half-hidden around the corner.

Still hiding from him. Why?

He started to go to her, until she looked up at him and he froze. She was pale, a bit more than usual, but roses bloomed in her cheeks. She didn't smile at him.

"Hello, Maxwell."

His senses went on high alert while his fingers curled into the brim of his hat. He'd meant to leave it in the front hall, but in his nervousness he'd forgotten and carried it with him.

"Evening. Can I help you into…?" He motioned to the parlor behind them.

She shook her head, pushing the wheels to move herself forward, maneuvering into the room with seeming ease. Except that, from slightly behind her, he saw her hands shaking between pushes.

Was she nervous that seeing her in the chair again would somehow change what he felt for her? She should know better, but based on his limited experience, he knew women weren't always rational. Maybe she just needed to be reassured of his feelings, that he didn't think less of her for having to overcome the obstacles she did. In fact, he thought more of her.

When she would've stopped her chair near the fireplace, away from any of the seating in the room, he gave the conveyance a gentle push and settled it right in front of the sofa, then took a seat so their knees nearly touched.

"Hope you don't mind."

He didn't think he could do this—share his feelings—if she was too far away. As it was, his heart was pounding, even as his pulse accelerated.

The pink in her cheeks intensified. He hooked his hat over one knee and clasped his hands loosely between his legs, leaning forward slightly on his elbows, bringing them even closer.

How to start? He couldn't just blurt out his feelings. Sam hadn't given him advice on how to do this with finesse. Now that he was here, he was afraid of saying the wrong thing, of messing everything up.

"I missed you at the clinic the last two days," he said, hoping that his words were enough to open the conversation, to ease the awkwardness building between them.

"I'm afraid I wouldn't inspire confidence in most of our patients at present." Her words seemed self-deprecating, and she raised her hands out of her lap. They trembled badly, the same way they had in the church the night she'd asked him for help.

He did what came naturally and reached out and took her hands, still leaning forward, and rested their clasped hands loosely between them.

"It doesn't bother me." He gazed straight into her face, hoping to show her his confidence. She looked down, hiding her eyes. She didn't move away, but neither did she return his handclasp or link their fingers together.

His nervousness increased. Something felt wrong between them. If it was about her condition, he wanted the record straight. How to best convince her?

"Hattie..." He swallowed nervously. "This condition doesn't define you. It is a part of you, but it isn't who you are. You're someone that I've...come to care about—"

Her eyes dropped, and she slid her hands from his. She was pulling away.

His pulse pounded in his ears and suddenly his head felt stuffed with cotton gauze.

"Maxwell—before you say anything more..." Her eyes still didn't come up to meet his, and his stomach swooped low.

"I've been thinking, and...well, I think we've let things between us get too far, too fast." She breathed in and finally met his eyes, and there was none of the warmth there that he'd seen before, during those late nights in the clinic or at his pa's ranch.

He felt frozen, unable to move, barely able to breathe. Her words registered, but he couldn't think. Was it because he'd kissed her? Had he gone too far, even though at the time she'd seemed open to his attentions?

"If this is because of Sunday afternoon..."

She shook her head, her face still averted. "It isn't that."

"Have I...have I done something else to offend you?" He thought quickly back to Monday and Tuesday, wondering if something had happened in the clinic. Had he been thoughtless and not even realized it?

She shook her head. "It's just, I have plans. For medical school and for the future, and I can't—"

She wrung her hands in her lap. He had the sense that this conversation was hurting her as much as it was him, but he couldn't catch his breath, couldn't figure out a way to fix things as they disintegrated around him.

"Do you want me to...do you want me to go?"

She didn't have time to answer as Doc Powell blustered into the room. "Hullo, Maxwell. The missus says supper is about on the table. You two had enough alone time?"

Not nearly enough. Part of him wanted to keep tossing questions at Hattie. Find out what he'd done to upset her.

And part of him knew why, or at least strongly suspected why.

His birth ma had been right, after all. No woman

in her right mind would want him. Wasn't this the ultimate proof?

He'd shared more with Hattie than he had with anyone else. They had so much in common, both with dreams of practicing medicine. During those long nights of working together, he'd thought they'd forged a bond…and then spending time with her this past Sunday had cemented his feelings for her.

Before he could ask Hattie to stay for a moment, she was already following her pa from the room.

Should he head home and save himself from further humiliation by having to sit through supper with her parents?

But the doctor didn't give him a chance to excuse himself, ushering Maxwell to sit down after Hattie and Mrs. Powell had been seated. Doc chattered about the day's patients and his wife asked after Penny and Jonas and the new baby.

Neither seemed to note the awkwardness between Hattie and Maxwell.

His skin burned when their hands brushed passing a bowl of potatoes.

She bit her lip when her mother referred to the next poetry-club meeting, which had been rescheduled after the cholera had passed. Now he couldn't see himself attending.

He was dying to escape and go home to lick his wounds—although he would have to find somewhere without any brothers present first—but both of Hattie's parents were more chatty than usual. Could they really not feel the tension between him and Hattie? Were they that unaware of their daughter's feelings?

Was their self-absorption why they still didn't know she wanted to be a doctor? It hadn't taken him but a few days working with her to see how she cared about the patients, to get a grasp on her intelligence and capability.

He shouldn't think about it, about her dreams and wishes, anymore, but he couldn't help the thoughts from coming.

When he'd put away all he could stomach, he excused himself before dessert was served. He couldn't be here any longer and maintain the facade that everything was all right, not when he was dying inside.

He shook the doc's hand, waved his hat to Mrs. Powell and Hattie, and escaped.

Outside, he couldn't get in the saddle fast enough, almost immediately let the horse have its head. The night air chilled his face as the dark landscape rushed past them in a wild gallop, making him blink over and over again as it bit into his eyes. He refused to think the moisture could be any other bodily function, like tears.

He'd started to believe that Penny was right, not his birth ma.

He'd wanted to believe it. That someone like Hattie, someone strong and smart and courageous, could love him back.

He'd been wrong, apparently.

But if she'd been right that no one could love him, what if she was also right that he'd never amount to anything?

It hurt less to think about his future as a physician, wondering if he could really make it. He wanted it badly enough, but now…could he do it without the dream of Hattie by his side?

Hattie only wanted to be alone after Maxwell had taken his leave.

She wheeled her chair out onto the back veranda and sat for a long time, looking up at the sky. Wondering if she'd done the right thing.

She hadn't wanted to hurt him, but the increased reserve in his manner throughout dinner had made it clear that she had. By the time he'd left, he wouldn't—or couldn't—even look at her.

She'd made a mess of the whole thing.

What had she thought? That he would understand her fears when she couldn't even understand them herself? Couldn't express them?

Talking with Emily earlier in the week hadn't helped at all. The other woman was content to be a wife and mother, to be her husband's helpmate. She hadn't really understood Hattie's need to practice medicine, to have a career of her own.

Hattie couldn't stop wondering—what if she did marry Maxwell, if their courtship continued, and she lost her dreams? She'd wanted to be a doctor for so long! How could she give it up—how could she even *risk* giving it up now that she was on the cusp of achieving what she wanted?

Even though her parents still didn't know about the possible scholarship. She needed to talk to them, at least convince Papa she could do it. Time was running out before she had to leave for her scholarship interview. But she wanted a few more days to get out of the wheeled chair before she spoke to her parents.

Mama would never agree if Hattie was relegated to the chair. Her nerves had been slightly better today, and if she could return to the clinic next week, then she was determined to speak to her father, to *make* him understand that she had to go.

She only hoped she would do better expressing herself than she had with Maxwell tonight.

Chapter Fourteen

Working with Hattie in the clinic had turned from a joy to the hardest thing Maxwell had ever had to do.

At least she was well enough to come back to work. That was something to be thankful for, even if it was difficult to be around her.

He was aware of her every movement, whether she conversed with patients in the outer vestibule or was at his side in the examination room, assisting him as the doctor looked on.

Those times were the worst. She was polite, professional. Distant.

Gone were the shared smiles, the understanding that had passed between them freely before he'd ruined things between them. Once, when he'd successfully stitched a young boy's nasty gash, he'd looked up, elated, only to see her turn away without meeting his eyes. His joy had turned to ash, and he'd had to take a moment outside, behind the clinic, to catch his breath before meeting the next patient.

He'd asked the doc to cut down his hours in the clinic, blaming it on the fact that his brother needed him to help finish the horses. It was true that Oscar wanted to attend a big sale in a couple weeks and wanted the horses broken first. But it was also an excuse.

Maxwell couldn't bear to be around Hattie with things so strained between them. He was angry at himself that he couldn't be satisfied with their friendship—he'd had to push for more and ruin everything. She'd said it wasn't his physical advances that had made her rethink their relationship, but what else could it have been?

He'd spent hours in the dark of night reliving those last few weekdays before she'd broken things off, trying to pinpoint anything else it could have possibly been, to no avail. He'd expressed everything he could to make her see that he didn't want to hinder her from becoming a doctor, even hinted that he'd like to work beside her. So it couldn't have been that—she had to know he supported her. No, it had to have been his kiss. Likely, he'd been too clumsy or too forward or too…something.

He didn't even know what he'd done wrong, and he was too humiliated and hurt to ask Oscar or Sam what it might've been.

Somehow his brothers, all of them, had figured out that things had gone badly between Maxwell and Hattie. They'd been tiptoeing around him for days, and he almost, *almost,* missed their teasing.

His ma had been distracted by the new baby and the adjustments in the household, and he hadn't told her yet that he and Hattie had parted ways. That was a conversation he'd avoid for as long as possible. He couldn't face his ma's indignation on his behalf, not when he was sure he'd done something to make Hattie push him away.

His pa hadn't said much, had only pressed his shoulder and said he was there if Maxwell wanted to talk. It was Jonas's way. He and Maxwell were a lot the same—they looked before they leaped, liked to think things through and make a logical decision. Held things close to their hearts.

Maxwell knew he could go to his pa if needed, or even to Oscar or Sam, but he was adrift, floating in hurt and disappointment until he barely knew which way was up.

It was all he could do to keep putting one foot in front of the other every day. But he would get through it. He had to. He *would* get back to medical school, if not in the fall then in the spring, and he would graduate and become a doctor.

He would prove his birth ma wrong on that point, at least. He could make something of himself. He might never find the love he was looking for, but he could be a doctor. He must. It was the only thing he had left.

"I'm sorry I'm a little late—Mama wanted to send over some biscuits, and I had to wait."

No one answered Hattie's call as she slipped through the clinic's back door, though she knew her father was already here, and Maxwell probably was, too.

Although she'd been running behind, it was still earlier than they usually accepted patients.

Except she heard voices in the examination room.

She left the biscuits on the storeroom counter and

went into the hallway, pausing outside the cracked door to determine if she should enter or wait.

"Nice stitching here." That was Papa's voice.

"It was all Hattie's doing." And there was Maxwell's. But who and what were they talking about?

She peered through the crack in the door and saw Maxwell's broad-shouldered form next to the exam table, blocking her view of whomever was in the room with them.

"She was calm and did what needed doing—I just acted the nurse," he went on.

Maxwell shifted slightly to the side, and she was able to see the head and shoulders of the patient laid out on the exam table—John Spencer. He must've come in to have his stitches removed. And her papa had complimented her work. But the words that repeated in her head were Maxwell's. *She did what needed doing.*

She should move—the direction Maxwell had shifted meant he could see her through the slit in the door if he looked up. She didn't want to be caught eavesdropping, but neither could she make herself move from this position.

"I had a hard time wrapping my mind around the fact that your daughter saved my life," admitted the man on the table.

"She's competent" came Maxwell's voice again. "Probably has more experience than a lot of nurses— even some doctors."

She couldn't really believe he was praising her to her father and in front of a patient, not after what had happened between them. He barely spoke to her anymore, only when needed. He was professional, never crossing into personal territory.

Had he guessed she hadn't gotten the courage to talk to Papa yet? Could he be...paving the way for her? She didn't know.

He looked up then, and their eyes met.

Instantly, she saw the deep hurt he'd been able to hide by not completely meeting her eyes since their talk. The connection between them flared to life. Her breath caught in her chest in a painful lump. She'd put that hurt in his eyes. Her fault.

And just as quickly, it was gone as he lowered his gaze and shifted slightly toward the patient on the table.

She knocked softly, pretending she hadn't been there and overheard.

"Papa? Do you need anything?" She pushed the door partially open and stuck her head inside. "Good morning," she murmured in Maxwell's direction.

He only nodded silently.

"We're doing fine in here." Papa's attention didn't waver from where he snipped the stiches in Spencer's side. "You might check the front room. It appeared a little disheveled last night before I left."

She did, only to find that someone—probably Maxwell—had rearranged the chairs and swept out the room, things she'd left undone and meant to do first thing this morning.

Another sign of his consideration, even after she'd treated him poorly.

She slipped back down the hallway and out the rear door, sinking to her haunches on the small stoop, pressing her hands to both temples.

Why did the man have to be so courteous? So considerate? Still wanting the best for her, even after what had passed between them?

Movement from beside her startled her. A small, shaggy white head appeared and was quickly followed by a wiggling body and thwapping tail.

"Oh, hello," she said to the dog, Maxwell's little friend. "Did you follow him to town today?"

She halfheartedly reached down to pet the animal, absently rubbing behind its ears. The dog seemed to sense her inner turmoil, because it sat beside her, raised one paw and planted it on Hattie's knee. She would have to remember to change her apron when she returned inside, but she welcomed the company for now.

It laid its head on her leg and looked up at her with mournful eyes.

They were on par with Maxwell's, as she'd seen moments ago. She realized it was the first time he'd looked her in the eye since Friday night—and he probably hadn't meant to do so this morning, wouldn't have done so if she hadn't been hiding behind the door.

Laying her hand on top of the dog's head, she closed her eyes. She hadn't meant to hurt Maxwell, only to protect herself. But now things were even more muddled, and she didn't know how to fix them.

And she found that she felt the hurt, too. When had she come to care so deeply for him? When he'd stood beside her as she performed surgery? Upon discovering there was more to him? Now her feelings ran deeper than she'd thought possible.

"Hattie?" A soft, feminine voice brought her head up.

"Emily." Hattie stood, dislodging the dog, who went to the newcomer with its usual exuberance. "Maxwell's dog," she explained when Emily looked at her questioningly.

"Hmm," her friend said.

"What are you doing here?" Hattie asked, hoping to distract her friend from the mention of Maxwell.

"I'm helping my father in the shop this morning for a bit and thought I might stop by to talk to you, after we ended things so abruptly the other day at lunch." She shooed the dog off and sat next to Hattie on the stoop. "You look about as well as Maxwell seems to be doing."

"Is he…all right?"

"You know Maxwell. He's reserved. Hasn't said much, even to Sam."

Hattie nodded, unsurprised. She stared over her knees at the ground.

"I wish you would've told me sooner that you had reservations about a relationship with Maxwell. I could've…I don't know." Hattie's friend blew out a breath. "At least I wouldn't have gone on and on and sounded so silly…."

"I really like Maxwell." She couldn't admit she loved him, not this moment.

Emily touched Hattie's sleeve. "Then I don't understand."

Hattie drew in another deep breath.

"I don't understand, but I'll listen," Emily prompted.

"I want to be a doctor."

Emily nodded. Waited.

"And Maxwell wants a family." It had become obvious to her after witnessing him with his own family on the homestead. And he'd said as much to her.

Emily hesitated, then spoke softly. "Being a doctor and a wife and a mother aren't mutually exclusive, are they?"

"For a woman? Who wants a wife who works long hours instead of keeping house? Who will watch the children, when they come?"

She dared to speak her real fear. "What if…what if I want to be with the children? What if my ambition goes away?"

Emily turned a frank, skeptical gaze on her. "Do you really see yourself wanting that?"

"With Maxwell…?" Hattie whispered.

Her friend seemed to understand what she couldn't say. That she *could* envision it happening. Hattie didn't know anything anymore.

"You've wanted to be a doctor forever, haven't you? Even taken steps to make it happen? Do you really think that desire to help people will just go away?"

Hattie shrugged miserably.

"Well, maybe you'd better figure things out before everything with Maxwell gets beyond repair."

Emily sat with her silently for a while, then had to leave. She gave Hattie a warm hug before she went. At least their friendship hadn't suffered, even after Hattie's abrupt departure from lunch the other day.

But Hattie's larger problems were ultimately unresolved. She *was* frightened to take a chance on loving Maxwell. And the only person who really seemed to understand her was the man inside with her papa. And she was no longer free to talk to him.

But maybe she could try to make things right. Make him understand she wasn't as callous as she seemed.

After Emily left, Hattie forced herself to go back inside. The clinic was still quiet, the flood of daily patients not yet arrived.

She went to find Maxwell and to ask for a moment to speak privately, but instead found herself eavesdropping again when she heard his quiet voice from inside the examination room.

"I wasn't exaggerating about Hattie's skill. I'm sure you've seen it plenty yourself, working alongside her."

Maxwell knew there was a chance he was overstepping his bounds, talking with Hattie's pa, but he also knew that her deadline for attending the scholarship interview was coming up quick and he suspected she hadn't settled things with her parents. And he cared about her enough to want her to get what she deserved.

"You've seen how she is with the patients. You know how smart she is—did you know she's read all of the medical texts you've got at home?"

He'd been absently writing in a journal, but now the doc's full attention turned to Maxwell.

"She's assisted you enough she could probably do most of the procedures on her own. I've never seen someone as cool under pressure as she was when doing that surgery. And she has a heart for the patients—I saw it in action when we were working with the cholera cases." He hesitated and then just put it out on the table. "You should allow her to attend medical school. You should encourage it. She'll be an amazing doctor."

The doctor set aside his journal. "And what about when she has can't help patients because of her nerves? What then? Who will care for her?"

"That sounds like something Hattie's ma might say. Not you."

The doctor flushed.

Maxwell knew the doctor's question stemmed from concern for his daughter. But he also knew that Hattie was capable.

"Being in the wheeled chair wouldn't hinder her studies—she could still attend classes and read her texts."

Now the man crossed his arms. "And what about when she moves to practice? Would it compromise her treatment of a patient?"

"Have you ever taken a sick day yourself?"

The man nodded, conceding the point.

Maxwell went on, "She is capable of handling herself. During the cholera outbreak, she knew her limits and traded off with me when she needed to rest. And if she was in a practice where she was a partner— perhaps with her father," he hinted, "she would have someone to lean on during those times."

"And what about the prejudice she would face as a woman doing a man's job?"

"With the right partner, she could overcome that. After working along with you and having people see her skill during your recent absence, the people of Bear Creek have begun to trust her."

The doc went silent, staring out the small window and considering Maxwell's words.

"And what do I say to her mother, to convince her to allow her daughter this career?"

Maxwell didn't have an answer for that.

"And how do I let my little girl go? Am I to assume from your persistence in this discussion that you share that struggle?"

It was Maxwell's turn to look away; he couldn't answer. If Hattie had felt differently about him, he would've found a way—any way—to make things work between them. Whether that meant corresponding via letter or him following her until they both got their medical diplomas. But she hadn't. "Hattie's been a good friend, but that's all that is between us."

No matter how much he wished the answer could be different.

Hattie scribbled a note as to her whereabouts and escaped from the clinic, nearly running all the way home, heedless of the greetings of others on the boardwalk. She kept her face down, hoping no one would notice the tears pooling in her eyes.

She didn't go inside but crept around to curl up in a small ball behind two of the rocking chairs on the back veranda. Hiding her face in her skirts, she finally let the tears fall.

She couldn't believe Maxwell had said all that he had to her father. Couldn't believe the depth of his faith in her. He'd obviously considered every angle of what it would take for her to attend medical school and be a part of a medical practice—not surprising, as the man had a tendency to think things through.

He'd laid out all of those arguments out so clearly that her father hadn't been able to argue with his logic.

She couldn't believe he'd done so on her behalf after how poorly she'd treated him, pushing him away without any real explanation. She didn't deserve a friend like him—had selfishly considered only her own feelings. Feelings that had moved beyond friendship to something much more. She was in love with the cowboy.

"Hattie?" her mother's voice called out from near the back door, and Hattie quickly wiped her face with her apron.

"Hattie, are you there? Your father is looking for you."

"I'm here, Mama." Hattie rose from behind the chair, hoping she didn't look as disheveled and red-faced as she felt.

"What're you doing hiding behind there?"

Hattie was saved from answering as she followed Mama into the kitchen. Papa waited in the doorway leading to the dining room. "You'd better join us, too, Mama. I've sent Maxwell home and put up the closed sign at the clinic. This could take a while."

Hattie was trembling as she sank onto the settee in Papa's study, Mama at her side. Would this discussion be fruitful or force her to break ties with her parents?

Her papa's first words were so completely unexpected that Hattie's eyes filled with tears again.

"Mama, it seems our little girl is meant to be a doctor."

It took the rest of the afternoon for the both of them to overcome Mama's railing and crying, but finally Hattie's dreams were on the verge of coming true. She was headed to Omaha for her scholarship interview. Even better than that was that her papa had promised to help her in whatever way he could—whether it meant digging into the family savings account or writing her a letter of recommendation.

Her papa's support meant more than anything. He really thought she could do it. All it had taken was Maxwell's convincing.

In her room, she sat on the bed, flushed and breathless.

And still aching inside.

She was on the cusp of a new journey. Of getting everything she'd wanted for years.

So why did she feel so empty?

Chapter Fifteen

Hattie didn't catch a glimpse of Maxwell until Sunday morning worship. His family had all traipsed in and taken their seats well before the opening hymn. She was seated with her parents near the front of the sanctuary but craned her neck continuously, trying to catch sight of him.

She really needed to thank him.

But he didn't slip inside until after the opening hymn and was one of the first outside after services were over. Hattie excused herself from her parents, waved off her friends, including Emily, and went to try to find him. She had to try to set things right.

She was intercepted just outside the door by his mother.

"Hattie." Somehow the woman still smiled at her, the baby bundled in her arms. "I wanted to make sure to greet you today. Everyone at home is still talking about your visit for lunch last week—it was good to have you out with us. We'll have to do it again sometime, won't we?"

And suddenly Hattie knew Maxwell hadn't told

his mother what had happened between them. He was sensitive enough, maybe he'd thought she was too busy with the baby to notice....

"Mmm, yes, sometime," Hattie hedged. She allowed herself to be pulled from the main flow of people coming out of the church to a quieter spot between the parked wagons and the side of the building.

The other woman touched her arm. "I'm so glad that Maxwell has met you."

Hattie shifted on her feet. Penny seemed oblivious to her discomfort, though, as she went on.

"When Jonas and I were courting, Maxwell was so starved for love—but he also held himself back so carefully...as if he was afraid to believe in it."

Hattie slid her eyes over to the horses standing placidly in their harnesses, waiting for someone to come retrieve the wagon. Hattie wished someone would come retrieve her. She already had enough guilt about growing her relationship with Maxwell and then breaking things off.

"It wasn't until later that I found out exactly how hard a childhood he'd had. His mother did severe damage to his confidence. I don't think he's ever told his father and me everything, but I do know that she told him multiple times that he wouldn't amount to anything. That he'd never accomplish anything with his life."

Hattie had seen a lot of things as she'd helped her papa in the clinic, but she had trouble imagining a parent so cruel. And she didn't know if Maxwell would welcome his mother telling her all of this, not now.

"Mrs. White, I really should be going—"

"Oh, I'm sorry. I didn't mean to hold you up. I just wanted to say…" Gracious, the other woman now had tears standing in her eyes. "Well, his father and I were worried about Maxwell coming home for the summer. In his letters, he seemed so discouraged about not being able to complete his education. But then he started working in your father's practice and…well, I've never seen him so happy, so settled as he was last weekend, even with his brothers teasing him so badly. And I wanted to thank you for bringing joy to my son."

She squeezed Hattie's arm and moved away before Hattie could say anything else or explain that things had ended between them.

Leaving Hattie's feeling more jumbled than ever. How could Maxwell have survived such a tough childhood and turned into the sensitive, caring man that he was?

How could she *not* be in love with a man like that?

But did it change anything? She still wanted the same goals.

Could she find a way to tell him that she believed in him, too, even though she just couldn't be with him?

The next morning, Maxwell braced himself to see Hattie, the same way he usually did.

She was in the examination room with her pa nowhere to be seen, and when she looked up and saw him, she smiled a warm smile that sent his heart swooping and soaring uncomfortably in his chest.

He glanced over his shoulder to see if someone else had come in behind him.

"Good morning, Maxwell."

The warmth continued in her tone, and he grew even more puzzled. They'd barely spoken in the week and a half since he'd made a fool of himself at her parents' place. Hope flared—had she reconsidered? Was there a chance she still wanted to be with him?

She clasped her hands in front of her apron and he couldn't help but note how the dark green dress beneath complemented her hair. She moved toward him. "I can't thank you enough for what you said to my papa."

And then humiliation flared and he realized what her reaction really meant. She was simply thanking him. "Your pa told you?"

"Actually, I overheard most of it."

Heat scorched his neck. He hadn't meant for her to hear him push for her. Hated feeling pathetic. He half turned away, patting his Stetson against his thigh. "So you're going, then?"

"Yes, thanks to you. Papa agreed to the scholarship interview, and with him on my side, Mama was brought around. Eventually."

He found himself responding to the humor in her voice with a small smile even as his heart crashed in his chest.

"I really think your words made a difference. I don't know that Papa would've listened to me without your influence."

It wasn't right that she had to fight so hard because of her gender, but he loved her enough that he could be glad her pa had come around.

"I'm getting to follow my dream, thanks to you, and I just… Thank you."

He didn't want her thanks…he wanted her love, but he couldn't have that.

"I think your pa would've come around regardless. You worked so hard during the outbreak, and you've got a proven record. But I'm glad for you," he said. He turned to move into the back hall, deposit his Stetson in the storeroom and get his bearings.

"Wait! Maxwell—"

He closed his eyes, still facing away where she couldn't see. It was too hard to be close to her—too hard to look into her face and see the joy there and want to be a part of it.

But he couldn't be rude, either, not when she meant so much to him.

He schooled his expression and turned back. She was looking at him with that adorable crinkle just above her nose. He swallowed hard, waited for her to say whatever she needed to say so he could escape.

"I wanted to… I just…" Now she looked nervous, her eyes darting down and away. He had to quell the urge to reach out for her, to comfort her in some way.

"I know I handled things badly the other evening, and I wanted to try to explain."

Mortification spread through him even worse and he turned his face away to stare at the paneling on the wall. "It's not that big a deal," he muttered. Lied. His pride couldn't take any more.

"It's a big deal to me. You've been a good friend, and I could see…I could see us growing into something more—"

For the briefest moment, his heart stopped completely, then began flying in his chest.

"Except for the fact that our paths seem to be going in different directions."

Hope crashed in his chest like galloping hooves. Different directions didn't mean the path couldn't be changed. Was she giving him a sign, trying to tell him that there was still a chance for their relationship?

She looked at him with those blue eyes, beseeching him for understanding. "You know—you're the only one who seems to understand how important it is for me to become a doctor. And courting...which leads to getting married...and *families*..." He didn't understand the soft emphasis she put on that word. "All of that would get in the way of what I really want."

Her words sounded as if she were trying to convince herself. She stopped speaking abruptly, brows furrowing, and her gaze seemed to focus internally.

He didn't know what to do or what to say but found himself speaking. "Hattie, I would never ask you to give up your aspirations."

"I know," she said softly, looking at the floor.

"I think we could make a good partnership. We work together well, we like each other." Though his feelings went so much deeper. "And it couldn't hurt to...to keep exploring things between us, could it?"

"Maxwell, I can't—"

He couldn't bear to hear another rejection from her, not with hope blooming. He was close enough to reach out and touch her arm, so he clasped her elbow and drew her in. Slanted his lips over hers as he'd wanted to do again ever since their first kiss in his pa's field, surrounded by sunshine and horses.

She responded with a lift of her chin, pressing her mouth more fully into his. He wanted to draw her closer but was afraid of scaring her off again. But the way she was kissing him back…he had the feeling she wasn't scared at all.

Then she pushed him away with a hand on his chest, her eyes wide and unfocused, lips reddened from his kiss. If this was what it took to convince her…

He reached for her again.

"Maxwell, no." The finality in her voice and the turn of her shoulder, so that his hand reached only empty air, brought him back to reality. Jarred him, as if he'd been bucked off a horse and landed particularly hard.

The hope that had momentarily expanded in his chest fell flat. Blood rushed in his ears so loudly that he almost didn't hear her next, soft-spoken words.

"I care about you, but friendship is the most I can offer. I think you're a wonderful, amazing man who will someday find someone that you deserve. But it isn't me."

Pride tattered around his feet, he wheeled around and ran out of the office.

Hattie stared after Maxwell as he retreated, pressing one shaking hand to her lips. Lips that had touched his only moments ago.

She shouldn't have kissed him back.

But his action had been so unexpected, and the feelings that reignited with his touch were so powerful that she hadn't been able to resist the pressure of his mouth. She loved him. So much. She was afraid of trusting it.

She felt overheated and shaky and went to the examination table to sit down.

That interaction hadn't gone over any better than the one at her parents' home when he'd come courting. The devastated look on his face, just before he'd turned away...

Her heart thrummed with a similar pain. She didn't want him to hurt, had been trying to *erase* his hurt, or at least ease things back to friendship between them, but she'd failed.

She felt like an awful person.

And the worst thing was, she loved him, too.

Even though her plans didn't include love or marriage or powerful kisses...

She loved him.

Dizzy, she pressed her other hand to her temple. She had to get herself under control before her papa came in and assumed she was having an attack of her nerves.

But even with every technique she could come up with to calm her breath, nothing stopped her racing heart.

She did want to be with Maxwell.

But she wanted medical school more. Didn't she?

Chapter Sixteen

Two days later, Maxwell worked a filly under the hot summer sun until she was flecked with foam and he was sweating through his chambray shirt.

His efforts physically exhausted him, but he couldn't get his whirling brain to stop.

Something wasn't right in what Hattie had told him on Monday. Oh, he understood the words, but *she'd kissed him back*. Passionately. Without reserve.

Hattie was a good girl, would never lead someone on if she didn't have real feelings for them.

She cared about him. He was sure of it. He'd seen something on her face when she'd pulled away from his kiss—a pain that matched his. He'd just been too caught up in his own feelings to register it right away. But after two days of replaying the whole interaction in his mind, he was almost sure of what he'd seen.

So why did she push him away?

He'd thought with everything they'd shared that he'd made himself clear. He wouldn't stand in the way of her dreams. Matter of fact, they shared the same dreams. But what if she didn't believe him?

How could he prove it to her?

Should he even try? He'd tried expressing his feelings, only to be rejected twice.

And facing Hattie's rejection was twenty—no, a hundred times worse than when Elizabeth had walked away from him in Denver. He was coming to see that he hadn't really been in love with her. Those feelings had been nothing compared to what he felt for Hattie.

And he knew Hattie was someone worth fighting for.

But he wasn't sure what to do, how to go about it.

He reined in the filly close to Oscar's barn, intending to give her a good rubdown while he kept thinking things through, working out a plan. But he was barely off the horse when several of his brothers marched around the corner of the barn and closed ranks around him.

"There he is!"

"Grab him—don't let him get away!"

The filly, one of the last to be trained, was nervous with the flurry of motion and sound, and balked, pulled back on her reins.

"Watch the horse," Maxwell told them, irritated that they'd interrupted him. He wanted to finish his task and keep working on the Hattie problem.

Two large hands—two different hands—clapped down on his shoulders and he was relieved of the horse's reins.

"I've got her," Seb called out confidently. "But don't be making any big plans until I get her cleaned up and put away."

That was when he realized the group was larger than he'd first thought. It included all six of his adopted brothers, along with Sam. The hairs on the back of his neck pricked.

"What's going on?" he asked, suspicious now.

"Whew—he's ripe today," someone commented as Maxwell was unceremoniously hauled backward, nearly off his feet.

"Hey!" He caught sight of Edgar, two years younger but with an inch on him, as one of the two holding his arms.

"A man'll work himself to death trying to forget a woman" came Oscar's voice, also from behind him.

"What is this?" Maxwell repeated, just before he was shoved forward and a bucket of cold water from the creek doused him.

He spluttered and spit, trying to come to his feet, but hands held him down to his knees.

"That's a little better on the smell," someone said.

They shoved him to his rear on the ground, legs sprawled out in front of him. Anger flashed through him.

"Don't move," Sam said.

Maxwell glared up at his friend. He'd stay where he was—for now. See what was what first. His brothers stood in a semicircle around him, except for Seb, whom he could hear rustling around and talking to himself in the barn.

"This is an intervention." Oscar squatted in front of Maxwell.

"Yeah, we're tired of you moping around here," put in Davy. "It's depressing watching you carry that long face around all day."

"We're determined to figure a way to get you back with Hattie," said Sam.

"Or someone else—" threw in Edgar.

Maxwell looked up at his next youngest brother, standing off to the side with the toe of his boot in the dirt. "You're in on this, too?"

"She's not all bad, I guess," Edgar grumbled under his breath.

"We know you're in love with her," said Ricky, ignoring Edgar's comment as if he hadn't spoken. "And we didn't even have to read about it in that secret journal you're always hiding."

Maxwell didn't blink. His brother might be bluffing about knowing about the poetry journal—or maybe not. But if he owned up to keeping one, they'd for sure josh him about it or even go on the hunt for it.

"Hattie's the right gal for you." Matty, who hadn't spoken until now, hanging back in the group, took his hat off and fanned away a buzzing fly.

"Yeah, you just gave up too easy!" Davy spoke again.

"I gave up easy?" Maxwell spluttered, because he'd tried to win Hattie twice, with disastrous results both times.

"Well, you ain't got a ring on her finger, have you?" came back Davy.

"All right. Enough." Oscar's voice rose louder than all the rest, shushing the conversation that had spread through the other brothers. "We know you love Hattie." He ticked off one finger, as if he was counting.

Maxwell couldn't deny it and nodded slowly, wondering just how bad this was going to be.

"And we think she likes you back," Ricky said.

Oscar ticked off another finger.

"We're relatively sure," Sam put in. Maxwell figured he would know as well as anyone, with Emily being Hattie's close friend.

"And somehow," Oscar continued, "communication got all mixed up between the two of you." Another finger was ticked. "And you're separated now. But not happy."

The whole group went silent, including Seb, who'd joined them during Oscar's last point. "And we've got to figure out a way to fix things," the oldest White boy concluded.

It was only because Maxwell had come to the same decision that he agreed. That and because he needed help figuring out what to do. Between his oldest brother and his best friend, who were both happily married and had won over their spouses somehow, surely they could come up with some idea of how he could get Hattie back.

"All right," he said slowly. "What did you all have in mind?"

"Depends," Matty said with a sly grin. "What you got written in that journal of yours?"

Hattie strolled down the boardwalk on her way back to the clinic after lunch, the summer sun warm on her face.

Only a week remained until her train departed for Omaha, to take her to the scholarship interview. She'd sat with her papa several nights in a row, discussing what questions might be asked of her and practicing concise, intelligent answers.

This would be Hattie's first trip on her own. Her mama had been flitting around, planning Hattie's wardrobe—although Hattie planned to take only a small valise—and talking nonstop about Hattie's manners and deportment.

Hattie thought perhaps her mama was more excited than she was.

She was too engrossed with figuring out the cowboy she worked with; that was the problem. She'd expected tense silence from him after their second shared kiss and her rebuff of his advances. Instead, he'd seemed…almost happy the next time she'd seen him in the clinic. He'd greeted her pleasantly, made eye contact and even talked at length about seeing little Bobby in church services last Sunday.

He made no mention of the kiss, or of anything remotely personal, but he'd been friendly and pleasant for days.

She was utterly confused. By all accounts, he should've been miserable. Or, at least, as miserable as she was.

She wanted to share her thoughts about the upcoming trip with him but was afraid he would misconstrue it as an overture on her part. She wanted his insights on whether or not she was prepared enough for the interview. She wanted to hear how his mother and the new baby were doing. If his brothers were constantly nosing into his business. If Walt and Ida were adjusting to life with their new baby brother.

But it wasn't her place to ask him, not when she'd been the one to push him away.

And it was her own fault.

She loved the handsome, quiet cowboy.

And now he seemed completely over her. No signs of hurt or confusion. Just a professional demeanor.

What had she done?

Voices outside the clinic had her hurrying up the boardwalk. She and Papa had closed the doors for the lunch break. Was someone waiting to be let in?

But she froze in place two storefronts down when she caught sight of Maxwell's tall form as he conversed with two young ladies. Annabelle and Corrine.

The sight of his dark head bent to their level, the smiles on the two girls' faces, suddenly cramped her stomach. Was this why he seemed happier in general? Had he already moved on to courting someone else?

With what she'd seen of his shyness and what Penny had revealed, it seemed unlikely, but here he was conversing with two beautiful young women. Then Annabelle reached up and touched his forearm, just a small, animated sweep of her fingertips as she expressed something while she spoke, and the tightness in Hattie's stomach worsened.

Was Maxwell sweet on Annabelle? Had he seen her socially since Hattie cast him off?

Feeling sick, she hesitated, wondering if she should backtrack to the end of the boardwalk and sneak around to the back of the clinic so that the trio wouldn't see her.

Unfortunately, Corrine chose that moment to look around and notice her. The other girl waved, which drew Maxwell and Annabelle's gazes, as well.

"Hattie!" Corrine cried.

She had no choice but to approach, as much as she didn't want to. She tried to find a smile that would seem genuine, but it faltered as she got closer and she had to force it to stay in place.

She accepted a light embrace from her friend, trying not to be aware of Maxwell, tall and silent, on her other side.

"We haven't seen much of you since things have gone back to normal," Annabelle said by way of greeting. "You've been busy with the clinic, I hear."

Had Maxwell mentioned it? A fleeting glance at him saw him watching Annabelle—it was only polite, since she'd been the one to speak last, but it galled Hattie.

"Yes, well…my parents have agreed to let me pursue my education further and I've been busy getting ready for that."

"Education? To do what?"

"I'm going to become a doctor." It was the first time she'd said the words to someone outside her family or Maxwell or Emily, and the pride Hattie felt was real. But there was still something missing.

And she guessed it was the man beside her, who hadn't acknowledged her other than a nod, though he didn't seem upset to see her.

Corrine gasped a little, and Annabelle's eyes went wide. "Really?" the taller girl asked.

Hattie nodded.

"She'll be a fine doctor," Maxwell said.

Hattie glanced at him briefly, but he was looking at Corrine now.

"She's had so much practice, no doubt she'll fly through the lessons at medical school."

The two other girls nodded as if what Maxwell said made sense, but Hattie noted their still slightly stunned expressions. Would this be the usual reaction she would receive from here on out?

They seemed to recover quickly. Annabelle smiled

first. "Well, you can't be too busy for the next poetry-club meeting," she said, obviously excited.

"It's tomorrow evening—the first meeting back since everyone was so sick," Corrine reminded them, as if Hattie wasn't aware of the fact.

Annabelle smiled up at the man beside them. "You're coming, aren't you, Maxwell?"

He nodded, surprising Hattie. She'd thought at the last meeting that he'd only gone because she'd suggested it as a way to get to know some of the girls in town. "I had a good time at the last meeting."

Was it her imagination, or did his eyes flicker to her? They'd just been getting to know each other at the first poetry-club meeting, but did his words have a deeper meaning?

"So you'll be there, Hattie?" Corrine asked.

This time she *felt it* when Maxwell's eyes rested on her. He squinted a little beneath his Stetson, his intensity aimed at her for a moment that stretched long.

"I don't know," Hattie murmured, unnerved. "It will depend on how busy things are in the clinic, if I have to help Papa clean up after the day's patients."

If she wasn't too exhausted, if her nerves cooperated…

If she needed to avoid Maxwell, avoid seeing him flirt with other girls.

"Oh, Hattie, you must come. We have a special reading planned," Annabelle gushed.

"We'll see." It was all the commitment she could give. If Maxwell was there, she didn't know if she could face it. "I really should get inside, ready things for the afternoon."

She excused herself, again surprised when Maxwell didn't offer to come in to help her but remained on the boardwalk with the other two girls.

What could he possibly be talking to them about? She stomped into the storeroom to don her usual full-length apron. She still didn't hear the door open to announce his presence.

She grabbed the broom and moved to the front room—though she'd swept it first thing this morning.

She didn't like the feelings swamping her just at this moment. The first was petty jealousy, plain and simple. She couldn't deny it.

It was what made her flick the corner of the curtain aside. Yes, he was still out there, but Corrine had gone. He conversed with Annabelle alone, their heads close together as if they spoke quietly.

Hattie almost, *almost* opened the door to brush the small amount of dust she'd swept up into their faces.

But she didn't.

Because the other feeling overtaking her was more than simple jealousy.

It was regret.

Chapter Seventeen

How had he let himself get talked into this?

Slightly nauseous and sweating through the Sunday shirt, coat and tie that his brothers had insisted he wear, Maxwell paced behind the small Bear Creek café, where tonight's poetry reading would be held.

He was thankful only Oscar and Sam would be here to witness him humbling himself in front of a passel of people. Oscar had ordered the rest of the brothers to stay home and threatened to tell Penny if they showed up anyway.

That wasn't really what Maxwell was worried about.

He was worried about putting his heart on the line for anyone who showed up to hear.

It might be embarrassing, but he was determined that he would do whatever he could—whatever he had to—to win Hattie.

She was worth it, even if it meant expressing his feelings in front of the whole town. Or, at least, anyone who showed up for the poetry reading.

"Any sign of her?" he said, startling Sam, who

stood in the partially open doorway, looking inside the rapidly filling room. Light spilled outward, illuminating his friend but leaving Maxwell in the gathering darkness.

Maybe it would hide the heat that scorched his face, neck and chest just thinking about what he was about to do.

Hattie was worth it. She was worth it.

He just needed to keep repeating that to himself.

"Not yet," came Sam's reply. "Emily isn't back, either."

Sarah and Emily had been included in the plans by necessity. The fact that the two women had approved had made Maxwell feel better. Marginally.

He'd been so nervous earlier that Sam had sent Emily to retrieve Hattie, on the pretext of walking to the poetry reading with her friend. Maxwell sure wasn't going to make a fool of himself if Hattie didn't show up.

"Full crowd in there!" Oscar said, coming around the side of the building and clapping his brother on the shoulder.

"Oscar," Sam growled.

Maxwell just moaned. His stomach threatened to heave, but he hadn't eaten any supper, so there wasn't much danger he'd make a mess of himself.

"You'll do fine," his older brother assured him.

But the delay was doing nothing for Maxwell's confidence. What if she didn't come, after all their planning?

"Hattie! You're not dressed!"

Emily's stunned and dismayed cry when Hattie had come to the front door was a bit much.

"Yes, I am," Hattie said, looking down at the serviceable dress she'd worn at the clinic that day.

"Oh, I guess it doesn't matter, but you're already late!"

To the poetry-club meeting. That Hattie had decided not to attend. She smiled as best she could at her friend.

"I'm not going."

"But you *have* to go." Emily nearly wailed the words. She flailed her hands, looking more upset than she had a right to be over a social event.

"I hardly ever go," Hattie reminded her friend. "I'm tired. I've worked all day." And she couldn't bear to see Maxwell smiling down at Annabelle, or anyone else for that matter.

"Shouldn't she go, Mrs. Powell?"

Hattie's mama sniffed a bit haughtily. "Hattie doesn't listen to my wishes on courtship or marriage."

Not all of the ruffled feathers from the medical-school decision had been soothed. Likely wouldn't be until Hattie got married. If that ever happened.

Emily turned from one Powell woman to the other, then back again. Her agitation seemed out of proportion with the level of distress that Hattie missing the event actually called for. "Oh, *please* come along, Hattie."

Hattie narrowed her eyes at her friend, suspicions rising. "Is something going on? And where's Sam, anyway?"

"He's already at the café," Emily hedged. "And..."

"Spit it out."

"...you don't want to miss the reading tonight. That's all I can say."

"Does this have anything to do with Maxwell?" Hattie pressed her friend anyway.

Emily's expression softened. She bit her lip but shrugged her shoulders. Hattie didn't want her friend to break a confidence.

But Hattie was a smart girl, and her mind was already flying forward. Maxwell. Poetry.

Would he make some kind of statement to Hattie at the poetry reading? Emily's insistence that she go was more than unusual for her friend.

Was it possible Hattie *hadn't* ruined things beyond repair? Heart racing, she reached for her shawl with shaking hands. She wanted this, wanted to be with Maxwell, if he would still accept her.

What did the night have in store?

Hearting pounding, Hattie didn't know what to expect when she stepped into the café. Everything appeared the same as it had at the last meeting, people filling the chairs and a few stragglers conversing in whispers near the food tables at the rear.

The meeting had already begun, with Annabelle presiding, making some announcement about the next meeting time and place.

Hattie moved to slip into one of the empty seats in the back, not wanting to draw undue attention until she had her bearings, but Emily grasped her arm with a surprisingly tight hold and ushered her to the second row of seats—where no one sat, either in the second or first rows.

Emily moved past her into the row, and Sam moved toward them from the other side, relief on his face. Hattie wanted to back up, go somewhere a little more unobtrusive, but suddenly Sarah and Oscar were crowding behind her, forcing her into the center of the row of seats.

Seeing no way out of it, she plopped down, Sarah and Emily on either side. Where was Maxwell? She surreptitiously glanced around the room, attempting to locate him. Instead, she met several pairs of curious eyes, all trained on her. Her palms started to sweat. Nervous anticipation tickled her spine.

She blinked and looked forward, wanting to escape from prying eyes, but Annabelle's smile twinkled from the podium up front—right at Hattie, and her stomach clutched up. What was going on?

"Everyone, tonight we have a special treat." Annabelle's face seemed to glow with pleasure as she spoke. "One of our very own residents is an aspiring poet…"

A buzz trickled through the crowd. Hattie heard several names whispered in conjecture.

"…and wants to share one of his poems…"

"His?" came a hiss from behind Hattie. "Who—"

"…with a special dedication." Annabelle finished with a rap of her knuckles on the podium, and the group went silent.

Noise roared in Hattie's ears.

"Without further ado, Mr. Maxwell White."

Annabelle left the podium to a smattering of applause and more whispers.

He strode to the front of the room without looking in her direction. Without looking at anyone, head tilted down so that his Stetson hid his eyes.

Once behind the podium, he removed his hat, then didn't seem to know what to do with it. Hattie was directly in front of him and close enough to see his hand shaking slightly as he first set the hat on the podium, then seemed to realize it would be in his way. He picked it up and hung it by his side, awkwardly.

Oscar stood from his place next to Sarah and reached out one long arm to his brother, who handed over the hat with a half relieved, half strangled look on his face.

Maxwell shoved one hand through his dark curls, face pink. "Sorry, I'm—sorry. Nervous," he explained.

No one laughed. Not even one giggle from the crowd escaped. It was as if everyone waited to see what he would do, or say, next. Most of the crowd had probably seen Maxwell and Hattie sit together in Sunday services two weeks ago. If she knew anything about the gossip mill in Bear Creek, no doubt they all waited anxiously to see what would unfold.

He took a small leather-bound book from his breast pocket, beneath his jacket. The same one Hattie had seen him writing in at the church late at night. He opened it to the page where a small ribbon marked his place and smoothed the pages beneath his long, elegant fingers.

Then his green gaze flicked up and landed directly on Hattie. She could read his intensity, his earnestness, his nervousness. All of it—for her?

He cleared his throat. "There's…someone special to me. I've tried to tell her my feelings twice before, but I think I'm not…not saying it right, so I want to read one of the poems I wrote about her."

Hattie tried to form a smile, encourage him in

some way, let him know that she welcomed his words, but her own nervousness made her lips tremble.

He looked back down at the book in front of him, face going even redder, if that was possible. "I've never shared any of my poetry with anyone else, so… bear with me."

He cleared his throat again, once, twice. Didn't look up from the podium.

He began reading, his voice low at first, slowly gaining volume until everyone in the café would be able to hear.

Flushed with embarrassment at being singled out and overwhelmed with emotion that he would do this for her, Hattie didn't hear every word. She caught phrases in snatches, certain words searing into her brain. "'I saw her beauty first in eyes of summer blue sky, Next in her hands so fixed and sure…'"

Hattie couldn't help glancing down at the very appendages he spoke of. Her hands weren't anything special; they were callused from washing up so often, not soft or pretty. But he was right, they *had* saved lives. And he'd noticed.

"'Her determination to overcome…'"

Her head came up. She'd been searching all her life—without even knowing it—for a man who admired her ambitions. And Maxwell did.

His eyes hadn't left the journal in front of him, but she willed him to know her heart was open, that she returned his sentiments.

"'Can a cowboy deserve her…?'"

Perhaps not just any cowboy, but she knew one she couldn't live without…

"'When she is weak, then she is most strong…'"

Now he had to be speaking of her affliction, though he didn't say the words specifically. He really thought she was *strong* when she needed to ask for help?

Heart overflowing, tears brimmed in her eyes.

"'Saying this makes me shake like a newborn foal, For this woman of valor, my love knows no end.'"

Hattie's breath caught. He'd actually admitted that he loved her, in front of this room full of people. She didn't know whether to jump up and go to him or wait to see what he would do next.

He finished reading, and the room was silent around them.

By that time, tears were overflowing in Hattie's eyes—she hadn't lost him. Whatever he'd been doing with Annabelle and Corrine on the boardwalk— planning for tonight's event, perhaps?—he hadn't stopped loving her.

Applause roared around them, started first by his brother, but Hattie barely heard it.

When Maxwell looked up, looked straight at her, she easily read the vulnerability in his face. Her tears spilled over. She shook her head slightly, unable to find words, unsure she wanted to speak in front of everybody.

He went perfectly still. Watched her for a moment that stretched long. Then nodded almost imperceptibly and began to turn away.

With noise, voices speaking, all around, she couldn't understand as he scooped up his book from the podium and turned away—had he somehow misread her expression? She stood to go to him, but the row of chairs was too tight, and she couldn't get past

Sarah, their skirts tangling together. Behind Sarah, the aisle was filling with other people.

"Maxwell, wait!"

Someone grabbed her arm from behind and she turned to find Corrine there with a half amused, half chagrined smile on her face. "That was certainly romantic, wasn't it?" the girl asked.

"Not now," Hattie said. By the time she'd turned back, Maxwell had disappeared. Into the crowd or outside?

She looked around frantically. "I need to talk to him—"

"Here." Sam came to her rescue, pushing the two chairs in front of Hattie out of the way so she could get through. "He went through the side door."

Heart sure this time, she went after him.

He'd made her cry.

Heart ripping inside his chest, Maxwell slammed out of the café, into the darkness, completely forgetting his hat, only wanting to escape.

He'd done it. He'd read his poem in front of nearly all their peers. Somehow he'd gotten the words out of a mouth that felt as if it was filled with cotton gauze, face flaming so hot he probably could've sterilized surgical equipment all on his own.

And Hattie had cried and shaken her head—as though she'd wanted to let him down easy. Well, at least he knew. At least he wouldn't regret trying everything to win the woman he loved. Not that it was much comfort when he felt so alone....

"Maxwell—"

He ducked to the side of the set of three stairs as

her voice rang out in the darkness. He didn't know if he could face her again—ever. How mortifying to make a fool over yourself for the same woman—three times. He'd have to find a way to let the doc down easy, couldn't even stomach facing her in the clinic.

She paused on the steps, probably to let her eyes adjust to the darkness after being in the lamplit room.

He shifted his feet, wondering if he should just dart around the corner of the café and find his horse.

She must've heard the slight noise of his boot against the packed dirt, because she turned in his direction. "Maxwell?"

He was breathing hard, as if he'd run a race. He didn't know if he could speak.

"Maxwell, I'm so…humbled by what you wrote about me."

He didn't want to hear about her being humbled. The only thing he wanted to hear—could bear to hear—was that she loved him back, after he'd laid bare his feelings like he had. "You don't have to let me down easy," he said, hating how gruff his voice sounded.

"I'm not letting you down," she said.

"I saw your face in there. You were crying."

She came toward him, but she must've tripped on her skirt or something. She wobbled on the step above him and then began to fall.

Reaching out for her was as natural as breathing, and she fell against him with a soft "Oomph!" His arms closed around her of their own accord.

She said something, but her words were muffled in his shirt. Holding her like this scrambled his senses and it was a moment before he could draw back, ask her to repeat what she'd said.

"I *said* that your words were so beautiful they made me cry and that I would prefer to make my return declarations in private. That's all that you saw on my face inside."

"Your what…?" He barely choked out the words, joy and hope zinging through him, racing like fire in his blood.

"For someone so intelligent…" she said softly, words burning against his chin.

He had a glimpse of her eyes in the lamplight spilling from the still-open door, and then her soft hands were on his cheeks, pulling him toward her.

She kissed him.

When he was so discombobulated he could barely remember his own name, she pulled back—slightly— in his arms and whispered, "I love you, too."

Which led him to crush her to his chest as he repeated it into her hair, over and over. He kissed her again, unaware of anything but the woman in his arms until a throat cleared nearby.

Maxwell shifted so that Hattie would be out of the line of sight of anyone who had come upon them. She didn't move away from him but did reach up to her hair to fix the mess he'd made of her pins.

"I think they've had long enough to clear things up," he heard Sam's voice say.

"Yeah, don't want to let them get too carried away…at least until after the wedding."

Maxwell growled. He appreciated Sam and Oscar's interference—to a point. A line that was perilously close to being crossed right at this moment.

"She hasn't agreed to marry me yet," Maxwell said.

"What?" Oscar's voice came again, disembodied in the night because Maxwell couldn't look away from the small slice of light falling on Hattie's face and illuminating her shining eyes.

"That can't be right," Sam teased. "They've been out here plenty long enough to get things settled. What d'you think they've been doing all this time?"

"All right" came a female voice from somewhere slightly farther away than Oscar and Sam. A school-teacher's tone. Sarah. "You two can tease all you want—later. Leave Maxwell and Hattie alone."

"We're just trying to make sure no reputations are tarnished tonight," protested her husband.

"Just wanted to tell them that the wagon is out front—in plain sight of anybody walking along the boardwalk or peeking out from a window. In case they wanted to sit there instead of hiding back here in the shadows. Ow—Emily!" Sam half howled.

Hattie grinned up at Maxwell, likely echoing the expression on his own face.

Maxwell knew they were right. He would never compromise Hattie. He gave her one last peck on the lips before taking her arm and carefully leading her through the darkness around the café—he couldn't quite find the courage to face the crowd inside, not yet. He didn't regret for one second showing Hattie that he loved her with his poem, but that didn't mean he wanted to go shake hands with all the other young folks.

"I guess your brothers had a hand in tonight's events?" she asked, clinging to his arm though he knew she could walk perfectly well. Her closeness was *right*. At last.

"More than you know."

He boosted her up into the wagon bed, then sat beside her, legs hanging down.

Light and voices spilled from the café's windows and open door, but he and Hattie were left in relative privacy as the other young people played their social games.

He clasped her hand in his. "Should I…ask your pa for your hand? Or is it…too early? I don't want to push."

After both of her previous rejections, he might've expected her to stiffen up or move away when he brought up marriage, but she leaned her head on his shoulder with a contented sigh.

"I'll agree to marry you—if we wait to settle the details of the engagement until we figure out about medical school. For both of us."

With her tucked beneath his arm, he felt her deep inhalation.

"I'm sorry about pushing you away before," she continued. "I was afraid that…that if I admitted I was in love with you, then eventually I'd stop wanting to be a doctor and just want to be your wife."

"I would never ask you to give up on your dreams."

"I know that. I know. I just got scared."

She turned her face slightly up toward his and he used the opportunity to steal a quick kiss. Or what he intended to be a quick kiss. Her hand met his jaw and he forgot everything else for a few moments.

A wolf whistle interrupted the moment, and they broke apart.

He recaptured her hand. "What changed your mind?"

"You. And your family, seeing how they interact. Or rather, remembering what I'd seen. Your father in the kitchen because your mother can't cook. Your brothers pitching in. I realized…that we can make things work, even after children come along."

The thought of having children—having children with Hattie—made his mouth go dry in a very good way.

"Once we get things worked out with medical school," she reminded him.

He held her close, willing to agree to almost anything for the woman he loved. The woman he could now hold close beside him.

Epilogue

Three months later

Hattie shook out one of her dresses, examining the wrinkles left from being packed away in a trunk. This one would have to be ironed. She laid it out on the boardinghouse bed, on top of two others that hadn't fared well on the train journey. Once she'd had time to go down to the kitchen area and iron them, she would hang them up in the small bureau.

She could barely believe it—she was here, newly arrived in Denver. Her first day of medical school would be tomorrow. Her first lecture, first chance to interact with classmates. A glance at her school texts, all lined up in an orderly row on the tiny desk beneath the window, brought a smile to her lips.

"Everything all right?" Maxwell asked, shouldering through the door, a small wrapped package in his hands.

And best of all, her husband—husband!—was right here with her.

They'd arrived between the noon meal and supper, but after days of train food, Hattie had wanted something better to eat. And her conscientious husband knew of a nearby bakery and set out to provide for her.

She greeted him with a kiss.

"I walked five blocks to get these pastries for you—don't distract me now," he teased, holding her in a loose embrace and feathering kisses across her cheek and ear. "Or rather, not yet..."

She pinched him on his side, the exact spot Breanna had shown her on one of the blissful days she'd spent with the White family before they'd had to leave Bear Creek. He yelped, jumping away with an overdone pout.

She didn't want to admit it, but she already missed both of their families and was glad to have him by her side for this journey—an unexpected blessing she never would have thought to ask for.

The scholarship committee had approved her for a tuition scholarship before she'd even left Omaha. And she'd been accepted to the same medical school Maxwell attended here in Denver. She would be nearly two years behind him in studies. But Papa and Maxwell had come up with the idea for him to seek a short-term partnership in Denver—there were many medical clinics and hospitals looking for doctors—until Hattie's graduation, when they would both move back to Bear Creek and take over Papa's practice. Her father had claimed he was ready to retire, though Hattie didn't quite believe him. Time would tell if he worked part-time in the clinic with them or not.

Things had smoothed over with Hattie's mama the instant she and Maxwell had sat down in the parlor and expressed their intention to marry. Mama had burst into tears, thrown her arms around Hattie and immediately started making plans.

And as for the White family...they'd taken her in as if she was one of their own. Maxwell's brothers had teased her until she'd retaliated by playing a prank on them—and then they'd begun pulling pranks themselves, until Penny had had to threaten them with harm if they mucked up the wedding.

Maxwell and Hattie had married several weeks before the semester was to start, so they could finalize their plans. He had planned to find work in the city, until a benefactor Hattie's father had contacted offered him a partial scholarship. With the funds he'd earned from working alongside Oscar throughout the summer, Maxwell would be able to finish his last two years of schooling.

And now here they were. Married. Getting ready to embark on the next adventure in their lives together.

She settled on the bed, smoothing her skirt before she reached for the pastry he offered her. "You promised to let me read another of your poems when we arrived," she reminded him. Since the poetry reading, he'd occasionally allowed himself to be talked into sharing some of his words.

Very rarely, in fact, but she'd argued that their arrival at school was a special occasion.

He sighed but settled against the headboard, long legs stretched out before him.

She snuggled next to him, pillowing her head on his shoulder.

"I'm glad to be here with you," she whispered before he began.

He put one arm around her shoulders and kissed her temple. "Me, too, darlin'. Me, too."

* * * * *

Dear Reader,

Thank you for taking the time to read Maxwell and Hattie's love story. I will admit I've had a soft spot in my heart for Maxwell since I wrote *The Homesteader's Sweetheart*. There is something about a sensitive, quiet hero that I love—not to mention how he's bravely overcome his past to make something of himself. I knew he would need a special woman to capture his heart, and when I "met" Hattie, I knew she was perfect for him.

This was a fun story to write, but it did take a lot of research into medical practices, and any mistakes are my own! I hope to be back to visit Bear Creek and another of Maxwell's brothers soon....

I always love hearing from readers and want to know what you thought about this story. Did you like Maxwell as much as I did? You can send me a note at lacyjwilliams@gmail.com or in care of Love Inspired Books, 233 Broadway, Suite 1001, New York, NY 10279.

Lacy Williams